THE

MISSING
WOMAN

An addictive crime thriller that will keep you guessing

JODIE LAWRANCE

Detective Helen Carter Book 4

JOFFE BOOKS

Joffe Books, London
www.joffebooks.com

First published in Great Britain in 2023

Cover art by Nebojša Zorić

ISBN: 978-1-80405-754-4

PROLOGUE

The only time he felt full of life was when he was taking one. There was no greater feeling. The very air of Waverley station, with its faint smell of diesel, pulsed with anticipation. He pushed through the crowd, his heart clenched tight, fearful of being caught. Thousands of people would be arriving and departing from this station during rush hour. The blare of a horn, ripping through the concourse, announced a through train, which roared past one of the nearby platforms, causing the plastic seat he had been lucky to find to vibrate.

With a clack, the departures board showed the next page — their train was due in a couple of minutes. Perfect. It was time. As he had learned, the greater the risk, the bigger the high, and this one promised to be the biggest yet. The sweetest drug in the world and he was an addict.

Smiling, he looked around the dusty waiting area. Moments like this were to be captured, treasured. His camera hung heavy around his neck. He lifted it and took a couple of shots, enjoying the cold feel of the metal against his face.

His chosen one was thumbing through the *Evening News*. He snapped again, a shot of his target in profile. No one looked — he was invisible behind the camera.

He stood to get a better shot. Travellers in thick winter coats shoved past, rushing to their platforms. Meaningless chatter swirled about him, the words just noise. He glanced over his shoulder, lowered his camera and moved toward the John Menzies. He couldn't risk his target giving him the slip.

Armed with papers and Opal Fruits, his target strode forward. He followed. It was fate that he had run into the man again.

A passenger announcement blasted from a tannoy just above him, making his stomach flip. He was annoyed at his reaction — he was more nervous than he had anticipated. He was out of practice.

He met the gaze of a police officer loitering on the platform, and the hairs on the back of his neck bristled. The young, freckle-faced lad looked like he'd borrowed his dad's uniform for Halloween. He kept moving, heart hammering, the target still a few paces ahead. They passed the officer and he let out a breath. The cop was now chatting to a young woman. He had timed this nicely — the train was pulling into the platform and the hordes were moving towards it.

He stepped up into the train, the door clunked shut and the whistle sounded. He snaked his way through the first carriage, grimacing when his knee connected with a suitcase jutting into the aisle. A haze of tobacco smoke thickened the air. The train pulled away, jolting him forward, and he only just managed to grab the back of a seat for support. The voice of the train guard crackled in the air. Several pairs of eyes looked up as the door to the next carriage slid open. A smile tugged at the corner of his mouth. *If only they knew.*

He sank into a seat and the smile turned a little wry. The train jolted again. He grasped the armrest, stilling his trembling hands. His target was skimming through the pages of his newspaper while chewing on a nail. *Not long to go.* Meanwhile, he turned his attention to the view outside. The sun had sunk behind the buildings leaving a horizon the colour of candyfloss. The luminous pink reminding him of the day at the fair, the only happy childhood memory he could recall with his real family. He wiped away the fractured feathered pattern of the frost on the window, lifted his camera and snapped. He glanced around the carriage, the woman closest to looked as though she was dozing. Perfect.

It didn't take long for Edinburgh to shrink into the distance as the train picked up speed, blurring the landscape. Suddenly nauseous, he slipped his camera under his jacket on the seat next to him and waited. The train slowed as it passed a small clump of houses whose chimneys were sending up smoke signals. It wasn't long after that the target stood up and tossed his paper onto the seat. He waited a few beats, then got up and followed. It was risky, but it was time to do what was necessary.

The chemical smell of the toilet hung thick in the air of the vestibule. He cranked the window down halfway and closed his eyes, letting the wind whip his hair back and forth, while the noise of the train racketing down the tracks filled the space. Perfect for drowning out any unwanted noise. He pulled his cravat from his neck and tied it in a loop.

The toilet churned. He glanced back down the carriage. No one stirred. No one was watching. Perfect.

The target emerged, fumbling with his zipper. Without loosening the knot, he slipped his tie around the man's neck and pulled him back towards the window, out of sight of the other passengers. His victim yelped and shoved an elbow into his ribs with an audible crack, pushing him back against the metal guardrail. He bit down hard on his lip and pulled, grabbing at the man's tie for leverage. His victim began thrashing wildly. *Come on. Come on.* The rocking of the train pulled them towards the door but he managed to get a grip on the handrail.

The man slumped against the window. His jacket lay in a crumpled heap at his feet.

'What do you want?' he gasped. 'Money?'

He pulled the window down as far as it would go. 'Money won't make this right,' he said in a hoarse whisper. 'I read your book, Stanton.'

Recognition dawned, too little and too late. 'I . . . didn't
. . . Look, let me help you.'

'Help?'

'We can set up something with my secretary.'

'It's too late for all that, the damage has been done.'
Who did this fucker think he was? He tightened his hold,
strangling his victim until he became limp. He grabbed him
by the scruff of his expensive shirt. Heavier now, but it still
took just one shove and he was gone. Just like that.

He grabbed the guardrail and pulled the window shut
with a thud that nearly knocked him off his feet. He looked
around but no one seemed to have seen. Grabbing the man's
jacket, he brushed off the dirt, draped it over his arm and
headed back to his seat, his whole body felt like it had been
doused in a bucket of icy water. The man's look of anger,
shock and pain played in a loop over and over in his mind.

Gasps erupted around him. He swallowed, tasting metal,
hearing a faint grinding noise under his seat. The voice of the
guard burst out from the intercom — a problem with the
line up ahead. Shit, this was not good. He sat forward and
tried to get a look at what was going on but the approaching
guard blocked his view.

CHAPTER ONE

Detective Sergeant Helen Carter sucked in a ragged breath and started back down the stairwell. Hot tears stung her eyes and she blinked them back. There was no way she was going to let herself cry. She was upset, but she was annoyed at herself too. Her emotional response had taken her aback, reminding her of things she hadn't thought about in a long time.

'I've got myself into a mess.' Detective Constable Terry McKinley had jumped to his feet and placed his empty beer glass on the shelf. The crumpled shirt he was wearing looked like yesterday's and his sandy hair lay flat again his forehead.

'That much is obvious,' Helen said after a heavy silence. She didn't know what else to say or do, all she could do was glare at him.

He had gestured for her to sit on the sofa but she had refused, unable to decide if she wanted to hear more.

'I know you're angry with me.'

That was an understatement.

'I've gone through it a thousand times in my mind.' McKinley dragged the heel of his hand down his face. 'I wanted to tell you—'

'But you didn't.'

'Will you let me explain then?' McKinley said, shaking his head slowly.

She nodded.

'It was an accident. Not something I set out to do. All right?'

'And that's the truth?' Helen's eyes narrowed. 'How can I believe you?'

'I swear.' For the first time in the conversation, he met her eyes.

'That doesn't mean much,' she scoffed. 'How could it have been an accident?'

'It was. Trust me.'

'How can I?' Her stomach tightened, her mind already on what she was going to tell the DI, because he wouldn't let it drop, even if she did.

'Well, there's a bible up on the bookshelf.' He slumped onto the sofa.

'That's not funny.' She knew he wasn't religious. Nor was she for that matter.

'It was around the time Sally was in some play, remember that Shakespeare thing she dragged me along to?'

Sally had been his on-and-off girlfriend, more off than on. She had been a typist down at the station for a while, and Helen had been glad to see the back of her and all her little passive aggressive comments about Helen's dress sense or her weight. She was jealous of Helen — not that she had any need to be.

'Sally had been going on at me, saying I was embarrassing her. We had a big argument. I was having a horrendous night. I had a few drinks too many. More than a few.'

'Then what?' Helen said, not hiding her impatience.

'Then I got approached by Jim Savoy. I opened my mouth when I should have—'

'What did you say to him?' Savoy was a shark when it came to getting his stories. Helen remembered him sniffing around her first crime scene on the day she joined CID. They had all been well warned about him.

6

'I can't even remember.' He shook his head. 'Or if I even got any money. If I did, it all went on drink that same night.'

'For goodness' sake.'

'It wasn't something I set out to do. I've been kicking myself ever since.'

Helen rolled her eyes.

'Out of them all, I thought you at least would understand.'

'What's that supposed to mean?'

He blew out a breath.

Helen felt her belly clench. 'Are you meaning my dad?'

'Well, look at you. You've stayed in the police to try and make up for the backhanders your dad took,' he said.

'That has nothing to do with what we're talking about now.'

'Can't you just forget about it? I'll probably be put back in Traffic, and I've worked so hard to get here.'

'I'll need to think about it.' She turned to leave.

Outside, she stood by her little red Mini and looked up at the living room window. The curtains parted and Terry looked down at her, meeting her gaze. All she could do was shake her head. A painful lump formed in the back of her throat, and she swallowed. Confronting him at his home hadn't been the smartest decision she'd ever made, but she needed answers. Terry had been the one person in the department she'd thought she could trust, and now he had put her in an impossible situation.

The evening sun threw an orange glow across the charcoal tenement, casting him in shadow. For a moment he looked like a photo negative.

He was the last person she would have expected to jeopardise their cases and ruin the department's reputation. According to him, he hadn't meant it. Now she didn't know what to tell Detective Inspector Craven, and he was going to demand answers sooner or later. He always did.

Helen pulled out from her spot and joined the queue of cars at a set of temporary traffic lights. She fumbled with the radio, then turned it off and drummed her fingers on the steering wheel. Despite her best efforts to distract herself, she kept going over her conversation with McKinley. Only now could she think of things she'd wanted to say to him, questions she needed answers to. Her eyes misted. Terry McKinley had been her only friend after a case had left her badly beaten and she didn't think she could return to work.

A gritting lorry just in front of her sprayed a wave of salt across the bonnet. Helen braked and swung into Ferry Road, only to be stopped at another set of lights. While she waited, a poster tied to a lamppost, old and faded, caught her attention, its edges fluttering in the breeze. It was advertising art classes at the community college, a few streets away from her flat. The light turned green and she moved forward through the grey slush from the earlier snowfall. Maybe she'd give that a go. Do something different.

An uneasy impatience niggled at her. The road sparkled, the wheels sliding on the turn. Helen kept a tight hold of the steering wheel. A sudden burst of chatter and static from the radio made her grit her teeth. She was needed back at the station.

* * *

Now occupying the seat that had belonged to his victim, he patted the pockets of the jacket. Empty. Damn! Surely his wallet hadn't gone out the window with him? He needed the train ticket. He ground his teeth. He didn't want to draw more attention to himself than he already had. The train jolted, picking up speed and throwing him forward. His eyes dropped to the worn maroon leather briefcase lying on the floor half-under the seat. He snatched it up. From the corner of his eye, he could see that the train guard had now stopped and was bending over a middle aged woman talking to her. Beneath the rattle of the hurtling train, he couldn't make out what they were saying. He risked a quick glance, not wanting them to see him looking. Maybe she'd seen — her seat was facing the toilet. No, he'd been careful.

He sucked in a breath and, fingers trembling, fumbled with the clasps. It took a couple of attempts to prise them open. He sensed eyes on him. Watching. Did they know? He reached in and pulled out the wallet. By the time the guard arrived at his seat, he was wearing his new jacket. It felt a little tight around the shoulders but the length was just right. He caught a glimpse of his reflection in the mirror. He looked different. Different, but good. He looked up from the newspaper he was pretending to read. The guard was at his shoulder, looking down on him. Chewing on an Opal Fruit — lime, his favourite — he handed the ticket to the guard and offered him a sweet. The guard, a stout man in his late fifties, looked like he was tempted but shook his head.

'Is everything all right?' He kept his voice low and calm, the way his victim would have.

CHAPTER TWO

One week later

His heart pounding from the exertion, he dragged the last bag down the stairs. The streetlights outside the block were out and the flat was shrouded in darkness, so he could take his time and get things right. He paused at the bottom of the steps, listening for movement outside. Nothing. It had been a while since he'd heard anyone. He felt on edge and he wasn't sure why. Maybe it was too quiet. The baby crying, the dogs barking, the faint mumbling of the TVs and radios, all had faded away into the night. This was good. This was as expected. So why did he feel so strange?

His heart no longer thudding, he made his way through to the kitchen, where he slid the knife back into the block with the others. His gloved hand on the cheap plastic handle, he listened again. Silence. The faint trill of a fire engine sent a jolt of electricity through his body. He waited for the sound to diet away then patted his pockets. He had taken Polaroids of the scene but the light was too poor, the vibrant colours too dull. He would have liked to see the blue of her eyes, the fear in them. The rich tone of the blood that poured from her

10

like red wine. Blood had always intrigued him, the different tones of reds and browns. The shape and spatter. He took out a handful of the photos and leafed through them, smiling in satisfaction. They wouldn't win him any awards but they would do. Shoving them in his pocket, he carried on.

He had barely finished moving everything down to the kitchenette when he heard the front door rattle. He stood unmoving in the doorway, wincing as red-hot pain shot down his side. His ribs still weren't right from the hit Stanton had given them on the train. The lights were off, so there was no chance he'd be seen. She was popular — this was the second time someone had been at the door this evening.

He waited for the shape to move away, then carried on with his work. He took the hardback from his bag and, sneering, he slotted it into the shelf among the others. Now, he had a phone call to make.

* * *

Detective Sergeant Helen Carter shrugged off her jacket and slung it onto the back seat of the Granada. She had only got it a couple of days ago. It was a baby-pink leather bomber that had been a sales impulse buy, and she didn't want to lose it to a crime scene like her old jacket.

Her colleague, Detective Constable Randall, whose broad shoulders gave him a looming presence, wore a permanent frown, which deepened as he turned into the housing estate. He pulled up next to a police van with a squeal of brakes. Facing them were rows and rows of flats squashed together in huge concrete blocks, some with metal balconies, others with tiny square windows. They looked like they'd once been white but time had faded them to grey. The façades were marbled with what Helen supposed was filler but maybe it was some kind of crazy design.

Randall lit a cigarette. 'The last time I was on this estate I was bitten on the arse.'

'By a dog, I hope.' Helen shoved her handbag out of sight under the passenger seat, wishing she had ignored his remark.

His lips turned up slightly at the corners. 'Chasing some wee shite through the estate.'

'Where you alone?'

'Aye, I was young and stupid back then. You do things when you're trying to prove yourself, don't you?'

She glanced at him. He'd had it in for her ever since she was promoted to sergeant, but he seemed different lately. Either he was beginning to accept her, or he'd resigned himself to his position. She suspected the latter.

His smile disappeared. 'Never caught the bugger and ended up with a chunk out of ma arse for ma trouble.'

'Painful.'

'Still got the scar.'

Helen blinked away the image Randall's words had conjured up and peered through the car window at the buildings. They looked more like a prison than places of residence. Most of it was in shadow thanks to the poor street lighting, making it easy for someone to come and go unseen. 'Place is built like a maze.'

'Did Dispatch give you breakdown of what happened?' Randall asked.

Helen shook her head. 'I didn't want to hear it. I want to make up my own mind. I think the address we're looking for is up there.' Helen pointed towards a block with a red door on the right-hand side.

'Fair enough. So, what about young Terry McKinley?'

Helen's stomach tightened. 'What about him?'

'He's called in sick the last couple of days, thought you might know what's up with him.'

'Not sure. A cold maybe?' She pulled off her seat belt. She wasn't going to tell him the truth — that McKinley was the department snitch, and she hadn't figured out what she was going to do about it.

Outside the car, Helen was hit with a gust of icy air that went right through her blouse. She rubbed her arms for warmth. The barking of dogs echoed in the distance and as they headed towards the block, Helen could feel eyes on her from the balconies above, so she kept her head down. The wind whipped up the rubbish, scattering crisp and fag packets. Randall kicked them aside.

'Ladies first.' The door groaned in protest as he pulled it open.

Helen checked to make sure they weren't being followed and headed inside.

The black door had a boot print on the bottom panel. It looked old. Helen's eyes fell to the handle that was speckled with rust. Randall pushed the door open with his boot. The flat was a maisonette spread out over two floors. There was a faint whiff of daisies in the hallway. Despite the forbidding exterior, inside the building was beautifully decorated with salmon carpets and peach walls. It was warm too, the central heating turned up high. A uniformed officer, who was busy filling in a report, stepped aside to let them through. She gave him a small smile. She thought his name was Mick, or was it Mack?

'What do we have?' she asked.

'This place is rented to an Ella White. Neighbour hadn't seen her for a while.' He looked down at his notes.

'Right, and why are we here?' Randall dragged a hand through his thinning hair. 'I'm not seeing any blood, there's no body.'

'Dispatch got a call at seven thirty this evening, reporting a murder at this address.'

Just over an hour ago. 'Do we—?'

'Call came in anonymously.'

'Does she live here alone?' Helen peered into the living room. She couldn't see a telephone.

'Yes, she does,' the officer said. 'The caller used the phone box up the road.'

'Make sure to get the names and details of anyone who tries to approach the scene, even someone just walking past,' Helen stated. There was a good chance that whoever phoned the police might return to watch. 'What about the neighbour? Which one's not seen her for a while?'

He tilted his head to the left. 'He's at home, he knows you'll probably want to speak to him.' He grinned. 'Wait till you see him — he could pass for Wurzel Gummidge's younger brother.'

Helen exchanged a look with Randall.

Randall tapped on the wall. 'Place is made of cardboard. If there was any disturbance, he'd have heard it.'

'Any sign of forced entry?' Helen asked.

The officer shook his head. 'The back door wasn't locked.'

'Right.'

'Forensics are up working in the bedroom.'

Helen pulled on her gloves and headed up the wooden stairs. The scenes of crime officer was crouching next to the bed. He appeared to be squinting at something.

Helen cleared her throat.

The SOCO looked up and gave a small nod. 'Evening.'

'You got something?' Helen asked. The room was barely wide enough for the double bed and wardrobe opposite. Randall had followed. And he stopped in the doorway and still Helen felt like the walls were closing in on her.

'I think there's blood down here,' the SOCO said. 'A small bit on the base of the divan.'

Helen remembered his name was Ralph. She was glad it was him. He had a reputation for being thorough.

'You think?' Randall quipped.

'Sometimes blood can look like other things. Oil . . . tomato sauce.' He sucked air in through his teeth. 'Not a huge amount. A transfer pattern. See for yourself.' He shuffled back so that Helen could get a better look. She could see a plum-coloured splodge on the fabric in the shape of a thumb. Male by the size of it, and it looked smooth.

'He was wearing gloves,' Helen said.

The SOCO nodded. 'There's some blood here, a couple of small crown patterns around here.' He jabbed a thumb towards a marked-off area next to the window.

Helen put the back of her hand to the threadbare carpet. She could feel a slight dampness through the glove and there was a smell of detergent. 'Someone's done a clean-up here.'

'Aye. Same with the walls.' The scenes of crime officer pointed to a patch next to the window that looked darker than the rest.

This looked well thought out. A clean-up of this size was no easy task. But why go to all the trouble of getting rid of all the evidence only to then call the police?

A sliver of plastic wedged under the skirting board caught Helen's eye. The edges of it looked stretched, as though someone had pulled the rest of it away in a hurry. She took an evidence bag from her trouser pocket while the scenes of crime officer used tweezers to retrieve it.

'From the lack of blood on the carpet I'd suspect they put a plastic sheet down.' She also knew that a spatter pattern like this was often consistent with a knife wound. 'Could someone have stabbed or killed her here and then moved her somewhere else and got their thumb print on the bed in the process?'

'Possibly, though there's not enough blood here to determine whether anyone was killed,' he said.

Helen nodded, making a mental note to follow it up with the local hardware stores and check any violent offenders who worked in the trades. 'Good work.' She got back on her feet and started on the rest of the room, working her way down from the ceiling. The bed was covered in a purple blanket that looked freshly changed, and the wicker laundry basket at the end of the bed was empty.

She got down and stretched out on her stomach to get a look under the bed. There wasn't much room under there, just enough to fit her hand. She reached forward and her hand connected with something hard. Grimacing, her head against the bed, she just managed to get her fingers round a book. The cover showed a picture of a dark-haired woman, her face depicted like the pieces of a jigsaw puzzle. The title was *Sybil*.

The SOCO peered over her shoulder. 'Read it then, have you?'

Helen nodded, turning over the faded dog-eared book in her hands. She had read it in her final year at university. It was about the treatment of a woman with multiple personality disorder. From what Helen remembered, it had been a chilling read.

'I've not,' the SOCO said, 'but I saw the film. Don't get much time for books. A true story apparently.'

'That's right.'

'Wasn't she possessed by a dozen personalities or something?'

Sixteen, as a matter of fact, but Helen didn't feel like correcting him. Instead, she dropped the book in an evidence bag. 'Let me know if you find anything else.'

'Aye, will do.' With a slight nod in her direction, Ralph turned his attention back to the bed.

Helen pulled open the wardrobe, which was full of clothes. It didn't look like anything had been taken from it. The rail was crammed with expensive-looking dresses, all neatly colour coordinated. She gave a wry smile. So, this was what a wardrobe should look like. She could feel the Ralph watching her, so she decided to look around the rest of the property and get out of his way.

She found the bathroom at the end of the corridor. The door was ajar, towels lay on the floor and there was an empty box of bath salts on the side of the tub, some of them scattered across the lino. The crystals sparkled like glitter. Helen closed her eyes. Maybe the victim had been taking a bath when she was attacked, and her struggle with her killer ended in the bedroom. Helen bent over the tub. She could see water still puddled around the plug and drops on the sides of the bath. The sink looked dry, there was a small mirror above the sink speckled with toothpaste.

Downstairs, the television was on low — the news. There was a half-drunk cup of milky tea, along with a mottled banana peel on the table.

She crossed to the window, which faced out to the laughingly named "village green", a concrete paved area. The blinds were partly drawn. The closed window showed no sign of damage. She stepped over to the fireplace and felt glass crunch under her boot. A tiny piece. She glanced around, but couldn't see what it might have come from. Everything looked to be in its place, apart from a tall floor lamp that was leaning against the wall.

She picked up the shard. It looked thin, like the glass from a picture frame, but the walls were bare. Come to think of it, she hadn't noticed any pictures or photographs anywhere in the house. She turned the glass over in her hand.

'I've found her driving licence and a logbook. She owns a blue Ford Anglia.' Randall was standing in the doorway, his face flushed from the cold, the documents in his hand. 'The car's not outside. I suppose there's a chance she could have driven off somewhere.'

'Maybe.' Helen wasn't convinced, and Randall didn't look like he was either. She dropped the glass into an evidence bag.

'What about you?' Randall said. 'Found anything?'

Helen shook her head. The oak bookcase on the right-hand side of the wall caught her eye and she crossed over to it. You could always tell a lot about a person from the books on their shelves — at least, that's what her father always said. 'There's a potential bloody thumbprint upstairs.'

'That it?' Randall scoffed, stepping into the room.

Helen ran her gloved finger along the books on the middle shelf. All of them were either about religion or true crime, a couple had been on her psychology reading list when she was at uni.

'Is Ella a student?' Helen asked Randall.

'Don't think so. I found some payslips in the drawer by the door. Works in a shop up town.'

A thick book on the bottom shelf looked out of place — there was dust on all the others but not this one. Helen lifted it from the shelf. *Catching Killers with Oliver Stanton — Volume 3 — The Button Killer.*

The hardback was heavy in her hand. She skimmed through it with an involuntary shudder. Mark Landis, aka the Button Killer, a name she'd never forget. She hated the moniker. Once the papers caught onto it, the name had transformed him into a celebrity overnight. She turned a page and found herself looking at a colour photo of the murderer. He was staring back at her with those dead blue eyes. Helen's blood ran cold.

Randall was peering over her shoulder. Helen wanted to drop the book, but she couldn't stop staring at the photograph. The images of the Button Killer's victims were still fresh in her mind, each grisly one of them. They were the first crime scene photographs she had ever seen, after she'd snuck into her father's office when she was small.

'There's a name I've not thought about in a while.' Randall said flatly.

'Me neither.'

'He's a right unremarkable-looking bastard, in't he?'

'Suppose he is.' Helen felt a sense of relief as Randall walked towards the door. The last thing she wanted to do was have a conversation about the Button Killer. His crimes had torn her family apart and he was best forgotten. She snapped the book shut. As she moved to put it back, her finger snagged the corner of something sharp, tearing her glove.

Dammit. Helen looked down as a line of red appeared on the tip of her index finger. Her eyes travelled to the floor and she noticed a train ticket next to her shoe. Finger forgotten, she picked it up. It was from a week ago. First class. Ella must've been using it as a bookmark.

Placing it in an evidence bag. Helen moved through to the kitchen, an open-plan space at the back of the lounge. The smell of bleach lingered faintly. The wooden worktops were spotless, a couple of plates sat on the drying board. A damp dishcloth had been folded next to the sink. Helen noticed two empty metal pet dishes on the ground in front of the bin. Animals were horrendous news for crime scenes. Helen would never forget the sight of a cat lapping up blood from the first crime scene she attended, nor the blood that had stained its matted tabby fur.

'She probably had a cat or a small dog,' Helen called out. Her suspicions were confirmed when she opened the cupboard under the sink and found a couple of tins of cat food. There was no sign of a cat though. Maybe it was outside. The kitchen cupboards were crammed with pots, pans, cups and plates, none of which seemed to match. Besides the cat food, the cupboard under the sink held bottles of various cleaning liquids and a small bucket with a pink rag draped over the rim. She felt it — damp. This was likely what had been used to clean upstairs.

Helen went over to the back door. It had a single glass panel, a cat flap and one Yale lock that looked intact. There was a small side window that looked out into the garden. She got down on her knees to look more closely at the black-and-white lino. It looked like the section in front of the door had been scrubbed with bleach.

CHAPTER THREE

The smell of bleach was getting to her. She opened the back door, which led to a small paved garden. There was a gate at one end that presumably led out into one of the many alleyways that interconnected these buildings. It was small, but Helen imagined it would be nice to sit out here in the summer. The high fences offered privacy, a rarity in Edinburgh. The garden was mostly empty except for a rusty washing line pole that swayed and creaked in the wind, and in the far corner a small tree with wilted leaves scattered around its base.

Helen was no gardener. The sliver of outdoor space that came with her flat was completely overgrown and had never been used. If she was going to give up and sell her flat, that was another thing she would need to sort. Helen guessed the tree in this garden to be apple. She crossed over to it, the paving slabs slick from the evening rain. It felt good to be outside, take a moment in the fresh air to catch her breath. She was just about to head back inside when something lying at the base of the tree caught her attention.

She crouched to get a better look. A couple of cigarette butts had been stubbed out on the ground. Helen pushed them aside with a gloved finger. There were a dozen or so, and all looked fresh. She stepped back onto the paving, not wanting to disturb the grass further. From this side of the garden, she had a good view of the kitchen and the bedroom window.

As she made her way back to the kitchen door, she noticed what looked like a shoe print under the window, with muddy water pooled in it. She guessed it had been there several days. Forensics would need to measure and photograph it. She called out to Randall, who jabbed a thumb back towards the road.

'I've been around all the nearby houses, no one has seen anything out of the ordinary. Ella White seems to keep herself to herself.'

Helen nodded.

'One of the neighbours also mentioned that Wurzel in there is a bit overfriendly. That's worth looking into.'

She pointed to the cigarette butts. 'Look at these. I found nothing inside to say she was a smoker, and I've spotted what looks like a shoe print over there. Someone might have been watching her.' Helen breathed in sharply to steady herself, the bitter gale icy on her face. 'From here you can see right into the kitchen. Better get Forensics out here.'

Scowling, Randall walked past her towards the gate.

'Something interesting?'

'I'm not sure yet.' He flicked on his torch and examined one of the posts. 'Take a look at this.'

He pointed to the bottom of the gate. A small piece of tape overlapped the bottom of the gate and the frame. This was a trick people sometimes used to see if a door had been opened. If it had, the tape would be dislodged. 'Looks like she was worried as well, maybe about someone coming into the garden.'

Helen slipped a pen out of her pocket and used it to check the edge of the tape. 'It's dislodged, true, but Uniform came in this way.'

Behind them, someone cleared their throat. It was the SOCO from the bedroom.

'I think we've found a shoe print outside the window. Make sure you preserve it,' Helen said to him. She noticed he was clutching a small tin box.

'Will do, but you might want to take a look at this.' Helen could tell by the grim look on his face that whatever was in that box, it wasn't good.

* * *

The police were still at the property. Not wanting to draw attention to himself, he sat in the car, his hands shaking uncontrollably. No, he told himself, everything had gone to plan. But why were they still there? His head was throbbing. He tried to remember the call he'd made to the police, but he couldn't bring back the words. A police van with blue lights blazing shot past him and into the estate. He sank back into his seat.

* * *

Helen set down the battered tin box on the worktop. Randall loomed over her while she tried and failed to prise open the lid. She could see Randall was struggling to stop himself whipping the box from her.

'Need some help?' Randall held out his hand, waggling his fingers. 'C'mon, love, we don't want to be here all night.'

'Give me a chance.' Helen shot him a look. Determined to do it herself, she managed to get a nail under, and on the third attempt the lid popped open.

'What's in it?' Randall asked.

'I'm not sure.'

The box contained dozens of yellowing newspaper clippings, some dating as far back as thirty years ago. Helen sifted through them. All of them were about murders up and down Britain, all from different tabloids.

'Morbid bitch, eh?' Randall muttered.

Ignoring his comment, Helen began to take out the articles, crinkling her nose at the smell of dust and damp that rose from the box. A familiar image in the final clipping sent a shock of electricity through her.

'Isn't that your father?' Randall reached for the scrap of paper.

Helen nodded, not trusting herself to speak, and swallowed the painful lump that had lodged in her throat.

'Where did you find this box?' Helen called out.

'It was down by the side of the bed,' the SOCO said.

The black-and-white image was grainy, but it was clearly her father, still in uniform, snapped at a crime scene. The headline underneath read, *Button Killer still at large*. At the very bottom of the box, Helen's fingers connected with something hard — a set of keys. Helen placed the lid back on the box. 'Let's go and speak with that neighbour.'

* * *

Thirty minutes later, Terry McKinley, his heart pounding and his mouth dry, rapped on the door of Helen's flat, desperate to sort out what had been said in their last conversation. Drink and lack of sleep had left his head foggy and a bad taste in his mouth. The flat was dark and silent, the only sound a faint mumble from the telly in the flat opposite. Sighing, he turned to go.

He shouldn't be surprised really. She seemed to use the flat only as a place to sleep. At the neighbouring property, he caught the silhouette of a figure outlined against the drawn curtains. Time to go.

It was raining when he got outside, but the air felt unseasonably warm. He headed for the nearest bus stop. He could always go home, he supposed, but he couldn't face the emptiness. Hospital visiting time was over, so he couldn't go there either. His mum had been over a month in that ward, and there was still no real answer as to what was wrong with her. She just got thinner and frailer with every passing week. Her hair, religiously coloured a rich copper tone, now had streaks of grey. The only other place to go — apart from the pub — was the station. Helen would probably be there. Despite what she might think, he needed to sort this out.

23

CHAPTER FOUR

'I take it you've not found her then.' The neighbour had opened his door just as far as the security chain would allow and peered out at Helen through the narrow gap.

'We're still investigating, Mr, er, List?'

He nodded slowly. 'Aye, but I go by Bert.'

'Can we come inside and have a word with you?' Helen slipped her warrant card back into her pocket.

'I already spoke to someone.' His eyes darted between them.

'I know, but we have our own questions to ask. It's just standard procedure.' She smiled. 'It would be better if we could do this inside.'

He closed the door. Unsure if he was going to open it again, she exchanged a look with Randall. Then the chain slid back.

'I cannae believe this,' the neighbour muttered. 'Just cannae believe it at all.' The neighbour, who looked to be in his late forties, was wearing a torn dressing gown with red stripes that didn't quite close over his gut. His dry fair hair stuck out from his head like straw, reminding Helen of a scarecrow. 'I mean, I was worried, but I thought I was overreacting, but this is like something you get on the telly, no' real life. Can ah get you a cup of tea or . . . ?'

'No, we're fine.' Helen looked around. 'Do you live here alone, Mr List?' She manoeuvred past a box of ancient-looking cameras and a rusted toolbox.

'Aye, since the place was built, and I lived in the prefabs here even before that wi' my mum.'

Randall groaned as his shoulder connected with one of the boxes, sending a pile of tools clattering to the ground. He stepped over them. 'Sorry about that,' he said casually.

The air in the flat was thick with cigarette smoke and the smell of fat. Through the open kitchen door Helen could see stacks of dirty dishes piled in the sink. A tabby cat sat next to the sink licking a paw and eyeing Helen suspiciously.

'Is that your cat?' Helen asked.

'No, it's Ella's.'

Randall made a face as they followed List through to the living room. The left-hand side of the room was completely taken up with heaps of faded newspapers and dusty carboard boxes.

Randall surveyed the room. 'What? Fifteen years, and you've not unpacked yet?'

List merely shrugged. He pointed to the threadbare sofa. 'Why don't you have a seat?'

Helen sat in the armchair opposite, while Randall remained standing.

'Sure I cannae get ye a drink?' He directed the question at Helen. 'I've no' got any milk though.'

'We're fine.' Helen took out her notebook and looked around at the dated pink carpets, the furniture covered in a faded floral pattern. The drapes looked yellow and stained with nicotine. The most modern item in the room was an antique Bakelite television sitting on the floor in one corner.

'This is a good area,' List said. 'You never get any bother.'

'Is it?' Randall thumbed through a paper with the headline "Buddy Holly dead in plane crash". 'You don't mind, do you?'

List shook his head. 'I've been meaning to throw they papers out.'

'So, when was the last time you saw Ella White?' Helen asked, not wanting to get sidetracked.

'Earlier on this afternoon, around four or five, I think.'

'Can you take me through it?'

He blew out a breath. 'I was worried about her.'

'Why?' she questioned.

'I hadn't seen her for days, which is unusual, so I went round, hoping to have a chat like.' There was a long pause during which he seemed to be thinking about what to say. 'She's nice and friendly, sometimes she'll give me a cup of tea. There's not many about here that'll do that.' His eyes darted between them. 'D'you think she's all right?'

Helen ignored his question. 'Do you have keys to Miss White's property? Or is there anyone close by who does?'

List shook his head. He reached for a packet of Marlboros on the coffee table, which was covered in ring marks from numerous cups. His hand shook as he put the cigarette to his lips. 'She rents the place. I don't know who'd have keys to it.' Helen noticed that the fingers on his left hand were tobacco stained, the nails bitten to the quick.

He fumbled in his dressing gown for a box of matches. Helen gestured to two mucky-looking nicks on his left hand. 'How did you get those?'

He sparked up his fag and looked down at his hand, as though noticing them for the first time. He shrugged. 'Don't know.' Smoke rose slowly from his nostrils as he answered. 'I was doing some DIY, must've been from that.'

'So, you saw Ella at home this afternoon?'

'Aye. She answered the door, but it looked like she had someone in the house with her.'

'Did you get a look at them?' Helen asked.

'No, not really. I could just sort of see this shape in the background.'

'Male? Female?'

26

He flicked his cigarette ash onto a saucer. 'Male. Tall, broad shouldered. That's about all I can tell you. She stepped outside to speak to me and spoke quiet like, as if she didn't want them to hear.'

'How did she seem?' she asked.

'Um . . . different. Look, I don't want to get her into trouble.'

Helen leaned forward. 'She's not in any trouble with us, we only want to make sure she is safe.'

'It was the way she acted. She seemed stressed, scared maybe. I don't know. I should've done something, I suppose. I just thought she didn't want me to see her with a boyfriend.'

Randall tossed the paper aside. 'Had you seen her with a boyfriend before? Nice-looking lassie like her, bet she's got loads of them.'

'No,' he spat, not hiding the bitterness in his voice.

'What about anything suspicious in the estate in the last few days — or weeks even? Any strangers hanging around?' Randall continued.

Slowly, List shook his head.

'You got a bathroom in here?' Before List could answer, Randall had disappeared down the hall. Helen knew he was going to take the opportunity to get a look around the place while she finished questioning List. There was something in List's expression that told her he was keeping something back. For a moment he looked like he was going to say something but decided against it.

'Anything at all, no matter how small,' Helen persisted.

'I'm probably wasting your time.'

'Let me be the judge of that.'

'I did see a man parked up across the way.'

'Did you get a look at him?' Helen rose and parted the curtain. From here, List would be in a perfect position to see all the comings and goings at Ella's place.

'He was sat out there for about an hour or so, then when he noticed me watching, he drove off,' List said. 'Never saw him again after that. I couldn't really see him then either, the streetlights have been out for a while.'

'What kind of car was it?' Helen asked.

'Ford Escort. Brown. Ella . . . She told me . . . She said she moved here to get away from something, make a new start.'

'From where?' Helen asked.

He shrugged again.

'Has Ella always lived alone?'

'For the most part.'

'The most part?'

'No, she . . . There was a man there last year. I don't know what happened to him. He left not long after she moved in. I didn't really speak to her then, he wasn't that friendly.'

'Did you get a name?'

He shook his head.

'Could that have been the man in the car? The one that lived with her?'

'Suppose so. Maybe . . .'

Helen made a move to leave. 'Thank you for your time, Mr List.'

* * *

'What do you think of him then?' Randall asked as they headed back towards Ella White's home. He was scratching his neck. 'That flat. Do you feel itchy?'

'No, why?'

He was now scratching at his back and stomach. 'I thought I saw fleas in there.'

So that was why he didn't sit down. Helen dragged a hand threw her hair. 'I think we need to keep an eye on him. He has feelings for Ella and by the sounds of it, they weren't reciprocated.'

'Aye, I thought that too. Maybe he didn't take kindly to being turned down, or he saw Ella with a boyfriend and saw red. There's something about him that's not right.'

'Maybe, but think of the crime scene. It's spotless. Someone took great care cleaning up and that Bert List, well, you could see the state of him. He looked like he hadn't washed in weeks and his hands were filthy.'

Randall was quiet for a moment. 'Do you believe he was doing DIY?'

'I saw no evidence of it, did you?' she said.

'No. I had a quick look round.'

Helen looked down at the notes she'd taken.

'We don't even know we're dealing with an active crime scene. For all we know, she's just left of her own free will. It's not likely, but it's a possibility.' She still struggled to get the image of the Button Killer out of her mind. 'This man he said Ella was with. We need to find out who he was.'

'Well, he's not made it easy for us.' Randall scoffed.

'I'm going to head back to the station.'

'I'll stay here, I've got a couple of things I want to check out.'

CHAPTER FIVE

A couple of the uniformed officers who had been checking door-to-door with the neighbours were now standing by the police van. One of them was stomping on the spot and both their faces looked red from the bitter cold.

Helen leaned into the car to get her jacket. 'Any luck?'

The taller of the officers shrugged. 'Most of the block is empty and the ones that did speak to us said they didn't see or hear anything.'

Helen zipped up her jacket. She hadn't expected anything different.

'I have been on this estate before,' the tall officer continued, blowing on his hands. 'Some creep pinching washing off lines. Never caught him though.'

'When was this?' Helen asked.

'Ach, a few years back.

'I'd like to check that, can you—?'

'Aye.' He pulled open the driver's side door. 'I'll dig out the report when I get back to the station.' The look on his face told Helen he regretted having mentioned it.

* * *

Helen switched off the engine and looked up at the modern edifice that housed CID. She took a deep breath. A polar low was creeping south, apparently, which meant more days of freezing weather. *Bloody brilliant.* She fumbled with the radio just as the presenter began to discuss James Callaghan's falling popularity. *Hardly surprising.* She clambered out of the Mini. Her breath smoked in the cold air, and she turned up her collar, trying to move as quickly as she could without slipping on the ice covering the puddles.

The front desk was empty but the full mug of coffee on the desk told her that the desk sergeant wasn't far away. She wasn't going to complain, having him glower at her was something she could do without. The faint aroma of fish and chips wafted towards her, and her stomach grumbled as she headed down the corridor.

The CID room — or the cleaning cupboard as she had heard it called — was a claustrophobic rectangular space jammed with scarred mahogany desks and dented filing cabinets on boot-stained carpet tiles. No one looked up when she entered. Most of the officers had their heads bowed over papers, cigarette smoke spiralling from the tinfoil ashtrays next to them. Keys clattered away on the typewriters. Even though it was open, the double window was misted with condensation. The latch had been broken even before she'd started with CID. A battered radio on the window ledge gave out staticky psychedelic tunes — was that "Crimson and Clover"? It was over before she could hear properly. The imposing DI's office was partitioned off at the bottom end of the room. Thankfully, the lights were out, giving her time to think about what she was going to tell him about Terry McKinley.

Detective Constable Bell aka Randall's right-hand man was perched on the edge of Helen's desk and half-smiled at her as she approached. He had a newspaper bundle of fish and chips in his hand and was stabbing at his chips with a little wooden fork.

'Evening.' He waved a chip at the bag on her desk. He was in his early forties, Helen reckoned, with thinning brown hair and a penchant for cigars, expensive watches and wives. Not necessarily in that order.

'Where's the DI?' Helen asked.

'Left about an hour ago, said he had something important to take care of.'

She had the tin box from Ella White's house in her hand, and she dropped it onto of a stack of folders. She could feel his eyes on her as she pulled out her chair. 'Is there something I can do for you?' she said through gritted teeth. She had just noticed that he had knocked her pen off the side of her desk and salt on her papers.

He shrugged and popped another limp chip into his mouth.

'Well then, is there any reason that you are at my desk and not your own?' She knew he was probably trying to see if she'd signed off on his overtime, which she still hadn't. It was somewhere in the pile on her desk.

'Yours is next to the kettle.' He was grinning now. 'I'm waiting for it to boil.'

Helen snatched up her pen.

'Need the caffeine to get me through the night shift,' he carried on. 'Heard it then, have you? I'll not forget that voice in a long time.'

'Heard what?' she asked.

'The 999 call.'

'No, I was at home when it came through.'

'It's on my desk if you want it.' Bell set his supper aside and sauntered over to his own table.

'Thanks, I would like to hear it.' Helen plonked herself down in her chair.

'I've got the transcript too.' He held it out. 'You're going to need it.'

Bell pushed down the "play" button on the tape recorder, and after a long pause, a loud crackle filled the silence. It was a while before the raspy low voice boomed out.

'I've killed again.'

Then the confused voice of the call handler. *'I'm sorry, did you just say——?'*

'She's dead. She's—— You need to send someone.'

'Who's dead?'

'You'd better send someone.'

'What phone are you calling from?'

Bell shrugged. 'I couldn't tell if that was a man or a woman.'

She gave him a look. She could do without a running commentary.

'You need to send the police.' The speaker's voice had become faint, and Helen strained to hear, though she could tell there was no real urgency in the voice.

Dispatch was having the same problem. *'Can you repeat that?'*

The caller spat out the address. *'You need to send police there. Now.'*

'Who's dead?'

The caller repeated the address.

'I . . . I didn't want things to be this way.'

Helen furrowed her brow. The speaker sounded almost regretful for a moment. Almost.

'Who is dead?'

'You'll find out soon enough.' The voice became clinical again.

There was a click and then silence.

Helen looked up at Bell. 'Is that it?'

'Aye. Do you want to hear it again?'

Helen nodded. Bell was right, she couldn't make out anything from the voice — age, accent. Nothing. Whoever it was had used some kind of voice distortion mechanism. She leaned forward, angling her head to hear better. The constant crackle made it even harder to make out the words.

Helen listened again and looked down at her watch. The call only lasted for a minute.

'Do you think it's a hoax?' Bell looked at his meal and made a face as she dropped it into the bin.

'I don't know,' Helen muttered. 'Can we get a voice expert on voices in to help us?'

'Aye, I'll see what I can do.' They both knew she was grasping at straws.

There was a long pause before Bell said, 'We should speak to Randall.'

'Why Randall?'

'Well, back in the day Randall was trained as a sparkie. He might know something about voice distortion.'

'I never knew that.'

'Aye, don't know why he gave it up really, good money.'

'I'll ask him. He said "again". We should also look at any criminals who've made threatening phone calls in the past,' Bell said. 'I'll get Terry McKinley to compile a list.'

Helen arched a brow. 'Terry's not on shift, is he?'

'He's in the records room. Arrived just before you did. Said he was feeling better.' He shoved his bundle of chips aside. 'We should look into violent offenders who have a background in electronics too,' he said.

'Good idea. We need to try and identify the voice.'

'That's going to be difficult.' Bell dragged a hand through his hair. 'There was no sign of forced entry, right?'

Helen nodded.

'Maybe this caller is an innocent bystander. He could have seen the door open . . .'

'No, I don't think so. Play the tape again.'

* * *

Not wanting to leave this any longer. Helen found McKinley in the records room. A large, musty windowless room with shelves stuffed with boxes and folders. He was down at the opposite end of the door, organising cards. He'd be tasked with seeing if police had attended Ella White's address previously or if she was known to police. It was a difficult job and a lot of it relied on memory. He would also liaise with other divisions across Scotland.

McKinley reached for the coffee on his desk and gave Helen a small smile. 'Have you heard the 999 call?'

Helen nodded and pulled out the empty seat at the desk McKinley was working at. 'I've never heard anything like it before.'

'It's a new one for me. Helen, I wanted to say—'

'I found a book there too, a book about the Button Killer at the crime scene.'

McKinley's brows lifted. 'Do you think its related to what happened to her?'

'I don't know.'

'That must've been a shock.'

'I don't think its related. I mean, it just brought back a lot of memories seeing that again.' Helen's lips thinned. 'I just wasn't expecting it.' Again, the Button Killer's victims flashed before her eyes.

'I understand that.' Scratching at his stubbly chin, McKinley sighed. 'I suppose he's a fascinating subject. A lot of people read those kinds of books.'

Helen looked away. They both sat in silence for a moment. Before McKinley spoke again. 'I hate the way we left things at my flat.'

Helen nodded.

'I want to apologise.'

'Let's talk about that another time.' She forced a smile. 'It's been a long night.'

'Have you seen DI Craven?'

'Not yet.' Helen pushed to her feet.

McKinley cleared his throat. 'Well, I'll have all the files you need on your desk first thing.'

'Thanks.'

* * *

It had been a good few hours since he'd watched Helen go inside the station, head down, clutching a box. He pictured her inside going through it. Had she liked what he'd left?

Had she found the book? Would she understand him now? If only he could be a fly on that wall. To pass the time, he thumbed through some of his photographs. The two Polaroids that he liked the most he slotted into cards, then plain white envelopes. Nondescript and impossible to trace. Just thinking about Helen opening them made him smile.

God, he needed a cigarette, but if he sparked one there would be a chance they'd see it from the window and it would raise suspicion, so he put it to his lips and left it unlit. Better than nothing. The radio was on low and tuned into the police wavelength. After the rush of a few hours ago, all had gone quiet.

CHAPTER SIX

It was well after two in the morning by the time Helen shoved open the door to her flat. She kicked off her boots. The balls of her feet throbbed. She groaned, pushing past the boxes and binbags full of old papers and books that lined the hallway. Most of it was from her dad's house, which was now rented out. Her spare room was piled high with the more precious objects — vases, crockery, and his favourite records. McKinley had been helping her sort through them. The cold hard face of the Button Killer filled her mind. Those empty evil eyes that used to haunt her childhood dreams. All her dad's notes on him were probably in there tucked away in some dusty old box. She pulled the door shut quickly. Out of sight, out of mind.

She pulled off her jacket and slung it over one of the kitchen chairs. The kitchen was in a state. The dishes needed doing and the remains of yesterday's takeaway supper still sat on the table. She picked up one of the plates, then thought better of it and chucked it in the sink. Tomorrow's job. She filled a pan with milk and placed it on the hob.

Her eye fell to the slip of paper she'd taped to the fridge. Stephen, the man she'd met at her mum's wedding. Tall, dark and handsome. She had been meaning to call him for weeks now but every time she remembered it was either too late at night or she was running late for her shift. She pushed the thought from her mind. Some digestives and a mug of extra-hot chocolate were what she needed, and then some sleep. But that wouldn't come easy — it never did.

* * *

Helen bolted upright, forehead and back slick with icy sweat, her senses on fire. She listened for noise, any indication of what had startled her awake. She looked around, feeling like a cornered animal. Nothing looked out of place and the only thing she could hear was the winter wind rattling against the windowpanes behind her. She snatched at the blankets that she'd kicked off in a panic. Her head was pounding.

She retreated into the warmth and curled into a foetal position, struggling to catch her breath. Another nightmare. Broken fragments, flashes of memory intermixed with fear. The Button Killer. Screaming. Blood. The figure at the end of her bed, watching her, but faceless. Flashes of crime scenes. Shuddering, she fumbled for her glass of water on the dresser and swore under her breath and she swiped it onto the carpet. She had thought her nightmares were a thing of the past. Giving up on sleep, she'd grab a quick shower then head to the station.

CHAPTER SEVEN

Detective Constable Randall was already at his desk when Helen entered the CID room, which was unusual. Ever since she'd been made acting sergeant over him, he had made a point of not arriving before or staying after his shifts.

'Finally,' Randall said. 'I've been waiting for you. I've already briefed the DI.'

Helen's pulse quickened. 'Briefed him about what?' Helen remembered he had stayed on at the crime scene. 'Did you find something?'

'You could say that.' Looking extremely pleased with himself, Randall showed her a manila folder. 'There were a few things about Ella White that didn't sit right with me.'

'Really?'

'We're wasting our time with that woman.'

Helen raised a brow. 'How do you mean?'

'It's obvious.'

'Not to me,' she said.

'You know the story of the boy who cried wolf?'

Randall was starting to irritate her now. She tried her best not to let it show.

'I got all the background information on her this morning. This is the up-to-date version.'

He handed Helen the folder. She could see DI Craven from the corner of her eye. He was standing at his door with a mug of coffee in his hand. Listening.

'Carry on,' Craven said.

'It's all in the file. Over the past eight years she's not stayed longer than six months at any one place,' Randall explained. 'She's lived up and down the country.'

Helen shrugged. 'Aye, but that doesn't mean—'

'She's had the police out to all her addresses. Sometimes on a weekly basis. First, someone was stalking her, but she could never give a description. No one else saw this stalker. Then there were the intruders. By the sound of some of the reports she's been beat up more times than Rocky Balboa.'

Sighing, Helen skimmed a couple of pages. 'You think this woman is a fantasist?' Helen paused on a photograph of Ella with a purple welt on her jaw.

'Aye, I do.' He gestured towards the photo. 'She could've easily done that herself.'

'Maybe.'

'Whenever the attending police visited her property, there was never any sign of an intruder. No sign of a stalker. No sign of forced entry. Neighbours never see anything.'

'We have to be careful, we can't just assu—'

Randall stood. 'On one occasion, while she was staying at a friend's property, she phones the police again, and same story — an intruder, broken in apparently and was standing at the end of her bed.'

Helen closed the folder and met eyes with Craven.

'The friend saw nothing.' Randall carried on. 'Even the wounds she sustained after the attack, well, the reporting officer thought they were self-inflicted. Don't believe me?' Randall arched a brow. 'Take a look at the photographs, make up your own mind.'

'I will.'

'I'm only giving my opinion from all my years o' service,' he said.

Helen held up the folder. 'I'm going to.'

'I mean, it wouldn't surprise me if it was her that phoned the police. All she would need to do was play a recording down the phone.' He was looking at DI Craven for approval. 'The woman's needing attention, right? Well, think about it, what better way to get it? Her face is going to be in the papers. She had us all running around in circles. I bet she's sitting in some bed and breakfast somewhere laughing at us.'

'Maybe.' Helen didn't remember seeing any medication in the house suggesting that Ella struggled with any mental health issues, and there was also nothing indicating that she had ever harmed herself.

'Do you want to know something else?' Randall said, and sniggered.

'Go on.'

'Even I was called out to see her.'

'When was this?' Helen asked.

'Ach, a few years back.'

'When, exactly? Can you be more specific?'

He made a face. 'Maybe five years ago, maybe more. I thought the name seemed familiar.'

'Why didn't you mention that last night?' Helen glanced at Craven.

'I wasn't sure until now.' He held up his hands in mock surrender. 'You can't expect me to remember all the folk I've ever been out to see, can you? Not when you've been in the police for over twenty years, love. I mean, I'm good, but I'm not that bloody good.'

Helen bit the inside of her cheek. It was too early in the morning to rise to Randall's bait.

'Even you must admit, it's all a bit of a strange set-up. A killer murders her then phones the police?' He scoffed again. 'I bet she'll turn up in a day or two.'

'Let's hope so, but we're still waiting on the forensics from the property.'

'And what about all those newspaper articles?' Randall was looking at Helen as if she was thick. 'And all those true crime books.'

Helen met Craven's gaze. 'If something has happened, I don't want to waste valuable time.'

There was a long silence. 'Fine,' Craven said. 'You've got a couple of days.'

CHAPTER EIGHT

Helen pushed at the door of the smart little boutique on Lothian Road where Ella White used to work, which opened with a tinkle.

'Let's get this over with,' Randall muttered. He flicked his cigarette into a puddle and followed her inside.

Helen glanced around. The shop was surprisingly quiet, the only customer a lone woman at the far end, frowning over the leather handbags.

Behind the counter, a woman with her red hair scraped into a topknot was boxing up hats. 'I'll be right with you.'

Helen held up her warrant card as they approached the woman. 'I'm DS Helen Carter, and this is my colleague, DC Randall. Are you Linda Rosco?'

There was a brief silence as the woman looked them up and down. 'I read about it in the paper this morning,' she said. She was wearing a rich-ruby dress fastened with a gold butterfly brooch. She had pencil-thin eyebrows that made her look angry.

'When was the last time you saw Ella White?' Helen asked.

Linda clicked her tongue. 'Ella was last in on Wednesday.' She paused for a moment. 'Aye, that's right, it was early closing day. Do you know what happened to her?'

'That's what we're trying to find out.'

'Terrible shame. You never believe these things can happen to people you know, it's always just something you read about in the papers. Edinburgh's no' what it was.'

'Was Ella due to come into work the next day?' Helen asked.

'Normally she would've, but she handed in her notice and took her wages. Told me that Wednesday was going to be her last. Left me in a right bind.' Linda turned her attention to a Rolodex next to the till and flipped through it. 'Sorry, I'm short staffed and I've got a ton of orders to get out this afternoon. I've put a notice in down the Labour Exchange, but it's hard to get the right people.'

'Carry on.' Helen leaned against the counter. Most of the clothes on offer here cost more than her monthly salary. She found it surprising that they couldn't get staff. She imagined girls would be queuing up to get a job in here. She would've when she was younger.

'How did Ella seem when she handed in her notice?' Helen asked.

Linda considered this for a moment and then sighed. 'I'm not sure.'

'It'll help us build up a picture of events,' Helen said, and waited.

'Aye, of course. Like I said I didn't really think much of it.'

'How long did she work here for?'

'Six months, give or take. She was a good worker too. I really hope she's OK.' She sounded sincere. 'She paid great attention to detail, was never late, never off sick, although . . .'

'Yes?'

'Well, in the last month things started to change. I suppose that's why I wasn't too surprised that she wanted to move on.'

'Change in what way?'

'She seemed stressed. She stopped going out at lunchtime. Hated being in the shop on her own.'

'Did she say why?'

'I tried asking her a few times but all she would say was that she couldn't tell me. I wish I'd pushed it further.' She shrugged. 'I got the impression she may have been involved in something, you know.'

'Do you mean some criminal activity?'

Linda shrugged again. 'Or she had family troubles.'

'Did she ever mention her family?'

'It wasn't my place to ask. Like I said, she did a good job for me and that was all that mattered.' Her lips thinned.

'Did she give you a reason for leaving, like she'd found a new job or something?'

'All she said was that she needed to get away from Edinburgh.'

'Oh, really.' Randall gave Helen a knowing look.

'Aye. I didn't ask her anything else, it was none of my business. Like I said, I don't pry.'

'Did she mention any friends? A boyfriend maybe?' Helen asked.

'No, sorry.'

'A stalker?' Randall said suddenly.

The woman's eyes widened.

'Just a thought.' Randall shrugged.

'How much were her wages?' Helen asked, with a stern glance at Randall.

'Thirty-five quid thereabouts.'

'Thanks.' Helen took a business card from her pocket. 'If you think of anything else, you can get me on this number.'

Linda appeared to hesitate.

'Anything you can think of might help us, anything at all,' Helen added.

Linda looked down at the card. 'There was one thing, though it's probably got nothing to do with her leaving. She brought her car to work to help me move some stock, and when she pulled out of the space, she bumped into another car.'

'When was this?'

Linda shrugged. 'It was a few weeks ago, a Monday, I think. As far as I could see it was just a bit of paintwork, but the man wanted her insurance details and everything. His car wasn't damaged. It seemed a bit over the top to me.'

'You witnessed it?' Helen asked.

'I saw them talking outside afterwards. I really don't know why he was making such a big deal out of it, though I suppose if the car was his pride and joy it would have upset him.'

'What kind of car was it?'

'I don't know. I'm not good with cars. It was dark green, I remember that much, and dirty. Ella seemed scared, which is why I kept an eye out.' She got on her knees behind the counter. 'Actually, I boxed up some of the things Ella left behind.' She placed a small basket on the table and rummaged through it, retrieving a business card. 'She got this from the driver of the car she hit.'

Helen took it and turned it over in her hands. 'Thank you, this is useful. 'Do you think you would recognise the man again?'

'It's hard to say. He was just normal looking, you know, one of them plain faces.'

'Thanks.'

'I don't know, maybe Ella had a bad marriage or something. It really wasn't my place to ask. She was a nice girl though. All the customers liked her, she was one of them people that never have a bad word to say about anyone.'

Helen noted that Linda had slipped into the past tense.

CHAPTER NINE

This was disappointing. He had scoured all the morning newspapers, but the only mention of Oliver Stanton was a few lines on page seventeen. He carefully cut it out and slotted it into the photo album next to the others and smoothed it down with his thumb. The radio was on behind him but there was no word of the psychologist who had fallen out of a train. Shame. Every so often he tuned in to the police airwaves, but there was nothing there either. Oliver Stanton was well and truly yesterday's news, replaced with strikes and inflation and the mysterious disappearance of Ella White from her home in the north of Edinburgh.

He closed his eyes, picturing the look of wild terror on Stanton's face as he'd known what was coming. God, he had missed this. He stood up, the album heavy in his hands. There were only a couple of empty pages left, and they would be filled soon enough. Then he'd have another book completed, another volume documenting his many successes. Smiling, he slotted the album back on the shelf. There wasn't a lot of time left, so he turned his attention to his Webley. The revolver needed cleaning. After all, a workman is only as good as his tools.

* * *

Randall patted his pockets for his cigarettes as they made their way back to the car. 'I suppose this prang could be a lead. But I still think we're wasting our time. The shop manager even said she was planning on leaving Edinburgh.'

'Right now, any lead is worth following up.' The air felt cool and fresh from the recent rain, and Helen took in a long breath.

'You're the boss,' Randall said, not bothering to hide the tone of sarcasm.

'Fine, it wasn't much of an accident but at least it's a connection to someone that might be angry with her.'

'Clutching at straws.' Randall put a cigarette to his lips. 'It's a big step from someone bumping your car to murdering them.'

'Aye, well, it seems she was running or hiding from someone, so a wee accident like that would be a good way to get her details without being too obvious about it.' Helen handed him the business card. 'There's an address written on the back of it. We can run that and speak to the driver.'

Randall sparked his cigarette and leaned against the car to smoke it. Helen didn't object. It meant not having to sit in a tin can with that stench.

'I've been meaning to ask you. Why did you decide to stop being an electrician?'

'Aye.' The smoke coiled slowly into the air. 'Who told you that?'

'It just came up in conversation, can't reme—'

'It was a long time ago,' he cut in. 'It wasn't for me.'

'What made you want to join the police?' she asked.

'I'm starving.' He motioned to the greasy spoon across the road. 'I could do with a bacon roll.'

* * *

He took the sharp turning into the police station car park, almost sliding on the slippery surface. The revolver in his jacket pocket thumped against the Anglia's door as he did so. Most of the parking spots were empty, the coppers having gone out on their rounds. There was a flurry of activity at the front door, though no one looked over as he drove by. His heart was thudding. There were another couple of cops standing by a van — he even managed to nod at one of them. His gut churning, he took the second left turn, some distance from the building, and parked in a bay next to a battered-looking plumber's van, out of sight of the main entrance.

Safely parked, he took one last look at his reflection in the rearview mirror and smoothed his hair. He was good at this, blending in. He was wearing Stanton's tweed jacket and it felt good on him. He sat for a while watching people come and go, wondering if he would see anyone from CID. After about half an hour, he reached for the map book under the passenger seat and slung it up onto the dash. Everything was set. He took his camera and headed into town.

* * *

'You were right.'

'Say that again?' Helen said with a smile. This made a pleasant change.

'The car Ella had the accident with was reported stolen two months ago, and it hasn't been recovered.' Randall put the radio handset down. 'And if you're driving a stolen car, you're not going to try and claim insurance when you have an accident.'

Helen slotted the key into the ignition. 'You certainly are not.'

'Let's not get ahead of ourselves though, we don't know who stole the vehicle.' Randall bit into his roll and swore as a blob of brown sauce landed on his white shirt. He dabbed at it with his handkerchief. 'We need to speak to the owner of the car,' he said. 'I'll get onto it. It's just a thought, but maybe this car thief used the interaction with Ella to squeeze some money out of her.'

'It's a possibility.' Helen glanced at him as she pulled out into the traffic. 'So, why did you join the police then?'

'The money,' he answered flatly. 'It was good in those days.'

She accelerated forward.

'What about you and young Terry McKinley?' he asked.

'What about him?' It was now her turn to feel caught off guard.

'Well, he's been avoiding you.'

'I don't know about that.' Helen looked away.

'I do. Where to next?'

'Let's pay Ella White's ex-husband a visit, see what he has to say about himself.'

CHAPTER TEN

The man looked to be in his late thirties, stocky with broad shoulders and tattooed forearms and a skull on his left hand. He was carrying a ladder into the building site for a development of a block of fancy-looking flats that, according to sign on the gate, would be finished in the near year. Helen approached him while Randall followed with his hands in his pockets.

'Ernie White?' Helen retrieved her warrant card from her pocket. 'Do you mind if we have a word?'

He eyed the pair of them and slowly nodded. 'What can I do for you, officers?' He placed the ladder against the wall. 'I can't talk long, mind. We're on a tight deadline. Can we walk and talk?'

She slipped her warrant card into her pocket as she explained the circumstances of Ella's disappearance.

He raked a hand through his thinning hair. 'I don't know what to tell you, but I've no' seen Ella for a long time though I really hope she's alright. I didn't even know she was back in Edinburgh.'

'You don't seem so shocked, Mr White,' Randall chimed in.

'Shocked would be the wrong word for it.' He led them into the Portakabin then slumped into a chair and placed his head in his hands. 'You've had a wasted trip.'

'When did you last see Ella?' Helen asked. Randall took one of the plastic seats while she chose to remain standing. The cabin stank of a mixture of fag smoke, sweat and turpentine.

'Ach, at least a year, maybe two. Something like that. We're divorced, we've had no reason to keep in touch.'

'Shocked is the wrong word for it?' Randall asked. 'What did you mean by that?'

He shrugged. 'Well, we got divorced because of all the drama. She'd do anything for attention. It was too much in the end.'

'What kind of things?' Helen asked.

'Ach, trouble seemed to follow us wherever we went. She'd get in fights with the neighbours, could never keep a job. Like I say, it got too much.'

'Do you know anyone who might want to hurt her?'

He shook his head again. 'We were only married six months. We were too young . . . too stupid.'

'We haven't been able to track down any friends or family, do you have their details?'

'Don't know about friends. But she doesn't have any family, her parents died when she was young. She was put into a children's home, but from what she told me, she wasn't the right type to be fostered out.'

'What does that mean?' Randall asked.

He looked grim. 'She's had a hard time of things. They didn't treat her well. I really did feel sorry for her but like I said, it just got too much in the end. I really do hope nothing bad has happened to her.'

'Has she gone missing before?' Randall carried on. 'Maybe disappear for a few days then turn back up?'

'No,' he sighed and his shoulders sagged. 'There's nothing else I can tell you.'

'Thank you, Mr White, if we need anything else, we'll be in touch.'

* * *

'Randall has noticed you've been avoiding me.' Helen found Terry McKinley in the records room again. He had his shirt sleeves rolled up to his elbows and his blond hair looked dishevelled. She pulled out a chair and gestured for him to sit at the table.

He nodded slowly. 'I suppose I have. I . . . I just didn't want to make things worse.'

'I get that, but—'

'I know I've put you in a bind. Thank you for not telling the DI. I know it must've been hard for you. I'll make it up to you, really I will.'

'It's not me you have to make it up to.' Helen drew a shaky breath. 'Like you said, you made a mistake.'

Helen knew both of their jobs could be on the line if the DI found out, and it wouldn't take much for Randall to put two and two together either.

'Still, I didn't think you would.' McKinley shifted in his seat.

'Neither did I.'

He reached out and placed his hand on top of hers. It felt warm. Soothing. He gave her hand a squeeze.

'Don't make me regret this,' she said.

'I won't.'

Helen pulled her hand away. She nodded towards the boxes McKinley had been going through. 'Any progress?' She tried to sound business-like.

'There're ten known criminals with an electrical or electronics background.' He shook his head. 'None of them are violent though but I'll get Uniform to follow them up.'

'Good work.'

'There's another fifteen that have made malicious calls. I'll get that list up as soon as I can. Ernie White is clean too, not so much as a parking fine.'

* * *

When she got back to the CID room, Helen found a note wedged under her Rolodex. 'Mother called — again!' She snatched up the note and shoved it into her pocket. It could wait until after her shift. She knew what it would be about anyway, plans for her birthday. Her mum always made too big a deal out of these things, probably from losing her brother when she was a child. Every birthday, every Christmas, was an important occasion. Although she could be calling to try to set her up with someone, which she'd been doing ever since Helen broke up with Ted. Helen skimmed through her in-tray. Nothing new to deal with, which was a pleasant surprise. She glanced over at Randall. He had a coffee in one hand and a Marathon bar in the other, a pile of reports spread across his desk.

She grabbed her jacket from the back of the chair. 'How did you get on with the stolen car?'

'Uniform spoke to the woman that owned the car. Her name's Agnes Saunders.'

'Could she—?'

Randall shook his head. 'It's a non-starter. She's a pensioner, lives alone. No family. The car was stolen from outside her house.'

'Great,' Helen muttered.

'Aye, she's sixty-eight years old.' He looked down at his notes. 'Really not much to go on. Not long before it was stolen, a workman came round offering to look at her roof. She reckons that was when her keys were stolen.'

'Could she give a description of him?'

'Nope. She's coming in to look at the book of known criminals, but I wouldn't put money on her recognising him.' He went back to laboriously typing a report, two-fingered.

Terry McKinley entered the CID room and smiled at her. Helen could feel Randall eyeing the pair of them.

'Are you thirsty?' Helen asked.

McKinley was clutching a box, eyes wide, like a rabbit caught in headlights. 'Me?'

'Aye. It's been a long day and I need a drink.'

CHAPTER ELEVEN

The bus stopped just short of the block of flats where Helen Carter lived. Very convenient. The sun had gone down, leaving an icy chill in the air. He shoved his hands in his pockets for warmth, his fingers connecting with the cool barrel of the pistol. He stopped across the road from Helen's home.

To his disappointment, there was no sign of life. It was a nineteenth-century tenement block. The dark grey block brought back memories of the slum clearances he had lived through as a child. He recalled the damp, rat-infested Victorian boxes that they were only moved out of when the buildings started to collapse before he was taken away.

The bus merged with the traffic, and the beep of its horn pulled him from his memories. He surveyed the street. Identical flats lined the road on both sides. The flat directly opposite Helen's had a "for sale" sign taped to the window, the lights were on, and the stairwell door was propped open with half a brick. He hesitated. He had no idea how many people might be in the property or who. He headed inside, his hand on the gun.

The front door of the third floor flat opened, causing his heart rate to ratchet up a gear. 'Sorry to bother you, but I noticed your "for sale" sign.' He flashed his best smile.

The woman was in her late forties, he guessed, with badly dyed canary-yellow hair and auburn roots. She stood eyeing him doubtfully, obviously unsure what to make of him.

'My wife and I are new to Edinburgh and we're desperate for a flat in this area.'

'There's viewings tomorrow, could you come back then?'

'I'd love to but we'll be travelling tomorrow. From the outside the flat looks perfect, and as I said, this is the very location we've been looking for a place in.'

She gestured to the camera. He'd forgotten it was still round his neck.

'Photographer, are you?'

'Oh, it's just a hobby.' He stepped back, not wanting to seem intimidating. 'I'm actually a policeman and my wife's a nurse. Anyway, I don't want to make you uncomfortable.'

'I just wasn't expecting viewers you see.'

'I understand though I want to buy somewhere quick. If the flat's still for sale by the time we get back to Edinburgh—'

'Come in, take a look around.'

'Thank you.' He glanced around the hall, which was freshly painted in magnolia.

He stepped over the threshold and was instantly enveloped in warmth and the smell of baking. 'I won't take very long,' he said. 'Do all the flats have the same layout?'

'Yes. Living room is through that way.' She nodded towards a door at the far end of the hallway. 'The bathroom has been recently renovated, the kitchen has all the mod cons, and I can leave the fridge if you want.'

'Do you live here alone?'

She stiffened, suddenly suspicious. 'No. My husband's away on business.'

He smiled reassuringly and pushed open a door to the left. A box bedroom. 'What are your neighbours like?'

'Nice and quiet. The ones downstairs are away on holiday right now.' She came in behind him. 'It's a good size for Edinburgh, this room.'

Good size? The room was crammed with a dressing table, a single bed and numerous boxes.

'We love it here. We're only moving because we need a bigger place. There's good schools and shops right on your doorstep.'

'Good buses too,' he said.

This made her smile. 'Did she not want to have a look around too? Your wife, I mean.'

'No. If I see a flat I like, I'm under strict orders just to go for it.' He frowned. 'Wasn't there a fire in this block?'

'No, that was the next one. There was no damage here, and the other block has all been repaired.'

He stepped over a pile of books and looked out of the window. Carter's curtains were open. He'd be able to get a good view from here.

'It's a good spot to watch the world go by.'

'I can see that,' he said.

He followed the woman to the lounge.

'There's new carpets.'

A three-paned window at the end of the room faced directly onto Carter's flat. 'Do you mind if I . . . ?' He gestured to his camera.

'Go ahead. Nice big windows, always let in plenty of sun in the morning, and it's nice and quiet too—'

'I'm really sorry.' He muttered after he got his photograph.

She looked puzzled. 'You don't like the flat?'

'I don't take any pleasure in this, you know.' He set the camera down and reached for the revolver. 'I'm just doing what I have to.'

She stared at him, uncomprehending, until realisation dawned. Her face contorted and her eyes darted about wildly.

'On a positive note, this flat is exactly what I need.'

* * *

Crack. One of the barmaids clearing the table next to Helen and McKinley knocked over a glass, which fell to the floor and shattered, sending tiny glittering shards over her feet. The revellers around them cheered and clapped. Under the applause, the young barmaid's face was as pink as the rosé Helen had been nursing. She half-rose from her seat to help the poor woman, but was beaten to it by one of the newer officers.

The Cask and Barrel was cheap, cheerful and only a few minutes from the station, so it had become the police's "local". Tonight, the pub was heaving, and the air was thick with fag and cigar smoke.

'So much for the quiet drink,' McKinley said. 'Must be someone's birthday.'

'Or retirement.' Helen smiled. Helen sipped her wine. 'I've needed this.'

'Bad day?'

'Long day.' Helen corrected him. 'Randall thinks Ella White will turn up in a few days.'

'Do you?'

Helen shook her head. 'I mean . . . It's possible.'

'So,' he asked, 'did you see that man again — the one . . .'

'What? From my mum's wedding?'

'Aye, the university professor?'

'Stephen.'

McKinley looked down at this drink. 'Aye, him.'

No. I mean . . . I wanted to, I guess. I suppose we've both just been busy, you know what it's like. Never-ending shifts don't make for a good social life.'

'Suppose not.'

'Anyway, it doesn't feel like that long ago that I ended my engagement to Ted.'

McKinley merely looked thoughtful.

'Truth is,' Helen continued, 'I haven't been sleeping very well these past couple of nights. So I thought it might do me some good to get out of the station for a while.'

'Is it because of the newspaper clipping of your dad?'

Helen's eyes narrowed.

'The one you found in Ella White's flat. I heard Randall talking about it.'

'What was he saying?'

'Nothing much. Just that there were some newspaper clippings and that book in her house, and it seemed to put you on edge.' McKinley looked apologetic.

'I'm sure he didn't put it as nicely as that.' Typical Randall. Any excuse to put her down.

McKinley looked at his pint. 'He said some other things too.'

'I don't want to hear it.' Helen drained her glass.

'Fine.' He reached forward and gave her shoulder a squeeze. 'If you ever feel like talking, you know where I am.'

'Thanks. I'll remember that. It's just this case. It's brought back things I haven't thought about in a long time.'

'Go on.'

'The Button Killer, for a start. For some reason Ella White has an interest in him and his crimes. You know who I mean, don't you? Though he was a bit before your time.'

McKinley nodded. 'He killed ten people before he was caught in the early sixties. They called him that because he used to take buttons from his victims' clothing and some-times, he'd leave a button in his victim's throat. He liked to taunt the police as well.'

'My father was the arresting officer,' Helen said quietly. 'And he probably killed more than ten, a lot more.'

'I read a book about it recently. My mum's into true crime. She's a big fan of that Oliver Stanton — got all his books.'

'Well, it was his book I found in Ella White's flat.'

'It was an interesting read.'

'I lived through it. Interesting is not the word I'd use.'

'Sorry.'

Helen rose from her seat. 'I think I'm going to go home. I could do with an early night.'

McKinley's face dropped. 'It's still early. How about getting something to eat?'

'Another time. All I want now is a hot bath and some sleep.'

'It's a shame what happened to Oliver Stanton. Still, you never know what people are going through, do you?'

Helen stared at him. 'What do you mean?'

'He jumped from a train a few weeks ago. Didn't you know?'

Helen felt like the air had been sucked from the room. 'No, I didn't.' She wasn't a reader of true crime, it was enough living it forty hours a week.

'I think it must've been Strathclyde that was dealing with it. It didn't happen in Edinburgh,' McKinley said. 'Was on the telly though.'

Helen stared at the paper cut on her finger, the one she'd got from the train ticket that fell out of the book.

'What's the matter, Helen? You've gone all pale.'

'What train was he on?'

* * *

'Thought you had gone for a drink,' Randall said. He strolled into the CID room, fag dangling from his lips, clutching a box. 'We've had no luck with the door-to-door enquiries around Ella White's place. Or any of the lists that Terry gave us.'

'I had but I want to check something,' Helen muttered. She shoved an evidence bag of newspaper clippings aside and began leafing through the crime scene photos to find the train ticket.

'Aye.' He sounded bored. 'Two neighbours in the vicinity came forward this evening, reported hearing a piercing scream around the time she went missing but they didn't see anything unusual in the neighbourhood and they couldn't tell which property it came from.' He glanced at her.

Helen sat hunched over the spare desk at the far end of the room, all the evidence from Ella's flat spread out across it. McKinley was down in records. She had a black coffee next to her and took a swig. She'd only had one glass of wine but she didn't want him smelling alcohol on her breath. 'Forensics back, are they?' she asked.

'Not yet. Wait — tell a lie, there is some.' He tapped a folder on his desk. 'Nothing useful though. It's from the phone box they called the police from, but it doesn't give us any leads.' There was a beat of silence. He was watching her intently.

'Have we been able to track down any family or friends?' she asked.

He shook his head. 'Maybe someone will come forward once they see her picture in the paper. Er, found something, have you?'

Before she could answer, McKinley appeared in the doorway, panting. He must have run up the three flights of stairs.

'Sorry it took me so long. They weren't answering the phone, and—'

'What did you find out?' Helen interrupted.

'The train ticket is from the train that Oliver Stanton jumped from Strathclyde are sending over all the information.'

Randall looked surprised. 'What have I missed?'

* * *

It took a couple of whiskies to calm his nerves. He had pulled up a chair by the living room window and was staring at the entrance to Helen Carter's flat. It was just gone ten and there was still no sign of her. He had the telly on just for some background noise and glanced at the screen. More strikes — nurses this time. According to the newsreader, the hospitals were only accepting emergencies. No wonder his work hadn't made the news. It wasn't just the nurses either. The camera panned across the rubbish heaped on Princes Street, rotting in the gutters. He leaned forward. Now that could be useful. He emptied his glass and poured himself another whisky.

* * *

DI Craven stood at the head of the briefing table. 'Oliver Stanton. Fifty-two. Married, no children. Spent twenty years as a psychologist.'

Helen had one of Stanton's books open on table in front of her. Terry McKinley had asked his sister to drop off a pile of his books. Helen looked at the photograph on the inside sleeve. Stanton had his hand on his jaw, in a pose of studied thoughtfulness. He'd been a handsome man, clean cut, with black hair slightly grey at the temples giving him a distinguished look. Strathclyde had also faxed through most of Stanton's paperwork.

'What about a disgruntled patient?' Randall asked. He was leaning back in his chair, arms crossed and the inevitable cigarette in one hand.

'I wouldn't think so,' Helen said. 'According to this, he stopped practising back in 1969.'

'That doesn't mean it's not a grudge. We're talking about nutters here.' Smiling, Randall looked to the others for approval. 'Maybe it was someone who wasn't happy with the treatment he gave them, that's all I'm saying.'

Helen rolled her eyes. 'What do you suggest? How are we meant to find the names of everyone he ever treated.'

Randall ignored her comment. 'I'd never even heard of this Oliver Stanton fella till now—'

'What was Oliver Stanton doing before he got on the train?' Craven interrupted.

'He was speaking at the university on a talk entitled "Getting inside the criminal mind". Strathclyde faxed through their report on the case,' Helen said.

'Well, he certainly managed to do that all right.' Randall quipped.

'What made Strathclyde think he committed suicide?' Craven asked.

'It's not clear from the report, but he had been treated for severe depression in the months leading up to his death. We know his home life wasn't all sunshine and roses, his wife said they had started divorce proceedings.'

'Still.'

'It's not much but he'd been described a benzodiazepine for depression a couple of months before.' Helen flipped to the next page of the report. 'It's odd though — they never found any of his possessions on the train.' Helen had been glad she had delayed her dinner while she looked through the photos of him post-mortem. 'His wife said he'd been carrying his briefcase when he left that morning, and he was wearing a tweed jacket. Neither were found on the train or at the scene.'

'Could the divorce have pushed him over the edge?' Craven asked.

'According to the report, the wife didn't seem to think so.'

'The Button Killer book was his last one,' Craven said. 'It suggests that Mark Landis, who is in prison for the murders, might be innocent.'

Helen scoffed.

'Some of the things he says about the Button Killer though, all the speculation about why he did what he did . . . If the Button Killer wasn't Mark Landis, he could've made the real killer angry,' Craven said.

Helen's mind was made up. 'I don't think he jumped. I think he was pushed. He suffered severe damage to his head. If he'd jumped, I would have expected more injuries to his legs and feet.' Helen had been glad she had delayed her dinner while she looked through the photos of him post-mortem.

Craven scratched at the stubble on his chin. 'What page in the book did you find the ticket in?'

'I don't know,' Helen shrugged. 'I found it on the ground.'

'According to her manager at the shop, Ella White was not on the train. She was working there, all day,' Randall added.

'We need to find out if there is a connection between Ella White and Oliver Stanton.'

CHAPTER TWELVE

Helen was busy, making the most of a rare chance to cook herself breakfast. She cracked a couple of eggs into her frying pan while baked beans bubbled away on the back ring. Sunshine filtered through the net curtains above the sink, and she found herself moving to the music that blared out from the wireless. Humming along with "I Can See Clearly Now", she halved a tomato and dropped it in next to the eggs. Swigging her coffee, she scooped the eggs onto a plate along with the beans. She was no "galloping gourmet", but it would do nicely.

The letterbox rattled. Wiping her hands on her apron, Helen picked up the box that had been left on the doorstep. She brought it into the kitchen and put it on the table.

She recognised the handwriting on the parcel at once. Despite the cooked breakfast, she had almost forgotten what day it was. She let out a sigh. The window above the sink was open a crack, letting in a cooling breeze. She pulled it shut. Turning off the stove, she sat down at the table and opened the box, pulling out a neatly folded bundle of fabric. A dress in tangerine silk. A quick glance at the tag told her it was at least a size too small — it might have fitted her when she was fourteen. She held it up against herself and thrust it back into the box. 'Thanks, Mother,' she muttered. She opened the card attached to the top.

For you to wear on the special day and to go with the shoes xx

At least she could squeeze those on without being charged with public indecency. She shoved them back in the box too.

She sat down at the table, having suddenly lost her appetite. She forced down a couple of bites of egg, then pushed the plate away.

* * *

Determined to have a few moments to unwind, Helen set her hot chocolate on the corner of the tub, sprinkled the last dregs from a box of Radox salts into the bath and lay back in the hot water. Spending most of her day slouched at her desk had taken its toll on her back. This was bliss.

She heard letterbox flap again. *If that's Terry McKinley* . . . She climbed out of the bath, tightened her towel around her and went into the hall. But there was no one behind the frosted glass of the door.

Her gaze fell on a small envelope lying on the carpet. It was white and looked like it could be a birthday card. Hand delivered, no stamp. She opened the front door to see if there was anyone in the stairwell. Silence. She peered over the railings but no one was there.

Helen took the card inside. The corners of her mouth lifted. Most likely it was her mum, a party invitation that had probably fallen off the box, but it couldn't have as she didn't recognise the handwriting. Strange. Heading back to the bathroom, she prised open the envelope with her thumb. Inside, there was a small card printed with a watercolour image of Edinburgh Castle. Helen turned over the card, gasped and dropped it on the floor. Two Polaroids had fallen out of the envelope. Shaking, she ran to the living room and grabbed the phone.

CHAPTER THIRTEEN

Feeling as though the air had been sucked out of the room, Helen rummaged around in the bottom of her wardrobe for her overnight bag. Her suitcase was on top, but it was too big and heavy, and she only planned to be away a night or two anyway. Her washing was still at the launderette, so she could pick that up on the way. She had a set of spare clothes down at the station too, and there wasn't much food in the fridge to worry about.

Bingo. She found it in the bottom of her handbag box. By now, the room was spinning. She sat down hard on the bed with the open bag next to her and tipped the contents onto the carpet. Wasn't much — some French francs, an ancient-looking French phrase book and one of Ted's shirts, which reeked of mothballs. How long had that been in there? Not that he'd miss it. He had more expensive suits than Helen had had hot dinners.

She needed a minute to think about this. She could hear McKinley moving around in the kitchen, and she took a long, steady breath. Slipping off her cardigan, she tried to avoid catching sight of her reflection in the wardrobe mirror. Her hair was a riot, her fringe stuck to her forehead and yesterday's mascara clumped under her eyes. She glanced around the room, at its bare mottled walls, the unmade bed and the stack of cardboard boxes that she had never got around to sorting and, if she was honest with herself, probably never would. The stack of brochures she had collected was next to her foot. Glossy photographs of sunny destinations, winter sun, white beaches and happy couples, *"Book for only £20"* and *"Get away"* emblazoned across them on a big red sticker. She flicked through the first couple of pages and found herself smiling. Malaga before her twenty-seventh birthday, celebrating her move to CID.

Discarding the brochure, she got up and crossed the room. There wasn't much in the chest of drawers, but she pulled them all open anyway. Finally, she threw in a couple of her turtlenecks, trousers, pants, and her nightdress from the back of the chair. That would have to do. She rummaged through her nightstand and chucked in the novel she was halfway through reading and a packet of Polos. Why not? She wouldn't need much, just a couple of tops, trousers, and her art supplies — notebook, watercolour pencils.

The aroma of coffee wafted under the door. She carried the bag to the bathroom and began ransacking the medicine cabinet. *Where the hell did I put the aspirin?*

'You going to be long?' McKinley called out. 'We need to talk.'

'I know. I need . . . I'm just going to have a quick shower.' Helen shut the bathroom door and leaned against it, her head and heart pounding. She couldn't go to the station looking like this. God, how careless she was. She'd opened the door without a second thought. What if there had been someone out there? In the kitchen, McKinley was busy clunking pots and pans. She pulled the plug on her now tepid bathwater and got under the shower, turning the temperature up as hot as it would go. As the warm water ran over her body, she stretched her left shoulder until it gave a satisfying click. She ran her fingers across her ribs, broken during her first case. It had taken a long time, but they finally felt like they had healed.

A knock at the door made her jump.

'What?'

'Do you want anything to eat?' McKinley called out. 'I've cleaned up your breakfast stuff.'

'No . . . and thanks.'

'I found a couple of tins of that salad stuff.'

'If I'm going to start eating salad, it won't be from a tin.'

Dressed, Helen found Terry McKinley in the living room, sitting on the sofa. There were dark patches under his eyes and a couple of days' worth of stubble peppered his chin. He was staring at the envelope, now in an evidence bag on the table.

'I'm sorry I called you the way I did,' Helen muttered, 'but I didn't know who else to turn to.'

'You did the right thing.' He dragged a hand through his dishevelled hair. 'I'm glad you've decided to stay with me.'

'I thought of going to my mum's, but I didn't want to worry her.' She shrugged. 'That, and—'

'You don't want to put her in danger.' McKinley smiled.

'I don't know what to do, Terry.' She slumped into an armchair, her eyes on the photographs. 'He's been watching me.'

'If I hadn't come home with you last night . . .' McKinley said.

Helen picked up the photos. The first one showed her heading into the stairwell on the previous night. 'How would he get my address? He must have followed me home and I've not noticed. How could I not have noticed?'

'Did you see anyone hanging around the crime scene that might've followed you here?'

'No. Anyway, I went back to the station.'

In the second picture a bloody woman who looked like Ella White was lying face down on a bed. Helen recognised her bedroom. 'I need to get to the station.'

CHAPTER FOURTEEN

'So, you have no idea who delivered this?' Craven picked up one of the evidence bags.

'I didn't see anyone.' Helen stood in front of the incident board. Terry McKinley had gone down to the canteen to get her a coffee and something to eat, though she'd said she wasn't hungry.

Craven was perched on the edge of a desk, looking at copies of the letter and photographs left at Helen's door. The silence hung heavy in the air, broken only by Randall talking quietly on the phone, a cigarette in his hand.

Helen jumped when the CID room door opened to admit McKinley. He was carrying a plate holding a selection of cheese sandwiches and chocolate bars. He set them down on his desk, giving her an anxious smile.

'I'd say go home but that probably wouldn't be a good idea,' Craven said.

'Before I came to the station, I asked my neighbours if they'd seen anyone in the stairwell, but no one saw a thing.' It wasn't that surprising — the stairwell door was often left propped open with a brick, meaning anyone could wander in off the street.

'How do you think he got your address?' Craven asked.

Helen shrugged. Her flat was on the other side of town, a good four or five miles from Ella White's place. 'I don't know.'

'Someone is taunting us.' Randall stubbed out his cigarette, got up from his desk and grabbed a sandwich. 'Well you, I mean.'

'Or they're making sure we treat Ella's death as suspicious. If you think about it, there wasn't a lot to see at the crime scene. All we had to go on was that phone call saying there'd been a murder there,' Helen said.

'Why bother cleaning the place up then?' Randall frowned. 'That doesn't make any sense. It takes a lot of effort to move a body and clean up so much blood. It also shows he wasn't rushed, he would've needed to take his time.'

Glumly, Helen nodded. 'All of this speaks of experience and confidence. Whoever did this called the police to that address. They wanted us there, poking around. That's a big risk to take and they were probably watching us. If Ella was murdered, and it looks increasingly like she was, then this is unlikely to have been their first kill.' Helen turned away from the board. 'We are looking for someone who is organised. The neighbour reported seeing someone in Ella's house, so we could be looking at a man who talked their way in. We didn't find any murder weapons at the location, so he probably came prepared.'

'If they are so experienced, what about the blood left in the room?' Randall asked.

'I think that could've been deliberate, you know, dangling a carrot in front of us. Give us enough so we go in and have a look, which is what he wanted.'

Randall didn't look convinced. 'Bit risky, isn't it?'

'Think about it. If no blood was found, we wouldn't have been called in. There were no fingerprints, no forensic evidence we can use. We've been left to stew a while, and now we've got another carrot showing us how smart he is.'

'A smart man would just get away with it,' Randall said.

'He wants to give us a message.'

'What, though?'

'That's what we've got to try and figure out.' Helen turned to McKinley. 'Go to records and pull up any cases where the killer stayed in the house or did a clean-up with bleach, also any unsolved murders.'

McKinley nodded.

'The Button Killer,' Randall said.

Helen stiffened.

'He used to taunt the police. He sent letters, didn't he?'

Helen met eyes with him. 'The Button Killer is in prison and the Button Killer never sent in photographs.'

Before Randall could say anything more, his phone rang.

Helen swallowed. The letter and photographs would go off to Forensics, but she wasn't going to hold her breath that they'd get anything useful.

Randall read out an address. Helen let go of her sandwich. 'Say that again.'

He repeated it, and Helen gasped. 'Oh my god!'

'What?' Craven stared at her.

'That's the flat opposite mine,' Helen said. 'It's directly across from me.'

'Well, there's been a 999 call from that address,' Randall said. 'The caller said that because we haven't stopped him, he's had to kill again.'

CHAPTER FIFTEEN

Helen's mind raced. The murky stairwell looked exactly like hers. She was standing outside a flat on the same level, with the exact same mud-brown door and frosted-glass panel. She could hear voices on the landing above. Randall was speaking to one of the neighbours.

'Are you up to this?' McKinley was behind her, his brow furrowed. How long had she been standing there? 'Maybe you should go back to the station.'

'I'm fine,' Helen muttered. Her pulse was racing and she struggled to take a breath. A sickly-sweet odour hung in the air, coming from the door she was facing.

'You don—'

'I'm fine,' she repeated, too loud.

A forensic officer who was dusting the glass for prints, looked up in surprise.

Helen forced a smile. 'Morning. Is she in here?' Without waiting for a response, Helen walked towards the only door that was open, which she knew would be the lounge. The layout of the flat was identical to her own, only more modern. The walls were a cream colour, and it was missing the fifties' pine wall panels. The same SOCO, Ralph, who had been at Ella White's flat was kneeling next to the sofa. He was

72

wearing white overalls and had a leather doctor's bag open in front of him. She could see part of the victim's leg draped over the arm of the sofa. Her nylons were laddered, her black brogue shoe suspended from her foot. Helen recalled seeing another victim lying just this way. In the crime scene photos from the Button killings.

The SOCO glanced up at her. 'You look like you've seen a ghost.'

'I may have,' she muttered.

McKinley whispered in her ear, 'Did you know her?'

'No.' She cleared her throat. 'So, what do we have?'

'Name's Irene Shultz,' the SOCO said. 'Forty-nine-year-old female found with her arms folded over her chest.'

Helen noticed a length of purple fabric in a large evidence bag. 'What's that?'

'The blanket that was covering her.'

Helen swallowed. 'How long has she been dead?'

'Around twenty-four hours.' He shrugged. 'Give or take a few.'

He got to his feet so that Helen could get a better look. 'She also has bruising on her temple that I'd guess came from the barrel of a gun.'

Helen was about to ask how she died, then saw the ligature mark on her neck.

Irene lay on her back, staring up at the ceiling. She was wearing jeans, a tan-coloured turtleneck and a black woolly cardigan, which had risen up her abdomen. Helen noticed some defensive wounds on the victim's hands and wrists. She slipped on gloves and examined the left hand. Irene had at least put up a struggle. Her manicured nails were chipped in places, and it looked like there could be some fibre under the thumbnail. She turned the hand over. Irene was wearing an expensive-looking diamond ring.

Helen looked at the family photographs adorning the mantelpiece. 'Where is her husband?'

The SOCO opened his mouth but the DI, who had suddenly appeared in the doorway, answered for him. 'He works on the oil rigs. He's on his way back now. And before you ask, robbery wasn't the motive. There's money in the bedroom and the jewellery box hasn't been touched.'

Helen glanced at the ring. She'd worked that one out for herself. 'Point of entry?'

'There's no damage to the door or any sign of forced entry.' Craven scratched at his stubble. 'She let her attacker in.'

Helen gestured to the "for sale" sign in the window. 'The killer could have come to view the flat.'

Craven nodded. 'Probably.'

'Who found her?' Helen asked.

'One of the neighbours. The front door had been wedged open.'

Like with Ella White, the killer had wanted her to be discovered quickly. Helen crossed over to the window and looked out. Straight into her own flat. Had he been watching her? She could see indentations in the carpet where a chair had been moved. It looked like it had been dragged over to the window, within arm's reach of an empty bottle of Highland Park Malt on the windowsill.

'If this is the man who sent you the letter, he could've been watching you for a while.' McKinley had joined her.

Helen turned away. What did this mean? Was Irene lying there dead because of her? Was she the target? Or was she giving her a message – this is what he was planning on doing to her?

'I've found something.' From the urgency in Craven's voice, she knew it was important. Bracing herself, Helen pushed open the door to the second bedroom.

Craven stepped aside. Helen gazed at the bed. Spread across the baby-pink blankets were a scattering of Polaroids. Helen stepped forward and looked more closely — some were of her, others of Irene. He'd caught Irene's face contorted in horror, her blue eyes bulged. She turned them over in silence. Two were of her and Terry McKinley going up her own stairs last night.

'Did McKinley stay the night with you?' Craven asked.

'No.' Helen stared at the image. 'He was at my place for about an hour, I think.'

'Why would whoever did this have an interest in you, Helen?'

Helen threw up her hands. 'I don't know.'

From his expression, Craven didn't seem sure whether to believe her. Not that she cared.

'This is looking like the Button Killer's M.O., isn't it?' he said.

'The Button Killer's in prison,' Helen answered.

Craven shrugged. 'So far, the author of a book about the Button Killer is dead, likely murdered. Another woman is missing, also presumed murdered. What do *you* think?'

'We're dealing with a copycat,' Helen said. 'This is someone that wants the notoriety of being the Button, being Mark Landis. We're looking for someone like Landis — in other words, charming, non-threatening. This is someone women aren't afraid to let into their homes. I'm going to have a look around.'

The SOCO was still working on Irene, so Helen headed into the Kitchen. A forensic officer was at the sink taking photographs.

'What have you found?' Helen asked.

'The remnants of a meal on this plate. Looks like Irene's killer made full use of the facilities while he was here, even cooked himself something to eat.'

'Helen! Get in here,' McKinley called from the lounge. When she entered the room, he was leaning over Irene and had pulled down her cardigan. 'Look, the bottom button is missing. The thread's not frayed — it's been cut off.'

CHAPTER SIXTEEN

Helen had to get away from that flat, out into the street. McKinley tried to stop her, but she brushed him aside. It was drizzling. She started towards her own flat, then stopped herself. Suppose he was watching? Her whole body tingled as though it has been in contact with static.

She glanced up and down the street, pulling her jacket tight around her body. Her ears rang and her head throbbed. The street was rammed with people making their way home, most of them students from the local college. She stepped back. Was he here somewhere, among all these people? She stepped forward, narrowly missing a woman with a pram. A hand grabbed her shoulder. She swung around.

It was Craven. 'You need a break. C'mon, you're coming with me.'

'Just give me a minute.'

He shook his head. 'I'm not asking.' He nodded towards her flat. 'I could do with a drink.'

Helen pulled at a hair that had blown into her mouth. Craven steered her across the road, his hand on the small of her back.

They went into Helen's block. There was a low murmur of music coming from the bottom flat. Craven closed the outside door. Away from the streetlights, the building was dark and gloomy. He trudged after her up the stairs.

Craven stood by the window. From here, they could see that Randall had arrived and was speaking to the SOCO. 'Aye, it's quite a good view from over here.'

Helen nodded. So that's why he had wanted to go to her flat. She was sitting on her sofa clutching a mug of the tea he'd made them.

'So.' He took a long breath. 'Are you going to tell me what's going on?'

There was a long moment of silence. Helen looked into her tea. What could she tell him? The real Button Killer was in prison, she was certain. Whoever this current killer was, he was not the same man.

'Put it this way, if you don't tell me, you're off this case.' He turned back to the window. 'Your choice.'

She cleared her throat. 'Well, I'll have to start at the beginning. My father was put on the Button Killer case when I was around eight years old. It became an obsession with him. He was determined that he'd be the one to catch this man.' She shrugged. 'The Button Killer liked to play games with the police. One of his victims was a neighbour of ours, Carla Jacks, who lived three doors away from us.' Helen had fond memories of Carla, she'd been a sweet woman.

'Bloody hell.'

'My mum was terrified. She and I left after that happened, we went and lived with my aunt for three years.' Helen pinched the bridge of her nose. Her headache was worse.

'I'm not surprised.'

'She couldn't sleep. Couldn't eat. I wasn't allowed out anywhere, not to see friends. Nothing.' It must've been at least a decade since she'd last told anyone about this. She hadn't even told Ted and they had been engaged.

My parents divorced not long after that. We never went back to the house.' Helen put her mug down on the table. She wanted to tell him the rest of it, but she couldn't get the words out.

'Was this around the time your brother died?' Craven asked quietly.

Helen nodded.

'I'm sorry.' He sipped his tea.

The silence hung heavy.

Helen looked down at her mug. She needed time to be alone and to think. She set her tea aside. 'Jack, I want to get back to the station. I need to be out there doing something.'

CHAPTER SEVENTEEN

A couple of hours later, Jack Craven drew to a halt outside his ex-wife's townhouse on the outskirts of Edinburgh. He leaned back against the headrest and caught sight of himself in the rearview mirror, hardly recognising the old man staring back at him. He grunted and glanced over at the house. Only a few years ago they had lived here as a family. It had been their forever home. A "for sale" sign, flapping like a flag in the wind, had been planted on the front lawn. That notice was the reason he was visiting now.

His mouth was dry and he swallowed. He couldn't get the image of that poor woman, Irene, from his mind. If there was a killer targeting homes for sale, Liz too could be in danger, along with his children.

Liz opened the door just as he was about to reach for the knocker.

'I saw you come up the path.' She looked him up and down, then abruptly turned on her heel, leaving him to catch the door.

'Nice to see you too,' Craven muttered. A whiff of her sweet lavender perfume reached him down the hallway.

'What do you want anyway? You said you'd be here hours ago.'

'A case—'

'There's always a case.'

Craven crossed the threshold and stepped onto the Terrano floor tiles. 'Aye, but this one . . . Oh, what's the use?'

Liz had already disappeared into the front room. He closed the door and took a breath. All the art was gone, a couple of nails still protruding from the walls the only proof that pictures had once adorned this house. Cardboard boxes were stacked at the side of the stairs.

'I thought you were going to rent rather than sell,' he called out after her, getting no response. 'How are you, Jack?' he mumbled to himself. 'Well, I'm fine, Liz, aye.'

He found her in the front room, standing before the mirror above the fireplace, putting on her makeup.

'When did you decide to sell?'

'A couple of weeks ago. Didn't want the stress of renting. The kids are upstairs.' She was tapping at her cheeks. 'Do you want a drink? Milton's got some wine in the fridge.'

'I'm fine.' *You won't catch me drinking that muck.* 'Has there been any interest?'

'Some. We've got to move on, Jack.'

'I'm not stopping you.'

She ran her fingers through her sandy hair. She had let it grow out recently and it suited her. 'There's just too many memories.'

He felt out of place here now, didn't belong. He sat on the sofa.

She turned to face him, looking him up and down. 'You look terrible, Jack.'

'I feel terrible.'

Her face softened slightly, there was almost a smile there. Almost.

She slumped on the sofa opposite. 'Jack Junior got in trouble at school.

'What for?' He resisted adding *this time*.

'Fighting. No thanks to you.'

'What do you mean?'

Before she could answer, Milton, his replacement, appeared in the doorway. 'Are we ready?' He frowned. 'Jack. Hello. Didn't realise . . . The kids are upstairs. We've got them Pong, can't get them away from the television now.'

Craven got to his feet. 'I'll go up and speak to Jack Junior.'

'Well, you see . . .' Milton looked like he was searching for the right words.

'What Milton is trying to say is that if Jack is having problems with bullies at school, he needs to speak to the headmaster, not take matters into his own hands.'

So that's what had happened. He had taught his own son to stand up for himself.

There was a long pause. 'About the viewings. Is it the estate agent doing them?'

'What does it matter to you?' She sighed. 'We've talked about this before.'

'There's something I need to tell you.'

CHAPTER EIGHTEEN

Helen's mind was a whirlwind, spinning with thoughts, fragments of memories and, above all, questions. She had her police manual out on her desk, the one her father had given her on her first day on the job. She placed a hand on it. He would've known what to do, he always did.

The CID room was mostly empty, apart from DC Bell, who was going through a pile of reports. Randall had gathered the other officers into the briefing room and for the time being, Helen was happy to let him take charge. She had some of the original Button Killer files next to her, including her childhood neighbour Carla Jacks and eyed them with dread.

'I haven't been able to find any connection between Oliver Stanton and Ella White.' McKinley pulled up a chair and handed her a manila file. 'I've spoken to colleagues of Oliver Stanton and nothing so far. The only thing I could get out of them was how devoted he was to his wife and that he was a very private man.'

'What about the wife? Or ex-wife?'

'She's been out of the country', McKinley shrugged. 'She's due back tomorrow.'

'Good. We need to speak with her.'

'The press appeared at the crime scene after you'd gone.'

Helen swallowed hard. She knew what was coming.

'I heard them say that Mark Landis is protesting his innocence from prison.'

'I know what you're thinking and I haven't said anything to Jim Savoy.'

'I wasn't thinking that.'

* * *

Jack Craven reached into his desk drawer for the bottle of single malt he kept for special occasions, like closing a case. There was no such occasion tonight, he just needed a drink. He poured a glass and sipped, savouring the flavour and warmth as it trickled down his throat. He could see Helen and McKinley deep in conversation at the far end of the office.

He had taken one of the viewing brochures from his old family home. If they managed to sell it, they'd be making a nice profit, amounting to nearly thirty thousand more than he and Liz had bought it for. He glanced at Helen again, then reached for the copy of *Yellow Pages* on the shelf behind him. He found the number he wanted, listened to it ring and was about to give up when a woman answered.

'Good evening, Hornby's solicitors and estate agents.'

'My name is Detective Inspector Jack Craven. My, er, ex-wife has a property for sale on Newbattle road, the five-bed townhouse. Elizabeth Cra— I mean Nairn. Elizabeth Nairn.'

There was no response. He waited, hearing her speak to someone in the background.

'Yes, we have that property on our books but—'

'We're investigating a serious crime and I have reason to believe that the perpetrator could have attended one of the viewings there.'

'Oh, my word.'

'Do you have a list of people who've viewed the property?'

'I . . . I'm sorry, but we can't give—'

'Listen to me. This person is highly dangerous. He's killed and will carry on doing so unless we manage to stop him. I don't think that's something you would want on your conscience, is it?'

There was no response.

'I also imagine it won't be good for business. Now. Do you have a list of the people who have attended viewings?'

'Well, yes. I . . . I have names, but—'

'I'll give you my number. Can you fax them through to me?'

'I can, but, Inspector, we don't check their identification or anything, we just go by the names we are given.'

As soon as he hung up, the phone rang again.

* * *

It was an hour past the end of their shift. Terry McKinley was the first to break the silence.

'Are you coming?'

Helen shook her head. 'I can't.' She gestured to the paperwork on her desk. 'I just want to get through this lot.'

'I can wait.'

'You don't have to.'

'I do.'

'I'm going to go back to my place tonight.'

McKinley was silent for a moment. 'I hope you're joking.'

'You see a smile on my face?'

'I don't think it's a good idea, you know. It might not be—'

'What? Safe?'

'Aye, of course.'

'I'm not going to let some stranger scare me out of my home. I just can't.'

'Helen, he's dangerous. He murdered your neighbour and is probably watching you. 'Why take that chance?'

Helen shrugged. 'What if it takes months to catch him? What if it takes years? Or we don't get him? I'll have to go back to my flat at some point.'

'Aye.' McKinley's face twisted in disgust. 'But not tonight.'

'Terry, I've spent the most of my childhood in hiding, terrified of the Button Killer, and I'm determined never to live like that again.

'I just—'

'I'll be careful.'

'I really don't like this.'

'He's letting us know that he is smarter than us. He's flaunting what he can get away with right under our noses. Anyway, I want to go through my dad's old case notes, see what I can find out about the Button Killer. My dad kept diaries, there might be something in them that we're missing.'

McKinley gave an exasperated sigh. 'I'm afraid you're making a mistake. We know this person is capable of murder, I listened to the phone call. He said he killed again. He's not going to stop — you've even said so yourself.'

Helen looked at the files on her desk. What kind of example would it set for the department? Especially if she wanted to keep the post of sergeant. Randall was just waiting for her to fail, and so far she was doing a good job of playing right into his hands.

'If it's just that you don't want to stay at my flat, why not go to a hotel?'

'Terry, I appreciate your concern. I really do.' But she knew that if this Button Killer copycat wanted to find her, he would, wherever she was.

CHAPTER NINETEEN

Whatever Jack Craven was reading must have been interesting because he didn't look up, even after she knocked, then popped her head around the door. There was an empty glass next to his elbow and she detected a faint whiff of whisky.

'Sorry, boss, is this a bad time?'

He shook his head. 'Take a seat.'

Helen pulled a little hard plastic chair up to his desk, feeling a lot like a naughty school kid. It was just this kind of chair she'd been made to sit on after the maths teacher labelled her troublesome.

He frowned and turned over the sheet of paper he was looking at. 'Liz, my ex-wife, has our house on the market. I've asked for a list of people who've viewed the property. Before you say anything, I am aware it's a probably a waste of time, but it's something.'

'Did you tell Liz?'

Craven sighed. 'Not all of it. I asked her to make sure she's not alone in the house with anyone and to get the estate agents to do the viewings. I didn't want to worry her, but I needed to do something.'

'It sounds like you did the right thing.' She noticed Craven had the crime scene photographs from Irene's house on his desk.

He lifted one of them. 'Are you thinking that could be you?'

'No.'

'Sorry.'

She sighed. 'I'll say it again. Whoever did this is not the Button Killer.'

He looked like he was considering this. 'Did you find out how the information was leaked to the press?'

Craven never was one for beating around the bush. It was one of the things she liked about him as a boss. She got up and moved to the window. On a clear day, you could see all the way to Edinburgh Castle.

'I'm sorry, boss.' She shook her head. 'Maybe whoever did it has had second thoughts. Maybe they've realised the risk to the department isn't worth the cost of a couple of pounds.'

'Let's hope so. I would've bet on it being Terry McKinley,' Craven said.

Helen said nothing. Terry's words about her also profiting from police corruption flashed through her mind. After all, what he had done wasn't nearly as bad — getting drunk and talking too much wasn't the same. People can make a mistake, they can change.

'Helen, I don't think you've heard a word I've said, have you?'

'Sorry.' She dragged a hand down her face. 'Say it again.'

'I was saying that I didn't just want to speak to you about that.' Craven's face was expressionless. 'I've just got off the phone with Jim Savoy.'

Helen's heart sank. Jim Savoy was a bloodthirsty reporter, so whatever this was, it wasn't going to be good. For a start, Savoy was the person McKinley had told too much to. If he had done it again, after all he'd said . . . She groaned inwardly.

'Oh? And what did Savoy have to say for himself?' she asked, trying to keep her tone light and probably failing miserably.

'It's not good.'

'It never is.'

'He was also sent some post this evening.'

'What kind of post?' Though she already knew the answer.

'Savoy didn't get any photographs. He got a typed note. Look.' He handed her a sheet of paper. 'That's a copy, by the way. The original is down in Forensics, hopefully we'll get something back from it.'

Helen was almost afraid to look.

Until the police apologised for imprisoning the wrong man, it read, he was going to keep on killing. Someone would be taken from the streets tonight and they'll be killed unless tomorrow's front page headline gives the correct story — that the wrong person was arrested for the Button Killer murders and the real killer is back.

'Shit.' It was all she could manage to say, and was surprised she even got that out.

'Indeed.'

'The right man is in prison. I'm certain of it.' Helen blew out a breath. 'I mean, I know. My dad put him there.' She looked at the carpet, picturing her parents arguing, her dad locked away in his office, always in a rage.

When she looked up, Craven was staring at her. 'If this is not the Button Killer, who is it and what does he want?'

Helen shook her head. 'Fame perhaps.'

'Then why copy someone else?'

'He was probably around when the Button Killer was terrorising Edinburgh. It would've excited him. He probably wants the same notoriety.'

'Who knows?' Craven said. 'But if it is the real killer from all those years ago, why now? Why suddenly announce to the world that Landis is innocent? It doesn't make sense. And the bigger question is, do we let Savoy run with this or not? If we do, we risk causing panic, and if we don't . . . Anyway, Savoy has agreed to hold off. I don't want to terrify the public over what could be nothing, and I don't want to give this nutter a platform. We can't risk doing something that could put a vicious killer back out on the street. Once we proclaim Mark Landis to be innocent, well, it'll be hard to retract.'

'Suppose he keeps to his word though, Jack? He's threatening to abduct someone this evening and we have no way of telling where he may strike.'

'I know, but if we run it, what's to stop him doing that anyway?' Craven shrugged. 'There's no real right answer here.'

'I'm going to visit Oliver Stanton's wife tomorrow.' Helen hid her trembling hands beneath the desk. 'He's the true crime reporter that fell from the train, and from what I understand, no one knew the Button Killer better than he did.'

'Well, take Terry McKinley with you.'

'What are we going to do tonight?' Helen asked.

'We've managed to get some extra police patrols, and this information has been circulated to all stations. With any luck Uniform will pick him up tonight.'

'Let's hope so.'

'It feels wrong to go home. I feel like I need to get out there and do something.'

'Go home. Get some sleep. You'll be no good to anyone otherwise.'

CHAPTER TWENTY

One of the worst things about operating from an Edinburgh tenement flat, he decided, was the obligatory curtain-twitching old witch who always seemed to be watching the comings and goings. The major positive was that in a block of this size, he was anonymous, just one of the many drifters who stayed for a while and then disappeared. He watched the old witch stroll down the street, dragging her battered old shopping bag and trying to get a look in each window she passed. He wondered where she was going at this time of night, until it occurred to him that he was acting just like her. She disappeared around the corner. Now he could slip out without running the risk of being cornered by her. Everything was ready — bag packed, tyre iron, rope, gloves, knives and bleach. His handgun was in his pocket. Time to go.

* * *

Helen couldn't just go home while a serial murderer was out on the streets. She was in CID, standing next to Terry McKinley, looking out at the nearly empty car park. The killer was in Edinburgh somewhere and she had no idea where. She had brought McKinley up to speed on her conversation with DI Craven. McKinley was looking rather sick.

'Growing up, most of my nightmares were about the Button Killer, Helen muttered. 'I used to think that once Dad caught the Button Killer, my life would go back to the way it was.'

'Did it?'

Helen shook her head.

McKinley snapped his fingers. 'I've just had a thought. I bet Randall will remember some of this.'

'Why would he?'

'He once interviewed the Button Killer — or Mark Landis. For another crime though. A break-in.'

'Really?' Helen raised her eyebrows. 'When was this? He's never said anything.'

'I think it was around five years or so before Landis was arrested for the killings.'

'I wonder why he didn't mention it before.'

'I don't know. He didn't tell me. I found it in one of the reports I was going through.'

'Where's the report?'

'On my desk. He probably forgot, it was a long time ago.'

* * *

When Helen got back to her flat, she double-locked the door and stood just inside it, holding her breath, listening for any sound in the stairwell, any indication that she'd been followed. Nothing. She had been on edge all the way home, watching every car behind her and taking a longer route. The fact that there was someone out on those streets stalking their next victim left her feeling helpless and hopeless.

A thud shook the ceiling above her head. She squealed. Then she realised it was probably her upstairs neighbour slamming his door. From their one conversation, Helen remembered him saying that he worked in a pub. She shook off her boots and dropped her satchel onto the floor. Unsure of what to do next, she peered out of the living room window, looking for signs of anything suspicious, a car that she hadn't seen before.

Nothing. Deserted. She glanced at the phone. It wasn't too late, she could still phone McKinley, get him to come and pick her up, or even to come here. He hadn't been happy about her going home by herself. The water pipes gurgled, and she jumped at the sudden burst of noise. Helen was beginning to regret the marathon sessions of horror movies she and McKinley used to watch.

Noise and light, that's what she needed to take her mind off her fears. She switched on the telly, just to have some background noise, and went to get a glass of wine — a big one. She didn't feel like eating, not that there was much in the fridge anyway. There never was. She glugged the wine and settled herself in the spare room, where she began rifling through the various boxes and crates. Her dad's notes about the Button Killer had to be in here somewhere. He was always so meticulous.

Over an hour and the rest of the wine later, Helen still hadn't found what she was looking for. She stretched and clambered to her feet, peeling off her blouse, which was sticky with sweat. She headed into the bathroom, tossing her clothes onto the floor. She caught a flicker of movement in the misted-over bathroom cabinet mirror and her heart gave a jolt.

She whipped round but there was nothing there. 'Helen, you're being ridiculous,' she muttered, and pulled the shower curtain back. Why had they ever watched *Psycho*?

* * *

He had waited until closing time before getting into his car. It would be easier to pick up the type he wanted then. Earlier, he had seen Helen Carter come home and stand at the window for a while, staring out. He hadn't been able to get too close. He couldn't risk her seeing him — there was a charged second where he thought she had. He liked watching her, and admired the fact that she'd come home alone. It was brave. She was a risk taker like him, and he liked that. A lot.

It took less than ten minutes to drive to Princes Street, the main thoroughfare, and that included a couple of detours to avoid the heavy police presence. They were out in full force tonight. The streets were filling up now as the pubs kicked out. His favourite was not far away, just up on the Royal Mile. The window was down a crack — he enjoyed the cold and the occasional burst of drunken noise and laughter. Two uniformed officers were standing sentry near the pub. He bit down hard. He knew letting the police know his plans would make things more . . . challenging, but this was really a bit much. He took a left turn and was forced to slow for a traffic light.

There she was, exactly what he was looking for, a solitary woman sheltering from the wind at a bus stop. She looked so alone, so scared. She would be perfect. As the lights turned green, she looked up and met his gaze. Pretty. Then he noticed two men heading towards him, so he moved off. Never mind, he'd circle back, and if he couldn't get her, there'd be others. And if he got really desperate, Helen Carter was at home.

CHAPTER TWENTY-ONE

Helen was sitting with her back to the door surrounded by a heap of papers, books, and dusty old folders. She reached for another box and knocked her wine glass over. Thankfully it was empty. Cursing, she started on another diary. She had only managed to flick through a couple of pages when she heard a soft click. Her hand tightened on the notebook as she strained to listen for any other sound. She felt woozy from drinking wine on an empty stomach.

Click. The front door. Someone was there. She heard the creak of the door handle moving and scrambled to her feet. Someone was standing on the other side of the frosted glass. Tall and broad, whoever it was took up the width of the frame.

Helen tensed, looking around for something, anything, she could use as a weapon. The clunk as the lock retreated into the barrel sounded thunderous.

The handle moved down again. Her chest tightened. She took another step forward and opened her mouth, but no sound came out.

* * *

Vera was grateful for the shelter of the bus stop, though if the timetable was to be trusted, she had probably missed the last bus by minutes. The icy North Sea gale rattled the glass panes of the creaking surround and whipped her hair into her mouth, but at least she could rest her rain-sodden body. She slumped onto the bench and wrapped her arms around herself. Mickey would be raging. Raging at the fact she hadn't left hours ago, raging that she was now alone on the streets in the arse-end of town. She glanced down at her engagement ring.

A faint silvery light illuminated the newsagents across the road. It was the kind of light you leave on when you want to give the impression that someone's still there though everyone's long since gone home. The newspaper headlines from the window display were visible from where she sat: *Is the Button Killer back?* Vera shivered. Remembering that she had a packet of fags in her pocket, she sparked one and inhaled deeply. Could she get a taxi here? She stood up.

The noise of a car engine filled the silence and Vera leaned forward to get a look. The headlights, on full beam, flooded the shelter with light. *Mickey, you bugger.* Vera flinched and raised her arm to cover her eyes.

Hang on. Mickey's car was blue but this one was brown. The Mercedes slowed as it passed her and the driver stared out. Yes, he was looking at her. Her stomach clenched. When he passed her a second time, still eyeballing her, she knew she was in trouble.

She clutched her handbag to her thumping chest. As soon as he was out of sight, she stood, ready to make a run for it across the road. A loud squealing of brakes stopped her in her tracks. *Thank God!* The bus was stopping to let passengers off at the top of the road. Once it was moving again, she waved frantically, making sure the driver saw her. The doors hissed open at her stop and, sighing with relief, she climbed on. Inside, it was deserted apart from the driver.

'Oh, am I glad to see you.' She fumbled in her handbag, looking for her purse. It was in here somewhere.

'Almost missed you.' He smiled. 'Don't worry about that.'

The driver didn't move until she had taken her seat, down at the back. Rain misted the windows. She wiped the condensation away with her sleeve and peered out, making sure she wasn't being followed.

CHAPTER TWENTY-TWO

Helen was curled up in her armchair, trying to get her breath back. 'What are you playing at, Terry? You scared the life out of me.'

'Sorry.'

'You could've given me a heart attack, you know.'

'Sorry.'

'Stop saying sorry.'

'The last thing I wanted to do was scare you.'

'Funny way of doing it,' Helen scoffed. 'Why didn't you just knock?'

'I thought you might be hungry.' He placed a bag containing two newspaper bundles on the coffee table. 'Sorry, I wasn't thinking.'

Helen closed her eyes for a minute. She recalled having given Terry a key to the flat not long after she had started in CID. It felt like such a long time ago now, another life.

'I thought that if you were sleeping, I would just lie on the sofa. I couldn't leave you alone, Helen. I know you wanted to be, but suppose something had happened?'

She rubbed her tired eyes. 'I don't mean to sound ungrateful, Terry. She looked up at him. He was smiling.

'You should have seen your face.'

Helen rolled her eyes.

'Anyway, I got a taxi here, so you can give me a lift to the station in the morning.' He set a heavy-looking leather bag down onto the carpet.

'What's that? Your overnight bag? Exactly how long are you planning on staying?'

His smile broadened. 'Long as you like. No, seriously, like I told you, my mum was a massive Oliver Stanton fan. I've got his whole life in this bag. I knew you'd be looking through your dad's case files anyway, so I thought if you were still awake, we could go through everything together. Plus, I knew you probably hadn't eaten.'

Helen's stomach rumbled. She took one of the bundles from the bag. 'Did you remember the salt? Sauce?'

'Aye, got them to put extra on.'

She wasn't going to admit it to him, but she would sleep better knowing he was here.

* * *

The bus had taken Vera most of the way home, but then it was another half-hour walk. She couldn't shake the impression that there was someone behind her. She kept glancing over her shoulder but even though she saw nothing, it didn't ease the feeling of being watched.

She yanked open the phone box, which thumped shut behind her, pressing her up against the shelf. She grabbed the receiver, noticing a man walking towards her, head down and hands in his pockets. She dialled Mickey's number and let out a sigh when he finally picked up.

'Mickey, it's me.' She squinted, trying to see through the grimy glass.

'Where the hell—?'

'Rehearsal ran over.' Vera pressed the receiver to her ear, struggling to hear his voice. She couldn't focus on the words. She shuddered, thinking about that Mercedes driver and his creepy eyes. She looked around. All along the road the streetlights were out, and it didn't help that the only nearby building was a boarded-up church.

'Be careful.' She could hear the unease in his voice. 'I knew I should've picked you up.'

'Can you come and get me?' She read out the address from the phone box. 'I'm sorry I walked out this afternoon.'

'Stay there. I'll—'

'Oh, no.' Vera's breath became ragged. Outside, the Mercedes slowly rolled up to the kerb. 'It's him.'

'Who?'

Vera's throat tightened. 'The man. The one in the car.'

'What man? What's he doing? Vera!'

'I don't know, I . . .' She watched the car come to a stop opposite the phone box. The engine died. She flinched as the full beams went on, flooding her in bright white light. She held up her hand to shield her eyes, blinking away spots.

'Vera. What's going on?'

'He's stopping.'

'What does he look like?'

'I can't see. He has his lights on full.'

'Hang up and call the police.'

'I'm scared.' Despite the cold, her forehead was slick with sweat and her pulse sounded like it was drumming in her ears. If another car came along, she would flag it down, that's what she'd do.

'I'm coming straight over to get you.'

'Hurry.' She heard the creak of the car door opening, sending her plummeting back into darkness. The road was wide, flanked on both sides by overgrown bushes and weeds. There was a house with its lights on at the end but it was a long way to run. Especially with this stupid skirt that held her knees together, and her boots with their heels. The dial tone sounded in her ear, and she dropped the phone. He was walking towards her, something bulky dangling from his neck. A camera.

Her legs trembled. The man was now standing across the road with his hands on his camera.

She lifted her handbag from the metal shelf and slung it over her shoulder. The snap of the shutter echoed in the silence.

CHAPTER TWENTY-THREE

'Any luck?' Terry McKinley was wiping his hands on a napkin.

Helen shook her head. She had demolished her fish and chips. They were exactly what she'd needed. She hadn't realised how hungry she was. In between mouthfuls, she had managed to find some of her father's old Button Killer case notes. Typically, they'd been buried under other boxes at the very end of the room.

There wasn't as much as she'd expected. She recalled the stacks of case boxes that used to be in her father's office, piled on the floor and covering the desk. *Where had they gone?* Helen groaned.

McKinley looked like he was thinking about what to say. 'Your mum couldn't have got rid of them, could she?'

'Well, she wanted them out of the house, but . . . No, she wouldn't do that.'

'When my dad left, my mum burned everything of his. Mind you, he did run away with his secretary, leaving my mum in the lurch.' He'd also left Terry with the responsibility of looking after his younger sisters while his mum went out to work. She knew it had been hard on him. He'd missed out on a lot, never had a proper boyhood.

'I hate asking but I need to know.' McKinley cleared this throat. 'Did you tell the DI about, er, well, what happened with Savoy and me?'

'No. But that doesn't mean I won't,' she said. 'You know what the DI's like, he won't give up till he has an answer.'

He nodded slowly.

'I know what it's like to have made a mistake.' She did, having pretty much decided to carry on working in the police to make up for the backhanders her father took. 'He suspects it's you.'

McKinley's eyebrows shot up.

She gestured to one of Oliver Stanton's books. 'We've got bigger fish to fry right now.'

'Of course. Changing the subject, I've got something I've been meaning to give you for ages.' He reached into his jeans pocket.

'Screwdrivers?' Helen took the two tiny screwdrivers attached together on a hoop.

'They're also a keyring. Multipurpose and useful.' He smiled. 'Call it an early birthday gift. Now you have no excuse for not doing the shelves in here and getting the place in order. And if you're going to move house, they'll come in handy.'

Helen smiled. It wasn't that long since she'd been preparing to move into Ted's house, so she'd let a lot of the things that needed doing here slip.

She clambered to her feet and balled up her fish and chips wrapper, getting to the door just as the telephone in the living room rang.

* * *

Randall was coming back from the canteen when he heard a shrill cry at the far end of the corridor. He hurried towards it. As he got to the foyer, one of the double doors burst open and a dark-haired man bounded in. Wild-eyed and panting, he grabbed Randall's arm. 'You a copper? You need to help me.'

Randall pulled his arm away. 'What's wrong, son?' He noticed a car outside, parked at an angle with its lights on and the driver's door open.

'You've got to find her.'

'No, I don't *got* to do anything, son.' He looked the lad up and down. He was in his early twenties, dishevelled, in old, paint-spattered jeans and an orange shirt. 'Calm down. Who are you looking for?'

'My Vera.' He ran a hand through his hair. 'She's gone.'

Randall caught a faint whiff of lager on his breath. 'Have an argument, did you?'

'No, we bloody didn't.'

'I'm sure she'll be home soon enough.'

'No,' he spat through gritted teeth. 'She called me from a pay phone and asked me to pick her up, but as we were talking, she suddenly said there was a man, he was watching her. When I got there, she was gone.'

'Right. Well, she probably got tired of waiting and—'

'No! She wanted me to pick her up. Said there was a man. She sounded really scared. Listen to me. He's got her, I know it.'

'When was this?'

'About fifteen minutes ago. When I got to the phone box I found this.' He pulled out a Polaroid from his back pocket. 'It was just lying there on the shelf.'

Shit. Randall headed for the counter, the lad following. There wasn't much chance they'd get fingerprints off it now. He lifted an evidence bag and gestured for the lad to drop it in.

The photo showed a young woman in a phone box, clutching the handset. She looked terrified.

'You look at that and tell me nothing bad has happened to her.'

Randall nodded. 'We don't know for certain that anything has, all right? What's your name?'

'Mickey. Mickey Armitage.'

'Right, Mickey, come with me.'

102

CHAPTER TWENTY-FOUR

Less than an hour later, Mickey was sitting in Interview Room Two, the only one in the station that actually had a window. He looked up as Helen entered. His hands were trembling and his eyes were puffy.

He sniffed. 'If only I'd picked her up from her class as I normally do, none of this would have happened.'

'If you don't mind me asking, why didn't you pick her up tonight?' Helen asked, taking a seat opposite him.

'I was tired. I've been having to do a lot of overtime. Pathetic excuse, eh?'

'It's understandable. It's hard when money's tight.'

'Aye. We're meant to be getting married next month.'

Helen's lips thinned. She slipped out a photograph of Ella White from the file. 'Do you recognise this woman?'

His eyes widened. 'I don't know her that's the woman from the papers that's gone missing. Vera doesn't know her either.'

'Thanks.'

'She's dead, isn't she? I'm going to have to tell her mum, how can I do that?'

'We don't know that, and I assure you, we're doing everything we can to find her, and I'll help you but first I need you to answer some questions.'

'Okay,' Mickey relented. 'What do you want to know?'

'How long had she been going to the college?' Helen asked.

'A year, maybe a little more.'

'Does she have any friends in the class?

'A few.'

'What course does she attend?' Helen put her drawing pad and pencils on the table.

'Acting classes.'

'Had she ever mentioned anyone following her before?'

'No, but then I always picked her up.'

'Can you think of anyone who might have a reason to hurt her?' Helen asked.

'No. This is all my fault. I need to get back out there and look for her.' He half-rose from his seat.

'You mustn't blame yourself. None of it is your fault. We are doing everything we can to find Vera. We have officers going door-to-door, and speaking to everyone in the area. The best thing you can do is stay here and help me build a picture of Vera's last known movements. Will you help me do that?'

Mickey nodded.

'When you spoke to Vera on the phone, she gave you a description of her potential attacker. We need to get that down on paper.'

'Are you an artist then?'

'I am.'

'I don't know if I can.'

'Yes you can. Take it slowly. I want you to tell me, word for word, everything that Vera said to you and I'll draw an image from it, one that we can put out on the telly and in the newspapers. It might jog someone's memory.'

CHAPTER TWENTY-FIVE

Back at her desk, Helen surveyed the black-and-white pencil sketches she'd made. One had the suspect sitting in his car, looking out of the window, and another showed him standing holding a Polaroid camera. With a sigh, she pulled open the pedestal under her desk and rummaged around in it for her packet of Polos. She noticed the old note asking her to call her mum, which she still hadn't done. She also needed to ask her about the missing Button Killer files.

McKinley came into the room and made a beeline for her desk. 'No cars matching Mickey's description have been reported stolen.' He peered over her shoulder at the flyer. 'You going to go to that?'

She jammed the leaflet into her pocket. 'Might do.'

'These are good.' He picked up one of the sketches she had done of the man in the car. The one she thought might be the most effective showed him looking out of the driver's window and holding up a Polaroid camera.

'We should send these to all the local photography groups,' McKinley said. 'Then there's the college, of course. Maybe we could show them to the photography students.'

'That's what I was thinking.'

'I know these aren't witness sketches, but don't you think they look at bit like your ex?'

'Who, Ted? Maybe vaguely but then again, they also look a bit like Randall or even you if you darkened and cut your hair a bit.'

'Aye, I suppose you're right.'

Helen grabbed her jacket. 'Where are we with the Forensics from Ella's place?'

'I got the report back on the shoe print found at the window. A male size eight training shoe,' he said.

'What make? Could they tell?'

'Couldn't get anything definitive on that.' McKinley blew out an exasperated sigh. 'The print was saturated with rainwater.'

'What about the bloody thumbprint found in Ella's bedroom?'

'Yes, we got that. All the blood found in the bedroom is the same — type O.'

'Do you know if Randall had any luck tracing the plastic sheeting that was found in the flat?'

He shook his head.

Helen sighed. 'Did Ella ever attend the college?'

'Not as far as we can tell. I haven't been able to find any connection between Vera and Ella.'

* * *

Helen hesitated for a moment, then pulled open the heavy door to the phone box Vera had called Mickey from. McKinley waited outside, gusts of wind whipping at his jacket. He always seemed to wear one that was at least a size too big. Maybe it had belonged to his father. Helen stood facing the telephone and closed her eyes, trying to get a sense of the place Vera was taken from. A faint smell of diesel lingered in the air. The phone box felt claustrophobic but at the same time the whole length of the person inside was exposed. Anyone in the road or car park opposite would be able to see exactly who was there and what they looked like. Helen rested her hand for a moment on the scratched metal shelf the Polaroid had been left on.

McKinley pulled open the door. 'Come on, it's bloody freezing. Let's go and have a look at the car park.'

The car park had served an abandoned factory that looked as if it had been destroyed by fire. Rubble and shrapnel lay strewn across the ground. They stopped where they had the best view of the phone box.

'He probably parked around here,' McKinley said.

'You wouldn't be visible from the road either,' Helen said.

'We've been door-to-door.' Randall was standing with his hands in his pockets, his face red from the cold. 'Big fat waste of time. No one heard or saw anything.'

'Surprise, surprise,' McKinley muttered.

CHAPTER TWENTY-SIX

Vera and Mickey's address turned out to be a top-floor tenement flat in the Easter Road area of Edinburgh. It was around a mile from the phone box Vera had called from.

Looking grim, Mickey had let them in and was now standing, arms crossed, gazing out of the kitchen window. A cup of tea stood untouched on a table beside him.

Helen felt the kettle with the back of her hand. It was stone cold. 'Would you like me to make you another one?'

He shook his head. 'She's been gone the whole night. She must be terrified.'

'We're doing everything we can to find her,' Helen said.

'I can't imagine what she's going through.' Mickey swallowed. 'Do you think he might've left the photo to tell us she's still alive?'

'Possibly.'

'Well, why else?' He asked her but his face to Helen. He already knew the answer.

'I'm going to have a look around the flat now,' she said. 'Is that all right? We'll be as quick as we can.'

'Why look around here? I haven't done anything with her.'

'The more we know about Vera, the better chance we have of finding her.' She started towards the doorway. 'Just one other thing. Have you or Vera had any post from someone you didn't know?'

He shook his head. 'No.'

'Any telephone calls?'

'No, there's been nothing.'

'Thank you. We'll try to be as quick as we can.' Helen paused. 'Do you have anyone who can come and stay with you? I can call them for you if you like.'

Another shake.

Helen found Terry McKinley in the bedroom. It was only a one-bed flat with barely enough room to swing a cat. 'Have you found a diary or anything?' she asked, keeping her voice low. She glanced around, looking for any clue that might tell them why Vera in particular had been taken. She also wanted an insight into Vera's life and whether she had any connection to Ella or Irene.

There was nothing anywhere in the flat to suggest that she hadn't been happy. Smiling photographs of her and Mickey on various holidays and outings adorned the mantelpiece and the walls. The bedroom was barely big enough for the bed and a pine chest of drawers in the corner. The space above the latter was taken with makeup and perfume. Helen rummaged through the drawers. There was nothing in them but clothes, a couple of paperback novels, and another photo album, again containing more pictures of a smiling, happy young woman.

'Any luck?' McKinley asked.

She shook her head. Next, the living room. It was smallish, not that different from her own. There were books about acting techniques on the bureau. Helen flipped through them. The top drawer was full of theatre ticket stubs. Stomach churning, Helen thought of the warning they'd received, describing what would happen if they didn't run the story. McKinley lifted a photograph from the shelf.

Mickey appeared in the doorway. 'You're wasting your time here. You should be out looking for her — there's nothing in this flat that can help.' He drew in a shaky breath. 'If you're looking for evidence that I did something to Vera, you're putting her life at risk. Somebody's taken her, and you need to find him.'

'We have plenty of officers out there looking for him, I can assure you. We're just trying to make sure we don't miss anything.'

'What do *you* think the photograph meant?' Mickey said. 'Why did he leave the Polaroid in the phone box?'

He's taunting us. He wants us to know it's him that's taken her. 'I don't know,' Helen said.

'I can't get it out of my mind. She looked so scared. I've never seen her like that before.' He sniffed. 'Are you any closer to finding that other woman?'

'Not yet.'

Mickey nodded towards the telephone. 'I've been waiting here in case he calls.'

Helen smiled a little.

'You don't think he will, do you?'

Helen blew out a sigh. 'I think if he was going to call, he'd have done so by now.' She noticed a pile of college brochures lying on the windowsill, all for places outside Scotland. Helen leafed through them.

'I know what you're thinking,' Mickey said, watching her.

'Oh? What's that?' Helen said.

'You're thinking that maybe I've hurt her so she can't go to one of those schools.'

Helen shook her head. 'We're just trying to get a better understanding of Vera's last movements.' She didn't want to tell him that she had nothing else to go on, or that they had no clue as to who had taken Vera. 'Thanks, Mr Armitage, we'll be on our way now.'

'Do you think he is involved?' McKinley asked, once they were out of the flat.

'No.' Helen took her car keys from her pocket. 'He looks genuine to me, and how would he know to leave a Polaroid photograph? That information wasn't released to the press.'

'Aye, I was thinking that.'

'Plus, she left her class at half past nine and by ten forty-five he was in the police station — it didn't give him a lot of time to work with.'

'Suppose not,' McKinley said.

She started the car. 'Let's go to the college.'

'Why her though?' McKinley said, echoing Helen's own thoughts.

'Maybe she was just in the wrong place at the wrong time.' Helen released the hand brake and pulled away.

CHAPTER TWENTY-SEVEN

The college drama teacher was a woman in her late fifties, dressed in a loose-fitting black jumpsuit. Her silver hair was wrapped in a scarf and she had a pair of reading glasses on a gold chain around her neck. She put her hand to her mouth when Helen flashed her warrant card.

'I couldn't believe it when I heard the news this morning.' She ushered them towards a circle of chairs. 'You don't expect someone to leave your class and not get home. It's terrible, just shocking.'

'Why don't you take a seat?' Helen pulled out a chair. 'Did Vera attend class on Tuesday?'

'She did.'

'How was the class? Do you teach a lot of students?'

'There's about fifteen,' the teacher said. 'It's a good group, and they all work well together.'

'So, they all get along?'

'I'd say so. I mean, I don't know what they get up to when they're not here.'

Helen looked back at her notes. 'Have you ever seen anyone around the college that didn't belong?'

'A lot of people come and go around here.'

Helen showed the teacher her sketch. 'Anyone who looks similar to this, for example?'

The woman stared at the drawing for a good few seconds, then shook her head. 'Doesn't ring any bells. Sorry. I've never seen anyone acting suspiciously, and none of the students has mentioned anything either. I mean if I had, I would have reported it.'

'I understand. How was Vera doing in the class?' Helen asked.

'We're preparing for our annual play, this year it's *A Streetcar Named Desire*. Vera is talented, I thought she would probably be chosen to play Blanche.'

'Do you work with any photographers — for the publicity for your plays, for example? Anyone who might resemble that picture?'

'No, sorry.'

'Is there anyone in the class that she is particularly close to?'

The teacher shrugged. 'I don't think so.'

Helen handed her a business card. 'If you do think of anything, let me know.'

The teacher hesitated. 'Well, I know there was a bit of trouble with the boyfriend.'

'Oh? How so?' Helen asked.

'It was only once and a while ago, but I saw them arguing after class. I have no idea what it was about.'

Helen and McKinley thanked the teacher and left.

'Well, that was a waste of time,' McKinley muttered. 'I still think Vera was just in the wrong place at the wrong time.'

'That makes it all the harder. We have no idea where to look or what to do, and time is running out.'

'What do you think he'll do?' McKinley asked.

'I think he will hurt Vera. Our only hope is to find her before that happens.'

'Helen?' Someone called out from behind her.

Helen glanced over her shoulder to see Stephen, who she had met at her mum's wedding. She had offered to show him around Edinburgh, but had never seemed to find the time to do it, or call him back.

'How are you?' He looked her up and down. 'It's good to see you again.'

Before she could answer, McKinley tapped her on the shoulder. 'I'll head back to the car.'

She gave McKinley a nod and waited until he disappeared down the corridor to speak. 'Sorry I didn't call you. It's just—'

'You don't need to explain.'

Stephen was somewhere in his late thirties, tall with short brown hair. He was wearing a tightly fitting suit that emphasised his broad shoulders. She could tell by the stitching that it was tailored. 'I know how these things are.'

'I still would like to though.'

'What? Explain?'

'Show you around. We could have a drink somewhere.' She could certainly use the distraction.

He smiled broadly. 'I'd like that. I really would.'

'I thought you worked at the university. I didn't expect to see you at the college.'

'Ah, I need the extra income.' He smiled again. 'I'm saving for a trip.'

'Anywhere exciting?'

'I'm not sure yet. Have you got any recommendations?'

They meandered towards the exit along the by now mostly deserted corridor.

'I saw a photo of you in the *Evening News*. You were at a crime scene.'

'Really?' Helen felt her cheeks warming. 'That happens from time to time.' She changed the subject. 'It's history you teach, isn't it?'

He nodded. 'For the most part.'

She noticed that his knuckles were scratched. 'How did you get those?' she asked.

114

'I was taking part in an archaeological dig.'

'Oh yes? Whereabouts was that then?'

He raised his eyebrows. 'Are you ever off duty?'

'Sorry,' Helen murmured. 'It's a habit. Comes with the job.' She gestured to the red Mini. She could see McKinley in the passenger seat. 'That one's mine.'

'Well, I hope you manage to solve the case, it was a nasty business.'

'Where's your car then?' Helen asked.

He laughed. 'I'm a teacher, I get the bus.'

'Can I give you a lift?'

'It's fine. Believe it or not, I actually enjoy riding on the bus.' He held up his hands. 'Seriously, it's my wind-down time. I have a book on Chichen Itza I'm looking forward to starting.' He stood regarding her, biting his lip. 'Um, I don't suppose . . . I mean, do you fancy going for a drink tonight?' He glanced towards McKinley. 'When you get off your shift?'

'I can't. Not tonight anyway.'

'Of course. Well, if you ever find yourself at a loose end . . .'

'I'm having — My mum makes me have a birthday thing.' Helen rolled her eyes. 'I don't know if you're free then?' Helen bit her lip, why did she have to mention that?

'Maybe . . . I—'

'Why don't I give you a call later?'

* * *

McKinley was putting the radio back on the receiver as Helen climbed into the car. 'We can eliminate Mickey. The telephone records show he did take a call from that phone box.'

She had thought as much.

McKinley glanced at her. 'He seemed nice. You never mentioned you knew a teacher at the college.'

'I didn't know he was one — at the college, I mean.'

'Is that the man from the wedding?' he asked.

Helen nodded. 'We'd better get back to the station.'

CHAPTER TWENTY-EIGHT

Back in the CID room, DC Randall was standing next to the window, gazing out through the grime and absent-mindedly stirring his coffee. He didn't seem to notice her come in. 'What's so interesting out there?' Helen asked as she slipped off her jacket.

Randall turned towards her. 'There's a car.'

'Well, it is a car park.'

'It's no' the fact that there's a car there,' he said. 'It's that it's been there two days now, and it's not one of ours.'

'Hmm.' Helen slotted her statements into the wire rack on her desk and leaned back in her chair.

'I'm going to run the plates,' he continued.

'Do you think that's really necessary?'

The trill of the phone cut through the office. Helen snatched it up, while Randall went back to staring through the window.

Helen listened for a few moments and then cupped her hand over the receiver. 'That car's going to have to wait,' she hissed and hung up. 'Why is Albert List in custody?' she said to Randall's back.

Randall placed his mug on the windowsill. 'Oh, that. The DI brought Worzel Gummage in for interview.'

'What for?'

'I had some concerns.'

'What kind of concerns?' Helen asked through gritted teeth.

'Turns out he's a budding author. The DI went to speak to him and found a couple of notebooks in his house.'

'What kind of books?'

'See for yourself.' He pointed to his desk, where Helen could see a couple of leatherbound books wrapped in plastic. 'It's no' Charles Dickens.'

Helen flicked through the pages. 'Quite the story. Graphic too.' The book seemed to consist of page upon page of descriptions of murders, all scrawled in smudged ink, and most of it badly spelled with sentences that led nowhere.

Randall grunted. 'It's not the best reading.'

'Do you think he's the person we're looking for?' she asked.

Randall shrugged. 'He lived next door, he had the opportunity, knew the victim.'

'Is her car still missing?' Helen asked.

'Aye.'

'He doesn't have a driving licence though.'

Randall shrugged. 'Doesn't mean he can't drive. We also found a load of old cameras in his house.'

'Polaroids?'

'No.'

Helen didn't find it surprising that they'd found cameras in the house — the man was a hoarder. With a dismissive gesture, she sat at her desk and dialled her mum's number, which rang out.

* * *

List was in Interview Room One sitting beneath the harsh, clinical strip lights. Their low hum filled the silence. He didn't look up when she entered.

'I'm not saying anything more without my lawyer.'

'That's your right, Mr List. But all we're asking is for you to help us and answer a couple of questions.' Helen pulled out a seat and sat facing him.

Craven remained standing, back against the wall. 'The solicitor will be here any minute,' he said. 'But if you've got nothing to hide, we shouldn't need to wait.'

'I haven't done anything.' List addressed his words to Helen. 'You have to believe me. My lawyer told me not to speak without him.'

'Why do you feel you need a solicitor if you've done nothing wrong?' Craven asked.

'I don't want to be blamed for something I didn't do.'

The door creaked. 'Apologies for the delay. Traffic was a nightmare.'

Helen straightened in her seat. She didn't need to look at the man who'd entered, she'd know his voice anywhere.

'I hope you aren't badgering my client. He's been through a lot.'

'Wouldn't dream of it. We were just offering him a drink,' Craven said.

Helen took a deep breath. She hadn't expected to see him again, and certainly not on the opposite side of the interview table.

His chair scraped as he sat down. Helen continued to stare at the table. Her head spun and she could feel his gaze upon her. After a moment or two, she forced herself to look up and meet his smile. 'Ted.'

'If drinks are on the go, I'll take a coffee.' he said. With a click, he opened his briefcase and sorted through the papers. His brown hair was styled and freshly trimmed, and his skin had a glow that spoke of a recent holiday. He was dressed in the pinstriped suit that Helen knew was his favourite.

'I'll go. Could do with the air,' Craven muttered.

The door slammed shut.

'We can continue the interview when Detective Inspector Craven returns,' Helen said to List.

They waited in a strained silence. When Craven returned with coffee, Helen slid the notebooks across the table. 'Why didn't you tell us about these?'

List gave a small shrug. 'They're just stories.' He looked at Ted. 'They're private.'

'What if they're not just stories? What if these are diary entries?' Craven tapped the cover of one of them. 'Hundreds of pages about murder.' He sucked air in through his teeth. 'I'm thinking writing about it wasn't enough after a while. You wanted to experience it in reality.'

'No. I just write things, I don't think about it, I just write what comes into my mind. I'm no' harming anyone.' List blinked back what looked suspiciously like tears.

'They're very detailed,' Craven said.

'Aye, well, I go to talks and that, and I read stuff.' List shrugged. 'I also watch a lot of telly.'

'Did you go to the talk Oliver Stanton was hosting?' Helen looked down at her notes.

'No, I've never met him before.'

'Quite a dark imagination you have,' Craven said.

'That's not a chargeable offence, Detective.' Ted interjected. 'Now, do you have any reason, apart from some made-up stories, for detaining my client, who, may I remind you, has been forthcoming in his responses to all of your questions. If that's all you have . . .' Ted pushed back his chair, preparing to stand.

'I told you I saw someone with Ella the night she . . .' List looked pale and waxy now. 'It's him you should be after, not me.'

'You keep saying you saw a man, but you can't give us a description of him.' Craven snorted. 'That's hardly something we can go knocking on doors with, is it?'

Helen's throat was dry. If Ted felt strange at seeing her again, he wasn't showing any sign of it. He seemed to be enjoying himself.

'Talk me through the last time you saw Ella,' Craven said.

'I don't know, I—'

But Craven gave him no time to reply. Instead, he slapped the Polaroid onto the desk. 'Recognise this?'

List recoiled, almost tipping his chair over.

'You took that.'

'No.'

'Take a closer look.' Craven slid the photograph towards him. List screwed his eyes shut, tears streaming down his face.

'What, you just like writing about it?' Craven said.

'Is that Ella? Take it away — please. I can't—'

Ted leaned forward and turned the photograph face down. 'Inspector Craven. That's enough.'

'You really liked Ella, didn't you?' Craven said.

'Aye.'

'I think you liked her as more than just a friend.'

'Didn't matter.' List sniffed. 'She wasn't interested in me.'

'I want to help Ella too, but if I'm to have a chance of doing that, I need you to not hold anything back, no matter how small it might be,' Helen said gently.

List wiped his nose with his sleeve.

'I know you also have a potential shoe print,' Ted interjected. 'My client has shown you his, so as to eliminate himself, and he is a size nine.'

'We don't know if that shoe print has anything to do with what happened to Ella.' Helen took in a breath.

'This could really blow up in both your faces. It's evident to anyone looking at it impartially that you have the wrong man here.'

Helen forced herself to meet Ted's gaze. 'Do you know this woman?' She slid a photograph of Vera Hudson across the table towards List.

List pursed his lips and shook his head emphatically. 'No. I've never seen her before.'

'You sure about that? Take another look,' Craven said.

He stepped forward and List flinched. 'I don't know who that is. I've never seen her before in my life. What does this woman have to do with me?'

Helen placed a photograph of Ella next to that of Vera. 'They both look similar, don't they? Same age, same hair colour.'

Ted sounded bored. 'We're finished here.'

CHAPTER TWENTY-NINE

Clutching her notebook, Helen ran up the stairs to the CID room, her pulse racing. It had been months since she'd last seen Ted.

'Helen, wait! I want to speak to you. Please.' His shoes clicked on the concrete steps behind her.

She reached for the handrail. 'I can't stop. I've got a lot of work to get through.'

'Helen, please!'

She turned to face him. He smiled, his green eyes boring into hers. 'Of course. It won't take long. You look—'

'You're the last person I expected to walk through the door this evening,' she said.

'You hid it well. Anyway, how are you?' he said.

'You've not missed a beat.'

'Oh that. That's just business. It's not personal. I was just doing what was in my client's best interest.'

'I thought you'd gone for good.' Keeping her voice low, she glanced over the banister to make sure no one was listening in.

'So did I.'

'You hated the job. You couldn't wait to get away,' she said.

'I . . . I do. I did, but—'

'You could at least have given me a phone call first. What are you doing back here anyway?'

'I didn't realise I was obliged to keep my ex up to date on my whereabouts.'

'You know I don't mean it like that, it's courtesy if we're going to be working in the same station.'

There wasn't time to call, it was a last-minute thing. A favour for a friend.'

'Right.'

'I had hoped you'd be on this case.' For a moment he looked like he was going to reach out and touch her arm but thought better of it.

'I was just passing through that side of town and I saw the house sale had gone through,' Helen murmured.

'Yes, well, sold within the first two weeks. Are you still living—?'

'In that old dump of a flat?' If she had a pound for every time he had called it that, she'd be a rich woman by now.

'I shouldn't have said that.' He stepped closer and his smile faded.

'It's fine, and I am. It's just . . . it's close to the station and I can't deal with the hassle of moving.'

'I said a lot of things I regret.'

'Water under the bridge.' Helen pursed her lips.

'Still, I feel—'

'Ted, it's fine. How long are you here for anyway?'

'Not long. I'm staying at a colleague's place.'

'Oh?'

'Just while he's away on business. Saves on paying for a hotel, and he has someone to water his plants.'

The last time they'd spoken he'd told her that he was going to Wales because his younger brother had died in a car crash. Helen had never met Ted's brother, only his children on one occasion. All Ted used to say about him was "He was the perfect one." 'What about your niece and nephew? It's terrible what happened. I've been thinking about them.' A painful lump formed in her throat.

'My mother is helping, but losing a parent so young . . . They're back at school, so they're doing as well as you can expect, I suppose. So I thought now would be a good time to get out from under their feet.'

'I know from my own experience, it will get easier for them. I wasn't much older than them when—'

'They've been asking about you,' he said.

'Send them my best and if there's anything I can do . . .'

'They'd love to see you again. They were talking about the time when you came down to stay with us and Wilbur pushed you into the pond.'

'Oh God, I forgot about that. I never should have taken that dog for a walk. Well, at least I made an impression.' She couldn't help smiling at the memory.

'You certainly did.'

'I've got to get this paperwork out of the way, Ted.'

'It's your hair,' he said.

'Pardon?'

'That's what's different, you've let it grow out.'

'Haven't had a chance to get it cut,' she said.

'It suits you. Look, could we talk?'

'We're talking now.'

'I mean properly, not here,' he said.

She looked away. 'I don't know if that's a good idea.'

'I've not been drinking either, not even a shandy.'

'That's good, I'm happy for you.'

'So can we then? Even after your shift if you like.'

'Ted.'

'It's about the case. I might be able to help, and you'd be doing me a favour — I really need another coffee.' He smiled.

* * *

'Are you sure you're not hungry?' Ted handed Helen a rather greasy mug of coffee.

Helen shook her head and took a sip.

'It's just, if you are, we could head to the wee Italian place around the corner.'

'No, here is fine.'

He looked down at his mug. 'Well, the coffee hasn't improved while I've been away. I reckon it's worse — if that's even possible.'

She took another swig. It was caffeine, and at this time of night that was all that mattered.

'I wanted to apologise,' he said.

'For what?' Helen cradled the warm mug in her hands. She had picked her favourite seat by the window. It was out of the way and offered a view out over the grass. The canteen was empty apart from a couple of uniformed officers eating fish and chips at a table by the door. The lights were dim and most of the tables had chairs on top of them, ready for the cleaners.

'I shouldn't have put so much pressure on you to leave the police. I do regret it.'

'It doesn't matter, Ted. It's all in the past.'

'Of course.' His coffee cooled on the table. 'It's just that I—'

'You lured me here on the pretext of giving me information regarding the case, didn't you?' Helen raised an eyebrow.

'I did.'

'So, what's this information you've got?'

'I wouldn't represent someone I didn't believe was innocent, you know that.'

Helen knew he was very proud of his sense of justice. 'I have to remain impartial on this, Ted.'

'I don't think it's List you are looking for.'

The double doors thumped closed behind Randall, who approached their table. With a sneer at Ted, he said to Helen, 'The DI is looking for you. We're needed upstairs.'

Helen pushed her chair away from the table.

Ted took a business card from his pocket. 'This is where I'm staying. Call me.'

CHAPTER THIRTY

Helen stared out of Craven's office window. The rest of the team had gathered and were waiting for Craven to start the briefing.

'We're letting List go for the time being,' he began. 'But I want a close eye on him.'

McKinley was handing out notes. Helen watched a squad car pull out from the car park, sirens blazing. She couldn't see Ted's car, but she guessed he had a new one now.

'We searched List's property and found twenty different cameras,' one of the uniforms said. 'And a load of electrical equipment.'

'I saw the look on his face when he saw the photographs. He was shocked and disgusted,' Helen added. 'I don't believe he took them.'

Craven rubbed a hand over his chin stubble. He looked like he hadn't slept in days. He was standing next to the makeshift board that had been set up.

'Mickey said that Vera mentioned a dark-coloured car,' Helen said. 'List doesn't have one, and the description of the perpetrator doesn't fit him either.'

'Aye, but how much stock can we put in what was said in a phone call?' Randall shook his head. 'I don't think we can eliminate him completely.'

'I know, but still.'

'Aye?' Randall sneered. 'Just because your old flame is representing him doesn't mean he's innocent.'

'That has nothing to do with it.'

'Anything from the door-to-door enquiries?' Craven asked Randall.

He shook his head. 'We've also spoken to the driver of the bus Vera was on. He said that she seemed nervous and jittery but didn't say much. That's what made him remember her, apparently. I think it's likely that whoever took her from the phone box was following her before she got on the bus. Which got me thinking.' He stood and pointed to Montgomery Street on the street map they kept on the wall. 'She got on here. Two streets away from the college. 'Well, number three Montgomery Street used to be the Anderson bed and breakfast. It's long gone now.'

'I remember that,' Helen added. 'It was where the Button Killer committed one of his murders. If he is focussing on old haunts. It could give us an idea of where he might strike again.'

Craven nodded.

'We've circulated the sketch to every photography shop in Edinburgh and nothing. It's like we're looking for a ghost,' one of the officers said.

'What about Ella White?' McKinley asked.

Randall smiled again. 'I've found a connection there too. Her flat didn't exist when the original killings occurred but there was a woman, Stacey Fisher, who vanished from one of the prefabs where Ella's flat now stands. She was never found. She went missing during the time the Button Killer was active. It was never pinned on him, but I think it's likely.'

'The Button Killer struck all over Edinburgh and the outskirts,' Helen said.

'Didn't he also kill a taxi driver?' McKinley put in.

'That was opportunistic. He killed the man for what little money he had in the cab, I believe,' Randall said.

'So we should contact the taxi companies too, make them aware of the danger. Right.' Craven clapped his hands. 'Get on with it.'

Chairs scraped as the meeting room emptied. Helen was at the door when Craven took hold of her arm. 'Helen, I need to have a word with you, in private.'

* * *

'You've got to be joking.' Helen sat down hard in one of the chairs.

'I wish I was.'

'Can't you send someone else?' she said.

Craven shook his head. 'I want you to go. You and Randall.'

'I can't do it. Send Bell or Terry instead.' Helen made a move to stand. 'I'm sorry, Jack, but not this time.'

'It needs to be you,' Craven stated flatly. 'Landis says he'll only talk to you.'

'Why me?'

'He mentioned your father.'

Helen sucked in a shuddery breath. 'I'd still rather someone else went.'

'This not a request.' Craven reached for his coffee cup. 'I wouldn't ask if I thought there was another way. Look, out of all of us, you're the one that has the best chance of getting anywhere. You know how his mind works.'

'He's wasting our time. There's nothing he can tell us that we don't already know,' she said.

'The department's under a lot of pressure from above. There's a growing number of people who think that Landis is innocent. They're calling for his release.'

'I know that.'

'Helen, if this carries on, he might just walk.'

Helen put her head in her hands. 'I can't think about that.'

'Well, you should. He's doing all the right things. He's been a model prisoner apparently, even runs the bible study group. Not to mention that there's someone out there on the streets claiming to be the real Button Killer.'

'That doesn't mean he's innocent,' she said. 'He's just good at playing the system.'

'I know that, but it's not us he needs to convince.'

Helen recalled that he'd very nearly got off the first time, it had been all over the papers for months. She remembered protests at the station her dad had worked from, celebrities and politicians all proclaiming his innocence. She got to her feet. 'If you really want me to speak with Mark Landis, I will, but he won't tell us anything we don't already know.'

She hesitated in the doorway. 'Did you get the list of names of people who viewed your ex-wife's house?'

'Yes. It was a dead end.

CHAPTER THIRTY-ONE

Helen hadn't looked happy when she'd got into the car. He smiled. The police weren't getting very far. Meanwhile, everyone was talking about him — they'd discussed him in the papers, on the telly, the radio. All because of him the city was gripped with fear. It was an intoxicating feeling.

Where was she going? Squinting, he pulled down the visor. The radio blasted out a Mozart symphony. He drummed his fingers on the steering wheel. He'd followed her Mini ever since she'd pulled out of the station, staying a couple of cars back in the long line of traffic snaking along Seafield Road. An uneasy feeling churned his gut. It had been interesting to watch them scrabbling for answers, but now he was restless. He needed to continue with his plan.

She took a right turn. Now he knew exactly where she was going.

* * *

'How the other half live.'

'Lived,' Helen corrected.

'Right.'

Oliver Stanton had lived in an architect-designed house in the Murrayfield area. The building appeared to be comprised entirely out of glass panels, with a flat roof and a row of palm trees on the front lawn. It didn't look like it belonged in cold Edinburgh. Oliver's wife, Judy, was waiting for them at the double oak doors at the front. In her mid-thirties, she was wearing thick-rimmed glasses, her fair hair in a light, wavy perm. Tall and slender, she could easily have passed for a model.

'Thank for you for agreeing to see us,' Helen said.

'Whatever I can do to help,' she muttered solemnly, leading them through to a library. 'Can I get either of you a tea, coffee, or something stronger?'

'No, thank you.' Helen gazed around the room. Ornate bookshelves and a mezzanine floor on which were displayed a number of sculptures and marbled busts complemented the modernist décor. Terry looked impressed — pity she couldn't have shown him Ted's old place.

'So, what can I do for you, officers?' Judy had a pronounced American accent. 'Can I tempt you to something stronger perhaps?'

Helen shook her head.

'I hope you don't mind if I . . .' Judy reached for a crystal decanter on a silver tray. 'It's for my nerves.'

'Of course.'

'Please, take a seat.' She motioned to a couple of reading chairs that looked antique.

'We'd just like to ask you some questions about your husband,' Helen began, while McKinley took out his notebook.

Judy frowned. 'I'm not sure what I'll be able to tell you.' She took a sip of her drink. 'I've just got back from Boston. I had to get away for a while.'

'When did Mr Stanton publish his book on the Button Killer?' Helen asked.

'Last year. His latest work was on Jack the Ripper. But Oliver was always intrigued with the Button Killer, he spent years investigating the murders.

'Do you have any of his research notes here?' Helen asked.

'I don't know . . .'

'We think that if anyone did hurt your husband, it might be someone who was part of his research, or someone he met in that connection. So, anything you do have could be incredibly useful to us.'

Judy sighed. 'Oli was so careful with all that stuff.'

'Did he ever talk to you about the work he was doing?'

Judy shook her head. 'I'm sorry. He liked to keep his work private.' She got up abruptly, looking as if she was blinking back tears. 'Let me go and see if I can find those files for you.'

While they were waiting, Helen looked around the room, which was about the size of her whole flat. Photographs of Oliver Stanton with various celebrities adorned the walls.

'Is that no' him with Oliver Reed?' McKinley motioned to a picture in a dark frame. 'And is that not Elizabeth Taylor?'

Helen gave a small shrug. 'It looks like it.'

'It is.' McKinley whistled. 'My mum absolutely loves him. I don't think she ever missed an episode of Stanton's show when he was on the telly. She was cut up when he died too.'

'I don't think I've seen an episode.' Helen could see the appeal of glamourising murder, but it wasn't for her.

Judy returned a couple of minutes later, lugging a very heavy box, which she set down at Helen's feet. 'This is everything.'

'Thank you,' Helen said. 'Did Mr Stanton mention anything strange in the days before he took that train? Did you have any unwanted visitors to the house, for example?'

Judy thought for a moment. 'No, but you must understand, it takes Oliver a long time to write these books. That one was maybe five, six years in the making. The only thing I can think of was the brother. I know Oliver met with him and interviewed him. He wanted Oliver to find Mark Landis innocent, but Oliver didn't see it like that.'

As far as Helen knew, Landis didn't have a brother.

'Did you yourself ever meet or see this brother?' she asked.

Judy shook her head. 'Hopefully it's there in the notes. Oliver was normally very good at documenting everything. I hope you find what you're looking for.'

'Thank you,' Helen said and heaved up the box. 'This is incredibly helpful.'

'The books are written for the general public, but don't be fooled. He was an expert in his field.' Judy gave them the ghost of a smile. 'I've stuck a copy of the book in too, just in case.'

'Thank you,' Helen took out a couple of photographs from her notebook one of Ella Smith and Vera Hudson. 'Do you recognise either of these women.'

'I don't and I can't imagine Oli would have either. He was very much a recluse when he wasn't working.'

'She was quite different from how I was expecting,' McKinley said when they were back in the car.

'In what way?'

'I'd always heard he was a bit of a ladies' man. Mind you, with all the money he was making and the lifestyle it gave her, maybe she decided not to make waves.' He shook his head. 'She's a right stunner, though. I don't know why he'd want to look anywhere else.'

Helen gave him a look.

'Sorry.' McKinley grinned. 'Where to next?'

Helen glanced at the clock on the dash. 'Back to the station. I need to arrange a visit to the prison.'

McKinley's eyes widened. 'To see Mark Landis?'

Helen nodded.

'Do you think it'll do any good?'

'I don't know, but someone's impersonating him, maybe he'll know why. At least, that's what the DI says.'

'He's not likely to say though, is he? He's always told anyone who'll listen that's he's innocent, and two of his victims have never been found, despite all the people who've tried to get more information from him over the years. Will he no' just say it's the real killer?'

CHAPTER THIRTY-TWO

As soon as Helen got back to her flat that night, she took Ted's business card from her bag and dialled his number. No answer. She swore. He had seemed so desperate to speak to her and now she couldn't get hold of him. She called Stephen and left a message on his answerphone, asking him out for that drink. Needing something to do, she went through to the kitchen and peeled a clementine. Maybe she'd wait an hour or so then try calling him again.

To pass the time, she decided to phone her mother, who picked up on the first ring.

'Helen, I thought you were never going to call.'

'I know, I'm sorry.'

'Did you get your package?'

'I did.' Helen looked out of the window and was relieved to see the street empty.

'And the shoes?'

She glanced over at Irene's place. Her flat was the only one with no lights on. Devastated, Irene's husband had gone to stay with family. She noticed that the "for sale" sign had been taken down.

'Have you been listening to anything I've said?'

'Sorry, Mum.' Helen yawned. 'It's been a long day.'

'You work too hard, darling. I worry about you, you know.'

'I'm fine.'

'I've been seeing all those Button Killer things in the paper,' her mother said.

'Hard to miss,' Helen muttered. 'That's what I wanted to talk to you about, actually.'

'Oh?'

'I wanted to go through Dad's notes on the case, but a lot are missing. I was sure he had boxes full of them.'

Helen heard static on the line.

'Mum?'

'I . . . Well, I got rid of them.'

'Why?'

'I just didn't want them in the house. Oh, Helen, you have to remember that it was such a bad time in our lives. I'm sorry, Helen, I need to go, there's someone at the door.'

'Thanks, Mum.' But Helen was speaking into the dial tone.

As soon as she put the receiver down, the phone rang again.

'Hello, Helen Carter speaking.'

'It's me.' Helen could tell from Craven's voice that something had happened. 'We've found a number of items in a wooded area.'

'What items? Are they Vera's?'

'Her handbag and her jacket.'

'Any buttons—'

'Aye. Missing from the jacket.'

'I'm on my way.'

* * *

Footsteps thudded above. Vera scuttled into a corner, screwing her eyes shut. He was going to kill her. Mickey would be heartbroken. Why hadn't she listened to him and called the police?

135

Her hands and ankles were bound. She struggled to loosen them but the harder she pulled, the tighter they got. She had no idea where she was or how long she had been here. *Oh God, he was coming.*

The door swung open. He stormed into the room and began pacing back and forth.

* * *

The place Vera's possessions had been found in was popular with hikers and dog walkers. There was a low winter sun just above the horizon, and temporary lights had been set up along the path, ready for nightfall. The woods had been cordoned off and the undergrowth rustled with uniformed officers and dogs.

Craven gave her a nod of greeting as she approached.

'Who found the things?' Helen asked.

'A dog walker. There's still no sign of Vera.'

At least they hadn't found her body — yet.

Randall was at the top of the path speaking to a couple of uniformed officers. He appeared to be in charge of the operation. He had a hand on one of the officer's shoulders and was pointing down the road with the other.

The path was steep, and Craven's breathing was becoming laboured.

When they got to him, Helen saw that Randall was holding a couple of evidence bags.

'Evening. We've found Vera's handbag. Even had a couple of pounds in it.'

'Where did you find it?' Craven asked.

'Lying at the side of the path. They hadn't even bothered to hide it.'

These woods were maybe a good twenty miles from where Vera was taken and it would take days, if not weeks, to search them thoroughly. Helen knelt to look more closely at what had been found. Her heart sank as she noticed blood on the collar of Vera's denim jacket.

'We've found something else.' The uniformed officer who had been at Ella's house hurried towards them. Why could she never remember his name? Mick? Mac? 'There's a rubbish bin further along the path. It must have got blown over in the wind and these fell out. Look.'

He handed her an evidence bag containing what looked like postcards and Polaroids.

'Thanks,' Helen sighed. Once she'd finished at the crime scene, she'd take these back to the station.

CHAPTER THIRTY-THREE

The following morning, McKinley entered the CID room holding a box brimming with manila folders. 'Morning.'

Helen was holding Ted's business card in one hand, the receiver in the other, just about to hang up. He still wasn't answering the phone. 'Terry, can you look through all the cases in the last ten years or so that either involved or took place near the Forth Bridge?'

'The Forth Bridge? Why?'

Helen picked up one of the photos that were lying on her desk. 'These were found in the woods last night. I went through all the Button Killer cases last night but I couldn't find a connection.'

'How did the search go? Has Vera been found?' he asked.

Helen shook her head. 'Here's another one. It's some tall column with a statue on top but I don't recognise it.'

McKinley took it from her. 'Aye, I do. That's the Marjoribanks Monument.'

'The what? Is it in Scotland?'

'Aye, it's in Coldstream, down in the Borders. I know a couple of the officers down there from my time in Traffic. I can give them a call.'

* * *

'Wow!' Helen parked her battered little rust bucket of a Mini between a brand-new Bentley and an Aston Martin. She couldn't decide which one was Ted's. It was no surprise that the address he had given her turned out to be a Georgian townhouse in the New Town, well beyond her salary scale. His last place had been as grand, but possibly slightly smaller — this one looked like it spanned four floors instead of three.

She rapped on the postcard-perfect red door and stepped back to get a better view of the place. She could see a grand piano and a crystal chandelier in what she guessed was the drawing room. Nice. A shadowy figure appeared through the frosted-glass panel. The door opened and there was Ted.

'Helen. This is a pleasant—'

She forced a smile. 'Have I caught you at a bad time? I tried to call you a few times but there was no answer.'

His shirt sleeves were rolled up to his elbows and he had a dishcloth draped over his shoulder. 'Oh, well, you know . . . Anyway, come in.'

Her mouth felt dry. She swallowed. 'I can come back another time if you like.'

'No, not at all. I'm glad to see you. Do come in.' He pulled the door open wide and gestured for her to enter. 'Excuse the mess, I wasn't expecting anyone.'

Helen followed him down a wide marble hallway towards a winding staircase. Art in expensive-looking mahogany frames adorned the walls. The only mess she could see were two suitcases at the bottom of the stairs. 'What a stunning place.'

'I know,' he said. 'I feel like I'm living in a museum, I'm scared to touch a thing. Can I get you a tea, coffee?'

'No thanks.' She stopped in front of an ornate grandfather clock. 'Your friend must *really* like you.'

'Colleague,' he corrected her. 'What about something stronger? There's a wine cellar in the basement.'

'I need to get back to work soon.'

'Oh. Yes, of course.'

He led her to a kitchen the size of a football pitch, complete with freestanding islands and an eight-person dining table positioned in front of two floor-to-ceiling sash windows. She could smell fresh coffee and regretted turning down his offer. On the worktop she noticed a wine glass and what looked like the remains of a second one in a dustpan on the floor.

'I just wanted to talk to you about Bert List.'

'I guessed.' He took a seat at the table and gestured for her to join him. 'You want to know why I'm so sure he is innocent, don't you?'

'Yes,' she said, sitting down. 'And I think you know more than you're letting on.'

'I can tell you don't think he's capable of murder either.'

She shrugged. 'It doesn't matter what I think.'

'It does.'

'You'd be surprised what people are capable of. I'm only interested in facts, not what I think.'

'Fair enough.'

'I know you, Ted. I've never seen you take such an interest in a case before.'

He seemed to be considering this. In all the years she'd known him, Helen had often felt that he tended to see the courtroom as a competition.

'I'm surprised to see you back in Edinburgh. You couldn't wait to leave.'

'That's true. I wanted to go to London, but I wanted us to go together.'

'London wasn't for me,' she said.

'I found you a good job. I wanted us to get married. You know, I still have your engagement ring.'

Helen rubbed her eyes. She was tempted to have a glass of wine but she had an empty stomach, and she was driving. 'On second thoughts, I'll have a coffee, and make it a strong one.'

Ted got to his feet. 'I remember how you like it.'

'So, why are you here then?' she asked again.

His back to her, he spooned coffee into the cafetière. 'A couple of reasons. I told you I was back for work, and that part is true.'

'But there is something else?' she said.

'Yes.' He came back to the table carrying two cups. He smiled. 'It's at times like these I regret giving up drinking.'

Helen glanced at the wine glass, but he didn't seem to notice. 'What's the other part?' she asked.

'I was engaged before,' he said.

'Before me?'

He nodded.

The knot in Helen's stomach tightened. 'OK, but what's that got to do with—?'

'In 1966 I was engaged to a woman named Simone Langford.' He took a breath. 'I was very young.'

Helen did the maths quickly, he would've been about eighteen. The name sounded oddly familiar, but Helen couldn't place it, though she could see he expected her to know it. 'OK.'

'I was just starting at university and managed to get a work placement at a law firm.'

'What happened?' Helen asked. 'And why would this Simone have anything to do with my case? Or Bert List for that matter?'

'Because Simone . . . well, she disappeared.'

Helen put her cup down. 'I don't understand.?'

'She went to work one day and never came home. There are too many similarities to Ella White's disappearance.'

'So, you think they're related?'

'I didn't want Bert List to be blamed for what happened to Ella White. There should be a proper investigation.'

'Take me through what happened with Simone,' Helen said.

'She disappeared a couple of days after we became engaged.'

'Right.'

'I thought maybe she had changed her mind and left me,' he said.

'How do you know she didn't?'

'I . . . I got something in the post.'

'A card?' Helen frowned. 'Like the card that was sent to me?'

He nodded. 'Exactly. Not long after that her jacket and handbag were found in some woodland. They were covered in mud and the jacket was missing a button.' He swallowed. 'That's when I knew . . .'

Helen ran her hand through her hair. 'Ted, I have known you for, what, more than five years?'

'Something like that.'

'Then why haven't you told me about this before?' Helen recalled all the occasions when she'd thought he was holding something back, but didn't know what. She had always put it down to insecurity.

'I . . . I don't know really. It was a long time ago. I blocked it out of my mind.'

'You can't just block something like that out of your mind. It's impossible.'

'I did, Helen. It was the only way I could carry on. It's not something that's easy to bring up in conversation, is it?'

'It's exactly the kind of thing that should come up in conversation, Ted. I don't know what to say.' She gritted her teeth. 'You should have found a way to tell me.'

He was nodding. 'When I heard about Ella White, I knew Bert List was innocent and I had to meet him. I had to find out more. I thought maybe he could lead me to Simone's killer.'

'Mark Landis is in prison. We're most likely dealing with a copycat,' she said.

'What if Landis is innocent?'

'Ted!'

'I think the Button Killer is still out there,' he said.

'Why?'

'Because when Simone was taken, Landis was in jail. Don't you see — Landis didn't hurt Simone, he couldn't have. And he's always maintained his innocence. Isn't that strange, even after all these years?'

'I'll look into the case,' she said.

'Landis has always said that the police fitted him up.'

'It's in his interest to say that. Criminals often do. It's not that unusual.'

He stared at her. 'Putting the Button Killer away brought your father his promotion.'

Helen stood up. She knew where this was going. It was a persistent rumour that her father had taken backhanders, but fitting up someone for murder, that was a different thing entirely.

'Helen, I didn't mean it like that. I know the police were under immense pressure at the time. The politicians, the public were all clamouring for a conviction.'

'That doesn't mean they got it wrong.' Helen was a child at the time, but she clearly remembered how much work her dad had put in to finding Landis.

'I have some files upstairs. I looked into the case myself,' he said. 'Will you look at them?'

'Of course. I want the truth just as much as you.'

CHAPTER THIRTY-FOUR

Ted handed her a faded, water-stained folder. 'This is everything I have.'

Helen flicked through it, glanced at the photographs. 'Ted, is this why you kept wanting me to leave the police?'

'It's one of the reasons.'

Helen sighed. 'I wish you'd just been honest with me.' He'd even found her a job in London, in a psychologist's office.

'I'm sorry. It's one of the reasons I drink — to block it all out.'

Helen shook her head. To her, Ted had always had it all — money, success. But at the same time, he acted like he carried the weight of the world on his shoulders. On another occasion when he was drunk. He'd confessed he was the black sheep of the family, but when she'd asked him about it when he was sober. He wouldn't say anything else about it.

'I've always felt guilty. I was meant to look after Simone and I failed.' He cleared his throat. 'I wouldn't want you to think badly of me.'

'Ted—'

'I was terrified that you would be hurt, like Simone was.'

'Take me through that day.'

'I'll try.' He got up and poured himself a glass of water. 'Do you want one?'

'No.'

He blew out a sigh. 'At times it feels like an age ago, yet it's still so raw. That's strange, isn't it?'

'Go on.'

'It was just a normal day.' He drained his glass. 'That morning we had breakfast together. We chatted about nothing much, then I said my usual goodbyes.' He looked down at this empty glass. 'I phoned her from work later — I often did that, but she didn't answer.' He held up his glass. 'God, I wish that was a whisky.'

'Was that unusual?'

'Not really. But when I arrived home that night, the house was cold and dark. She was gone.'

'Did you phone the police?'

He shook his head. 'She'd been depressed for a while, but back then people were just told to buck up or something. I thought she'd just left me.'

'Did she take any of her things?'

'No. Which was strange.'

Helen's chest tightened. From her photos, Simone looked incredibly similar to Ella. They could easily have passed for sisters. 'Then what did you do?'

'The next morning, I called her parents. I expected to have to do a little grovelling but—'

'She wasn't there?'

'No. Her parents called the police, who weren't that worried. She was an adult. But look at the photos in the back of that folder and tell me that wasn't the Button Killer's work.'

Helen asked for more coffee, waiting until he'd turned his back to look at the crime scene photos.

Yellowing black-and-white images of an expensive violet coat. The luxurious fabric was caked in thick mud. The second photo was a close-up of the bottom of the jacket, showing a missing silver button.

'Bert List is too young. He was in high school when Simone vanished.' Ted handed Helen a glass of water and sat down opposite her. 'That's why I know Bert is innocent.'

Helen closed the file.

'Mark Landis had already been arrested for the Button killings when Simone vanished. I think that's partly why the police just weren't interested.'

'I'll take the file if I may,' she said.

'Please do.' He walked to the door with her. 'Oh, I almost forgot. Wait here.' A few seconds later, he returned clutching an stained-oak box with a gold handle. He gave a small shrug and held it out to her.

'What's this?' Helen said.

'Acrylic paints, the best you can get, or so I was told.' A little colour returned to his face.

'I've not used those in a long time,' she said.

'I remember you wanted some. Anyway, it's just a little thing for your birthday.'

'You didn't have to.'

'I know, but I wanted to.'

CHAPTER THIRTY-FIVE

Helen peered through the smeary windscreen at a long line of traffic building up at the bottom of the street. It had only just begun raining but was already lashing it down. *Typical Edinburgh, four seasons in one day.* Helen glanced down at the folder as she pulled into the stream of cars. Ted was watching from the front-room window and she gave him a cursory wave.

All the years they had been together, and not once had he given any indication that his previous fiancée had been murdered. At least it explained some of the fear he'd seemed to have of her getting hurt and the pressure he'd put on her to take a "safe" job.

She was almost halfway to the station when the radio chirruped, startling her out of her thoughts. The caller, a voice she didn't recognise, informed her that her presence was needed in CID immediately.

* * *

'We need to do something.'

The door to the incident room was ajar. Through the gap she saw Randall pacing, a cigarette dangling from his lips and his blue eyes blazing with anger. McKinley was hunched over some papers on his desk. Helen heard a grunt that sounded like it could've been the DI. She was still reeling from what Ted had told her, and the last thing she wanted was to walk in on a briefing.

She took a breath and pushed the door open. 'What's going on?' Helen put Ted's file down on her desk. All the other CID officers except Randall were seated around the table looking grim.

'Can someone get me up to speed? Randall?'

'I had a call come in a few hours ago,' Craven said. 'The caller told us that if we don't broadcast the news that the real Button Killer is back, he is going to kill Vera. Tonight.'

'I think we need to do what he wants,' Randall said. 'We don't have a choice, do we?'

'Has he given any indication as to why he is supposedly back?' Helen asked. 'Giving this killer the attention he craves will just encourage him. We don't know that Vera is still alive. All we would really be doing is causing panic. If she is still alive, it may only be because of the lack of attention on him.'

'He wants you to give a press briefing,' Randall said with a sneer.

'Why me?'

Craven shrugged. 'Maybe because you're a woman, or have family ties to the case. Maybe he's thinking it might make people take more notice. He's even given us a script.' He nodded to a sheet of typed paper on his desk.

Helen picked it up and read:

We made a mistake when we arrested Mark Landis. He is an innocent man, imprisoned by a corrupt system. To punish us for our mistakes, the real Button Killer has taken a victim. If things are not made right, this victim will die.

'What does he mean "make things right?"' McKinley asked.

'I think he is saying we should release Mark Landis.' As she spoke, the air around her went cold, her head light. 'I can't say this.'

'That's never going to happen,' Craven muttered.

Helen inhaled slowly to steady herself. 'Even if I did read this to the press, I don't think whoever has taken her will let Vera go.'

Randall cleared his throat.

'And we don't know for certain that the person who wrote this is the one who took Vera. He's always left Polaroids before, but there's none with this letter.' Helen knew from experience that a high-profile case often brought false witnesses and even fake confessions. 'I do this and we can make things worse.'

'If you're wrong on this, Helen . . .' Randall growled.

'I know what's at stake. Do we have anything else to go on?' Helen met Randall's eyes and could see the weariness there.

'We circulated Vera's image and the sketch of the suspect,' he said.

'And?' Helen asked.

He shook his head.

'Brilliant. What about a connection between Vera and Ella?' Helen perched on the end of the desk.

Randall sighed. 'They're roughly the same age and type as the Button Killer's original victims. That's the only connection I've found. Vera's mum is downstairs. She's in bits.'

Helen put her head in her hands. 'I think we should try a different tack.'

'Oh? What?' Craven asked.

'I do the briefing but we get Vera's mum on with me. I think our biggest chance of saving Vera — if she's still alive — is to humanise her. We get her family to ask the killer directly to let her go.'

'Right, let's try it your way.' Craven said.

CHAPTER THIRTY-SIX

After the briefing, Helen took McKinley aside and handed him Simone's folder. 'I need you to pull out everything you can find regarding this case, but keep it between us for now. It's from 1966.'

'You looked good up there,' McKinley said.

'I just hope it was enough.'

'I don't think I could stand up in front of the cameras like that.'

Helen shrugged. 'I didn't really have a choice.' Her heart had been hammering the whole time. Helen was full of admiration for Vera's mother, who had spoken with compassion and love. She'd addressed the cameras directly, telling the assembled reporters that she did not hate the man who had taken her daughter.

'All those cameras. The lights,' Terry went on.

'Thanks, Terry.'

'Sorry. I forgot to say, your mum called again.'

Helen didn't feel up to phoning her mother right now. Besides, she was still annoyed at her for getting rid of her father's case notes.

Terry looked down at the folder. 'Why does it need to be just between the two of us?'

'Do you remember Ted, the solicitor I was engaged to?'

'Yes.' McKinley made a face. 'I heard he was representing Bert List.'

'Well, Ted was engaged to Simone, the woman in the case file.'

His eyes widened. 'Oh. I'll see what I can find.'

'Thanks, Terry.' Helen lowered herself into her chair. Her head was pounding and she was on tenterhooks waiting for the phone to ring.

'Um, you think you and Ted will . . . ?'

'I can't think about that right now.' All she could think of was Vera. Time was running out.

* * *

'Did you really mean what you said about not hating the man who took your daughter?' Helen asked. She and Vera's mother were sitting in DI Craven's office. Helen guessed her to be in her late sixties, though she could be younger. A delicate gold cross dangled from her neck.

Vera's mother sighed deeply. 'I love my daughter with all my heart, but giving way to hate does nothing to help the situation. Hate only hurts the hater, and I'm damaged enough already. Vera wouldn't want that for me.'

'I understand,' Helen murmured.

'From your experience, Sergeant Carter, do you think he will let her go?'

Helen reached out and gave her hand a squeeze.

* * *

Vera jerked awake. She could hear a TV on upstairs. It was her mother, begging for her release.

She shivered. The concrete was damp and hard, and her hip ached. The wind whistled through a gap in the bottom of the door. She wasn't sure how long she'd been here, or why he was keeping her. Days, hours, all blending into one long nightmare.

The door creaked open. Blinking away spots from the sudden burst of light, she strained to see what he was doing. 'What do you want from me?'

The camera flashed, a click followed by a brilliant white light.

Hot tears stung her cheeks. 'Why are you doing this to me? What do you want? Let me go, please!'

The flash flared, again and again.

CHAPTER THIRTY-SEVEN

'I've got something,' McKinley announced. He had the top two buttons open on his shirt, his sleeves rolled up to his elbows and was holding a heavy-looking plastic box. He and Helen were in one of the empty meeting rooms so they wouldn't be disturbed.

With a thud, McKinley dropped the box on the big table that dominated the room. 'There was a lot of information on this case, a lot more than I was expecting.' His face was pink from the exertion.

'This is good, thanks.' The more the better as far as Helen was concerned. She pulled out the first file and handed a second to McKinley.

'I'm guessing Ted never told you because he was one of the main suspects,' McKinley said.

Helen had guessed as much. She opened her file. It seemed the most recent findings were at the top. According to the file, Simone was reported missing by her parents on 8 June 1966 after she'd failed to get in touch with them. She was last seen leaving her workplace on the fourth. Her fiancé confirmed that he hadn't seen her after the morning of the fifth, when she'd said she was going for a walk — which wasn't unusual for her.

Helen turned to the next page, which gave details of an argument they'd had on the evening of the fourth. Ted had assumed she'd gone home and didn't know she was missing until the police visited him a day or two later. The report made for hard reading.

'Ted was never discounted as a suspect,' McKinley muttered.

'I can see.' Helen's gaze dropped to the file in front of her. 'I don't think Ted had anything to do with her disappearance. After all, I knew him, I was engaged to him.' Then again, what did she actually know about him?

'No, I know.' He blushed. 'That came out wrong.'

Helen nodded. In cases like this, nine times out of ten, suspicion fell on the partner and often rightly so, so it was hardly surprising that they would have looked closely at Ted. Helen frowned and looked at her empty coffee mug, she must have drunk it all without realising. She stuffed the file back in the box and pulled out a second.

He shrugged. 'Landis was in a cell around that time.'

'What do you mean around that time? Was he or wasn't he?'

'Landis was arrested on the fifth. But the last time anyone saw Simone alive was twenty-four hours before that.'

'Ted said he last saw her on the fifth,' Helen said.

McKinley sucked in air through his teeth. Helen knew exactly what he was thinking — that there was no proof that Ted was telling the truth.

'So, potentially Simone could have been a victim of the Button Killer?' Helen blew out a sigh.

He shook his head slowly. 'Trouble is, we don't know exactly when Simone went missing. If Ted is telling the truth, then no, she couldn't.'

Helen took an unsteady breath and flicked through some of the crime scene photographs of Simone's discarded, muddy and bloody jacket. Some of the buttons were clearly missing. She shuddered. 'Ted believes she was murdered by the Button Killer. Do you know why that line of enquiry wasn't followed up?'

McKinley shrugged. 'The only similarity to the Button Killer murders were the buttons missing from her jacket, but that was all. By then, everyone knew that the killer took buttons from the clothes of his victims.'

Helen flipped over to a shot of the handbag. It was open, showing it to be empty.

'Look at this.' McKinley gestured to the photograph Helen had. 'The Button Killer wasn't motivated by robbery.'

Helen shook her head. 'He did murder and rob a taxi driver.'

'I forgot about that. What's the plan now?' McKinley asked.

'Simone Langford's mother lives in Coldstream. I think we should go and pay her a visit and let's go see that Marjoribanks Monument.'

CHAPTER THIRTY-EIGHT

It took them well over an hour to get to Coldstream, a small-ish town in the Scottish Borders some forty or so miles south of Edinburgh. They had driven a lot of the way in silence, listening to the radio with the occasional chat.

They drove past a building set back in the trees, whose sign read, "Coldstream Community Hospital".

'Where is this monument then?' Helen asked.

'Keep going once we get to the shops.' McKinley's stomach rumbled right on cue. 'Hopefully there's a wee café on the way.'

'Bound to be in a place like this.'

Helen hadn't felt like eating after Ted's revelation, and was suddenly aware of how hungry she was. She gave way to an oncoming bus headed for Kelso and then turned into the high street. It was narrow, curved and jammed with little shops. McKinley tapped her on the arm and pointed to an empty parking space behind a Land Rover, opposite a church. The little café looked deserted, though the lights were on, and a woman stood behind the counter.

'This looks all right. I'm starving,' McKinley said.

Helen glanced along the busy street before they went in. 'It's a nice wee place this.' She smiled at a group of young children excitedly crowding the sweet shop a few doors down.

'Aye, my dad used to take us fishing here when I was younger — that is, before he walked out on us,' McKinley said.

They found seats at a table by the window.

'How's your mum?' Helen asked in between bites of her cheese sandwich.

'She has her good and bad days. More bad than good recently, but we've been told to take each day as it comes.'

* * *

'Mrs Langford?' Helen leaned over the gate, while McKinley waited in the car. In front of a small bungalow just off the high street an elderly woman was carefully trimming some rose bushes.

'Bloody vultures. Don't you ever give up?'

'I'm sorry?' Helen fished in her pocket for her warrant card. 'Mrs Langford, I'm not a reporter. My name's DS Helen Carter and if it's all right with you, I'd like to come in and ask you a few questions about Simone.'

The woman looked like she was considering this, then relented. 'I don't know what I can tell you that you don't already know. My memory isn't the best these days — the joys of old age. Have you travelled down from Edinburgh then?'

Helen nodded.

Mrs Langford opened the gate. 'Come in. Can I get you a cup of tea?'

'Thank you.'

'I've been following what's happening in the news, then the calls from the reporters started.'

'I'm sorry to hear that,' Helen said.

'So, how can I help you? What do you want to know?' She handed Helen a delicate floral-patterned tea cup.

Helen cradled the cup, warming her hands. 'I'm investigating a murder and the disappearance of two women in Edinburgh.'

'Terrible business.'

'The man who was Simone's fiancé at the time brought her case to my attention — Theodore Holland. Ted.'

The woman nodded slowly.

'I understand they hadn't long been engaged,' Helen said.

'No, they hadn't. A few weeks, that's all. It came as quite a surprise to us.'

'Oh?'

'Well, she'd never mentioned him before. Don't get me wrong, though, he has been wonderful. He's really done a lot for us over the years. He gave me this place after my husband died.'

It was a picturesque little cottage and obviously well cared for.

'Were you living in Coldstream before?'

'Oh, no. This place was Ted's before that.'

'What a lovely gift,' Helen said.

'I've lived here more than four years now.'

Four years. Helen had already met Ted at that point, and she'd had no idea. Her head was spinning. 'Does Ted still visit?'

The woman's smile faded. 'Not anymore, not for a couple of years anyway. I expect Ted has moved on with his life.' She looked down at her hands. 'It's not really surprising, is it, after all this time.'

'I've gone through Simone's case in detail,' Helen said.

'Yes?'

'Are you able to take me through what happened? I understand that it wasn't Ted who contacted the police?'

'No, it was me. Simone always phoned me, every week without fail, and when she didn't, I tried to call her and got no answer.'

'Did you go straight to the police?' Helen asked.

'No. It was Theodore encouraged us to. The police didn't take it seriously at the time, on account of . . .'

'Yes?'

Simone's mother looked away. 'I can't remember.'

'That's OK, Take your time.'

'I forget things, you see.'

'You were telling me the police weren't taking it seriously?'

She put her hands to her head. 'I'm tired now.'

'Let's talk another time.' Helen took a business card from her pocket. 'If you remember anything, just give me a call — day or night.'

CHAPTER THIRTY-NINE

Anton sipped his wine. It was a good choice, nice and sweet. Just the way he liked it. He swirled it around in his glass and looked out at the garden. Palm trees were swaying in the breeze, giving the illusion of a tropical paradise. Then he noticed it, a figure lying in the grass.

No, that couldn't be right. He blinked but it was still there. 'There's someone lying on the ground out there,' he said to the waiter, who was just then serving him his *crème anglaise*.

The waiter looked in the direction Anton was pointing. In the winter garden outside the restaurant, scarlet fabric was visible between the palm trees. Other patrons had noticed too. A woman in a black cocktail dress stood up and held a hand to her mouth.

Anton shoved his napkin aside and got to his feet. 'I'll go check,' he muttered.

'Call an ambulance,' a woman at another table said.

Before Anton could extricate himself from his table, a diner in an expensive suit was already kneeling at the prone figure. He seemed to be feeling for a pulse and was shaking his head. He headed towards the door.

* * *

'Well, this is one way to make sure you're on the front page.' Pulling on her gloves, Helen approached the crime scene with Randall. She glanced around and could see the restaurant patrons staring at what was going on. There must have been ten or fifteen people watching them.

'Can't get much more public than this,' Randall murmured.

Helen turned to one of the uniformed officers putting a cordon around the crime scene. 'Get rid of the onlookers. Tell them the restaurant is closed. But before they go, take statements from them all.'

The officer nodded glumly.

'Surely you can't just dump a body here and no one see it?' Randall said. The garden was flanked on all sides by the glass windows of the restaurant.

'This was done for maximum attention.' A lump forming in the pit of her stomach, Helen parted the fronds of a large tropical plant and looked down at the victim's face.

Shit.

'Is it . . ?'

'Vera Hudson.' Helen shook her head. All the happy smiling photographs of Vera came into her mind. What a waste. The girl's lifeless eyes stared into the sky. She was wearing a gold turtleneck sweater and jeans, which looked clean. Helen gently turned down the collar to reveal blue-and-green bruising at her neck. Her nails looked recently manicured. There appeared to be no debris under them and no sign of any defensive wounds.

Rigor was just starting to set in, so she hadn't been dead long. Helen glanced back at the restaurant. Was whoever did this watching in order to get an extra kick?

'Hello.' A man tried to approach but was stopped by a uniformed officer. 'I'm a doctor. I'm the one who found her.'

Helen motioned to the cordon. 'Let him through.'

The doctor looked to be in his mid-forties with black hair starting to go grey at the temples. He was wearing a white shirt, the sleeves of which were rolled up to his elbows.

'I, er, this doesn't look like an accidental death.'

Helen looked at him. *How about telling us something we don't know?* 'Were you dining at the restaurant?' she asked.

'I was. Anton McCallister.' He held out his hand, and then saw her gloves.

'So, you're a doctor, Mr McCallister?'

'I'm a surgeon.'

'What kind?'

She noticed his cheeks redden. 'Veterinary.'

'A vet? Did you move her?'

'No. I just checked for a pulse. Well, double checked for a pulse.'

'Double checked? Did you see anyone around or near the body?'

'There was a man but he was gone before I got out here.' He shook his head. 'This is a first for me.'

You're not the only one. 'We're waiting on our forensic team to arrive.' She looked down at Vera. For a second time it felt like the wind had been sucked out of her body. 'Did you get a look at this man?'

'He had his back to me. I never got a look at his face.'

Vera's lips were blue, her skin mottled. Her eyes were glassy and bloodshot, and the ligature mark around her neck suggested that, most likely, death had been caused by strangulation.

'I, um, I opened her jacket to examine her,' the doctor added.

'Thanks.' Helen patted Vera's pockets and found a small leather wallet. Inside, three pounds, a library card and some crumpled receipts. She placed it in an evidence bag. Something crinkled in her other pocket. A letter, A4 size. Helen unfolded it and swallowed hard.

I'm the Button Killer and you never caught me.
I'm the Button Killer and I'm still free.
I'm the Button Killer, come and find me.

162

'Poetic,' Randall murmured, looking over her shoulder. She placed it in a second evidence bag just as Forensics arrived. Alex Winston was lumbering towards them with his medical bag. Helen stepped back to make way for him. She would use the time he was here to wander around the crime scene.

The doctor had backed away from the scene and appeared to be on the point of leaving. 'We're going to need a statement from you before you go anywhere,' Helen said.

'Of course.'

CHAPTER FORTY

Helen moved around the surrounding area, scanning the ground. The paving stones were clear of debris and looked well worn. There was only one path from the street where he could have brought the body in. Helen followed it down to the restaurant car park. There were around twenty cars parked there, some of which were close to the entrance, so he wouldn't have had to carry the body too far. There would have been quite a lot of coming and going even before the restaurant opened, so how did he manage to remain inconspicuous? Helen made a note of the car registration numbers.

When she got back inside, the manager was waiting for her. 'I've been manager here for twenty years and I've never seen anything like this before.' He looked over at the window and shook his head. 'I can't get that poor woman's face out of my mind.'

'I understand. We'll have to have a look at your list of bookings.'

He opened his eyes wide. 'Surely you don't think anyone having lunch here would have . . . ?'

Helen held up her hands. 'It's just standard procedure. I also need the details of all your staff on duty today.'

'Right.' He went over to the reception desk. 'I should have all the information here.'

'Thanks.'

He handed her a red leather folder. 'You'll find all our bookings in there and staff information in the back. I, er, I don't mean to be crass, but do you know when I'll be able to open the restaurant again?'

Outside, the press had arrived and were clamouring for information. Hardly surprising but sooner than she'd expected. The scene was well cordoned off and mostly blocked from view by a strategically placed police van. She left just as the television camera vans were pulling up.

* * *

'Is there anything else you can tell us?' Helen asked.

Winston was kneeling over the body. A crime scene photographer was busily snapping photographs around them and another was dusting for prints.

'Yes,' Winston said flatly. 'See that slight bulge in her throat?'

'Yes.'

'There's something stuck in there. Judging from lividity and rigor, she died very recently, possibly this afternoon.'

'Thanks.' Helen waved to one of the uniformed officers, who had his notebook out.

He looked exasperated. 'We've taken statements from all the punters and nothing.'

Damn. 'If that changes, let me know.'

Randall had his hands in his pockets. 'So, if we had run that headline, this poor lassie would probably still be alive.'

'We don't know that,' she said.

He shook his head and started back towards the car. 'Come on then. We've got the job of telling a young lad that his fiancée won't be coming home this evening before he sees it on the news.'

* * *

Helen sat in the canteen, her tea untouched in front of her. Her eyes were stinging, but she couldn't afford to let herself cry. Instead, she gazed out the window watching a dog handler training two Alsatians in the fields. One of them had a good grip on his padded arm and the trainer was almost spinning it around. Helen couldn't stop hearing Randall's words. She wasn't responsible for what happened to Vera, she wasn't.

It was no good. She still felt guilty about it. She decided to go back upstairs and call Stephen. With any luck he would be free for a drink tonight, she didn't want to be alone and she didn't want to bother Terry with her problems either. He'd make her talk about them.

CHAPTER FORTY-ONE

Making his way towards his car, Randall noticed the Ford Anglia he had seen yesterday still parked in the same spot. He frowned and glanced around the car park. No one else here. The vehicle was the same model as the one registered to Ella White, but this one had different licence plates. Ach, what harm would it do to take a look?

The rear tyres were bald and there were speckles of rust on the back sills. He peered in the driver's window. A fat fly was crawling over the windscreen. The windows were grimy but he could make out some balled-up papers on the floor and a pair of sunglasses on the passenger seat. He tugged the door and it gave way. Inside, the keys were dangling in the ignition. Randall took a pair of gloves from his pocket and slipped them on. The interior looked as if it had been recently wiped down, and the seat was pushed as far back as it would go. The car smelled musty and sweet, reminding him of rotten bacon.

The hairs on the back of his neck bristled. He ran his hands around under the seats. Nothing. He opened the boot.

Shit. Dried blood and plastic sheeting. He slammed it shut. Next, he knelt down and peered at the licence plates. It looked like a 1 had been altered to make a 4, the O now a C.

He scraped at it with his thumb, and bits of black came away under his nail. It had been crudely altered using stick-on lettering.

* * *

Randall paced impatiently while a scenes of crime officer took blood samples and another dusted the car for prints. It sounded like they weren't having much success so far, and they were taking bloody ages. 'Anything?' he asked the officer, who just shook his head.

He pinched the bridge of his nose. Most likely the driver had worn gloves. You wouldn't dump a car in a police station car park if you weren't confident you'd covered your tracks.

To give himself something to do, Randall took the papers that had been lying on the dash. HO/RT/1 forms. She would only get these if she'd been stopped by the police and hadn't been able to produce her driving licence. to the incident, however minor, should have been recorded, which might give them something to go on. He'd speak to the issuing officers.

He glanced around and saw PS Robert Keaton heading towards him.

'Any idea how long the car's been parked here?' Keaton asked.

'I noticed it a day or two ago,' Randall said.

Keaton frowned. 'I didn't see anyone come into the car park who shouldn't have been here.'

'Well, no one leaves their car here for more than twenty-four hours,' Randall said.

Keaton shook his head. 'No, they don't.'

'I think this is Ella White's car. The plates have been tampered with.' He pointed. 'It looks like a bit of an amateur job, it only passes at a distance.'

'Do you think that's deliberate?' Keaton asked.

'Aye. It's all part of some big game we're playing, only we don't know the rules.' Randall blinked away spots. The bright lamps that had been set up around the car hurt his eyes. He supposed he should've called *Sergeant* Helen Carter, but he'd decided to wait on the DI instead. He was due in the next thirty minutes, and there was no way he was having Carter take the credit for his big break. Carter was only acting sergeant but if he cracked this, it would put him in the running for the position that should've been his in the first place. He would never get used to having to defer to her.

He lifted the bonnet. The serial number would be on a small plate near the engine. He'd be able to use that to find out exactly whose car this was.

* * *

After a drink with Stephen at the local next to the station. Helen headed home and sank into the bath. He'd only been able to stay for one as he was teaching that evening. She leaned her head back against the tiles. Idly she splashed the water and watched it ripple. She found herself smiling for the first time in a while. Her favourite Dave Clark Five record filtered through from the lounge, fighting a losing battle with the blaring television upstairs. She closed her eyes and listened to the beat that intermixed with the groaning wind. She felt herself drifting until she heard a pinging noise. A second later, the room went dark and the flat fell silent. She sat up, listening, sending a wave of foamy water onto the lino. All was quiet. She climbed out of the bath, wincing as her shin hit one of the taps. She fumbled for her dressing gown and flicked the light switch a couple of times. Nothing.

Helen sighed loudly. Bloody typical. She felt her way through to the living room and peered out of the window. The entire length of the street was in darkness. The builders who'd been working on the block opposite were now standing around in the road.

She lifted the window latch and called down to them. 'What's going on?'

'Power's out. Nothing to do with us though, love.'

Helen pulled her head back. She was sure she still had candles from the last power cut. They'd be in the kitchen. She rummaged through the drawers — they ought to be in the bottom one, which was where she generally kept her odd bits and bobs. Her wet hair clung to her cheeks, and she brushed it away with the back of her hand. *Where the hell are they?*

Eventually, she decided to get dressed and head to the station. She was tired but her brain was far too active for sleep.

CHAPTER FORTY-TWO

When Helen rounded the corner, she saw DC Randall in the car park standing by the boot of a car. He was stomping on the spot and blowing on his hands to keep warm. Wasn't that the one he had mentioned the other day? She frowned. It looked like it was being examined by Forensics. A scenes of crime officer was leaning into the boot. Wondering what was going on, she slowed to a stop.

She could see the annoyance flicker in Randall's eyes as she wound her window down. 'What's happened?'

Randall was definitely put out. 'I thought you'd gone home for the evening.'

'I had but there was a power cut in my block, so I thought I may as well come back here and get some work done.'

Randall grunted.

'I'll park up, then you can fill me in on what you have,' she said.

'I noticed this car parked here yesterday, and when it still hadn't moved over twenty-four hours later, I went to investigate.' A trail of vapour accompanied his words.

'Good work.' She shoved her hands into her pockets. Her hair was still damp and clinging to the back of her neck.

'This vehicle belongs to Ella White,' he said.

Helen looked down at the licence plate. 'It's been altered. Smart.'

Randall tutted. 'Not that smart. They haven't exactly done a great job of it, though it's passable from a distance.'

Helen nodded. 'Why are scenes of crime here?'

'I found traces of blood in the boot.'

An icy shiver ran down Helen's spine. The Button Killer would sometimes drive around with his victim in the boot of his car for days or even weeks. It was just one of the things he got a kick out of. This couldn't be a coincidence. The image of a car from her father's crime scene photos rose into her mind. She blinked it away.

If the car was empty, he had most likely already dumped the body. The Button Killer used to leave his victims in secluded woodland areas.

'Right. Well, there's nothing I can do here, so I'll go inside and grab a coffee.' She patted Randall on the shoulder and headed into the station.

* * *

'You look a right mess.'

Helen had just caught sight of herself in one of the grimy mirrors above the sinks. She puffed out her cheeks and tilted her head to get a better look. Her wedge hair cut had grown out to just above her shoulders. She dragged a hand through it in a vain attempt to repair the damage the bitter wind had done on the way up here. Her cheeks were pink from cold, which didn't improve matters. She splashed some water on her face and sighed.

When, coffee in hand, she entered the CID room she was surprised to find that she was the only one there. However, a lit cigarette left on a tin tray on Bell's desk told her he couldn't be far away. McKinley was also meant to be on shift, but he would be down in records. She crossed over to Bell's desk and stubbed out the cigarette, grimacing at the stench.

Back at her desk, she found a note informing her that Vera's post-mortem would take place the following afternoon. Hopefully, that would give them more answers. She would go home in a while and try to get a few hours' sleep before then. Meanwhile, all the official case files on the Button Killer had been left in boxes on the table next to so her, so she carried on going through them.

CHAPTER FORTY-THREE

Crunching on a Polo mint, Helen pulled open the door to the mortuary. This was a modern but unassuming flat-roofed building in the Cowgate area, a handy twenty minutes from the station. She followed the long corridor down to a room on the right. Alex Winston or Winston as he liked to be called was scrubbing up at the sink. He glanced over his shoulder. 'I wasn't sure if you were going to be gracing us with your presence.'

A young lad who looked barely out of high school was down at the other end of the room, clattering the metal tools no doubt needed for the autopsy. He looked up and frowned at Helen.

'Traffic was a nightmare.' It was a lie. She'd got distracted researching Mark Landis. As she stepped further into the room, she detected a faint smell like pickles, probably from the formaldehyde and other chemicals they used.

'All right.' Winston didn't look convinced. 'Just give me a moment then.' He was wearing a faded brown apron with a crisp white lab coat underneath and pulling on gloves that came up to his elbow. Helen had a good look at the victim for the first time. She shivered. Vera, only twenty-four, who went to a college class and never came home, was lying on the last of three metal slabs covered in a white sheet under lights that were just that bit too bright.

Winston gave Helen a thin smile. 'Let's get started then.'

Helen nodded and followed him over to the body. He rolled the sheet back to just under her shoulders and cleared his throat.

The lump in the pit of Helen's stomach was there again. Vera had had so much ahead of her, so much to look forward to, and now she was here, just another body on a slab. Her face looked waxy and her blue lips were slightly parted. The skin around her shoulders and chest was mottled and marbled. Helen looked at the tiled floor as Winston prepared for the first incision. The sound of bone crunching filled the silence.

'What about her neck?' Helen swallowed hard. 'I remember at the crime scene you said there was something in her throat?'

Frowning, Winston pointed a scalpel at Vera's bruised neck. 'That's right. I think there's something lodged in here.' He pressed the sides of her neck as though he was looking for a pulse.

'Can you tell what it is?' she asked.

'Something hard. Something round. But better than that, I'll show you.'

A few minutes later, he dropped the hard, round thing into a bowl. 'It's a button. A metal one.' He held the bowl out for Helen to see.

A chill ran down her spine.

He glanced at her. 'You look like you've seen a ghost.'

'I've seen this before, a long time ago.' The hard lump in her stomach turned into a wave of nausea.

CHAPTER FORTY-FOUR

Helen ran up the stairs to the CID room, arriving just as the afternoon briefing was about to start. She was desperate for a coffee but that would have to wait. She had just enough time to check what was waiting for her on her desk. The forensic report on Vera Hudson's crime scene had been rushed through, and she found that at the top of the pile. There was a note attached to the inside of the folder for her to give the forensic analyst a call. She dialled the number while skimming through the file and was about to hang up when someone answered.

'This is DS Carter — Helen Carter — I have the forensic report here for—'

'Vera Hudson?' The speaker on the other end of the line shuffled some papers. 'Gimme a minute. Right. I've found what I'm looking for now.' He tutted.

'There was a note on the report saying to give you a call.'

'Aye, that's right. I found something interesting.'

Helen's pulse quickened. 'Oh? What?'

'Hang on, I've got it here.'

Helen gripped the receiver, wanting to tell him to hurry up, but knowing that would only slow him down even more. She looked at the clock. The briefing would have started by now.

'Right . . . Sorry. So, I managed to get some fingerprints from the letter, or poem, found at the crime scene, you'll be pleased to know.'

'Good.'

'The prints aren't on record, but they were found at a previous crime scene.'

'What crime scene?' Helen groaned inwardly.

'One of the original Button Killer murders, Eunice Hanson.'

'I don't understand. How can that be?'

There was a moment of silence again. 'Yes, that's right, prints were found on the handle of a knife at that scene. The letter looks like it was written recently. Potentially, you are looking for someone who was present at both crime scenes.'

Helen gripped the receiver so hard her knuckles ached. 'Are you sure? Surely that's a mistake.'

'I'm sorry, Sergeant, I've checked it twice. I also put Eunice's file on your desk. I thought you'd want to see it.'

The phone slipped from Helen's hand as she put it down. If the same person was at both crime scenes decades apart, that strengthened the argument that Mark Landis wasn't the Button Killer. *Damn!* It made no sense.

Helen shoved a few folders aside and found the one she was looking for. Needing to sit down, she pulled her chair up to the desk and opened the file. Her heart constricted. Eunice could have passed for the sister of either Ella or Vera. They all had the same green eyes, long brown hair and slender build. Maybe that's why Vera was chosen — for her close resemblance to Eunice, who was young, only twenty-five, went to a dance hall for an evening of dancing and drinks and never came home again. It was the same M.O. as that of the Button Killer — her handbag and jacket were found in woodland, the jacket missing a silver button. Her purse was full of coins. She was seen leaving the hall with a dark-haired man. Helen turned the page and shook her head. The police sketch made the man look like some Martian. Thankfully things had moved on a bit since then.

Eunice too had been strangled and found with a button in her throat just over twenty years ago. Helen looked down at the note. How could that even be possible? How could the same fingerprint be found at two crime scenes twenty years apart when the killer was in prison? She leaned back in her chair, recalling that Mark Landis had used that unknown fingerprint as part of his defence. The print that didn't match his. The print that proved that someone else was at the crime scene, the *proof* that it wasn't him.

They had had enough other evidence at the time to convict him, but this would no doubt give rise to a lot of further questions, even now. Eunice had been his second victim and Vera was the second victim of this Button Killer copycat. That couldn't be a coincidence.

Heart hammering, Helen crossed to the spare desk, where the Button Killer files had been laid out. Near the bottom of the second stack, she found details of the first murder Landis had been convicted of. The victim's body was never found and so far, Ella White's hadn't been either.

CHAPTER FORTY-FIVE

He knelt in front of the television fumbling with the knobs, but it kept giving him static. Stupid bloody thing. He thumped the top of it with his fist. Bingo. The credits for the evening news were playing. He turned up the volume and sat back to wait. So far, nothing had been mentioned. He dug his nails into his palms. He kills someone and dumps the body right in the middle of bloody Edinburgh and they can't even be bothered to report it on the news? It should be the main headline.

When he'd got rid of that stupid Stanton bloke, he'd thought they were going to do a minute's silence the way they overplayed it. Even then they had managed to pass it off as an accident. He wanted to scream, to smash something. He would need to escalate this. He would have to force them to take notice.

He grabbed the newspaper from the coffee table. There was no mention of Vera Hudson until page six. Page bloody six! And that was one paragraph, with a tiny photograph of her, along with another small one of the crime scene showing Detectives Helen Carter and Robert Randall at the scene. *Police are appealing for witnesses . . .*

He looked up at the TV. Finally, they were showing a picture.

* * *

Randall came into CID with a cigarette clamped to his lips and a bundle of folders under his arm. 'You missed the briefing,' he muttered.

'I know.' She was still going through all the case files. 'And I had good reason to.'

'Oh, aye.' He slung the files onto his desk. 'Well, I have the lab report back on the blood from the car. It's the same type as Ella White's. No surprises there.'

Helen nodded. She had spread some of the files out on the carpet and was kneeling in front of them. 'If this is a copy of the Button Killer murders, I don't think we're going to find Ella White herself. That car was probably used to move her body from the crime scene. Mark Landis sometimes used to enjoy driving around with his victims in the boot of his car for several days after the murders. He enjoyed the risk that came with it.'

Randall rubbed his bleary eyes. 'I wish I'd looked up the car before.'

That had been the challenging thing about capturing Mark Landis. His M.O. continually developed.

'Vera Hudson's post-mortem took place this morning.' Helen sat back on her heels. 'Winston found a button in her throat.'

Randall scowled. 'Then why wasn't Ella White found with a button in her throat?'

She slid the file around. 'Because the Button Killer's first victim was never found.'

'What about Oliver Stanton?' Randall shrugged. 'Landis never threw anyone out of a train.'

'No, I think that was the trigger. I think something in Stanton's work started it all,' she said.

'But what?'

Helen shook her head.

Randall scoffed. 'Maybe.'

'The letter that was found on Vera's body, they managed to get prints off it. They're the same prints that were found at the scene of one of the Button murders nearly fifteen years ago.'

'How can that be?' Randall blew out smoke. 'What if Landis is telling the truth? What if he is innocent?'

Helen looked away. She had to believe that her father hadn't made a mistake. 'He must've been working with someone. A brother perhaps.'

'Landis's victims were discovered in remote woodland. Why has this one been more public then? Delivering a bloody car into the car park of a police station and a body at a public city centre restaurant? I mean, that's not Landis's style.'

'No, this killer is sending a message. They want to draw as much attention to themselves as possible. They want the world to know the Button Killer is back. That's why they sent the letter to the press.'

'If your theory is right, who is the next victim?' he asked.

'It will be a male, late thirties. The original victim was a taxi driver.'

'We can circulate the sketch to the taxi companies.' Randall frowned, looking at the photographs from the original crime scene showing the vehicle left by the side of the road and a man lying face down in the dirt. 'I'm not sure how much good it will do though.' He frowned. 'This was an opportunistic killing.'

'We're meant to see Landis in prison tomorrow?'

Helen nodded again. She had put it off as long as possible.

She pushed all the case files back into the box as more of the team started to filter back into the office. Someone turned the radio up again and chatter rippled around the room. Time to find some peace and quiet.

CHAPTER FORTY-SIX

'I knew I'd find you here.' Terry McKinley was standing in the doorway of the interview room Helen had retreated to for a bit of quiet. It was hardly ever used because the radiator wouldn't switch off, so it was always stiflingly hot.

'I didn't hear you come in.' Helen rubbed her bleary eyes. 'How long have I been here?'

He glanced at his watch. 'A few hours I think.'

'And with nothing to show for it. What about you?'

He shook his head. 'We've had lots of people phoning in with tips . . . The copycat's telephone call has gone out on the news.'

'That's good.'

He came into the room and closed the door behind him. He looked like he was thinking hard. 'Helen, can I say something to you?'

'Of course.' She bundled the files back into the box. 'What is it?'

'If you're not careful, you're going to burn yourself out.'

'I think we're all in danger of that with this Button Killer copycat out on the streets.'

'It's not healthy to work the hours you do.'

Helen nodded. He was right, of course. 'I know. I just . . . I need to stop him before he hurts anyone else and I need to prove the right man is in prison.'

'Keep working like this and you'll be no good to anybody.'

Helen smiled. 'You sound like my mum.'

'I hate the fact that you're going back to that flat.'

'We've been through this.'

'Why don't we go for a drink?' He held his hands up. Get something to eat? We've no' done that in ages.'

'I can't.'

'Why not?'

'I've got this . . . birthday thing.'

'Eugh . . . Helen, I forgot.'

She shook her head. 'My birthday's not until next week but my mum likes to have these birthday dinners.' She pushed her chair away from the desk. 'Though I could do with some Dutch courage. I've got my outfit in my locker, so there's time for a quick one.'

* * *

The Cask and Barrel was crammed with drinkers. Terry McKinley pushed his way to the bar while Helen made a dash for a free table in the corner. He joined her a few minutes later, clutching a pint in one hand, a Babycham in the other, and a packet of crisps between his teeth.

Helen took a large gulp of her drink. God, she needed that. Idly, she picked up a beer mat from the sticky table and tore at the corner. This wasn't her favourite pub in Edinburgh, but it was mainly frequented by cops, so it was a safe place to talk shop. 'I can only stay for one, mind.'

'How is it, being back at the flat?' McKinley wiped foam from his lip with the back of his sleeve.

Helen considered this. 'I make sure my doors are double-locked and keep an eye out for anything suspicious.'

'You can stay at my place tonight if you want. Come over after your dinner.'

'Aye, and how will that look down at the station?' Aside from that, she knew it would only complicate matters between them. Helen spotted Randall over at the dartboard, swigging from a pint glass. He turned his back on her.

'Have you, er, called that man you met at the college?' McKinley asked casually.

'The history teacher?'

'Aye.'

'We've spoken. It's just with everything going on, I didn't want to—'

'Put him in danger?'

Helen made a face. 'I don't think I'd do that.'

'I just meant that—'

'He's coming to my birthday thing tonight. I didn't really mean to invite him . . . it just kind of happened. I'm meeting him here shortly.'

There was silence between them as McKinley drained his pint.

'You don't mind, do you?' Helen asked. 'I don't want things to be awkward.'

'They're not.' He wiped his mouth with the back of his hand.

'You've done a lot for me, and you've been there when I've needed someone. I appreciate it.'

'Helen, I . . . I like you.'

'Thanks Terry, I . . .'

His brows raised. 'Stephen's here, that really was a quick one.'

'Terry.'

'I hope you have a lovely time tonight.' He stood up. 'I'd better get going.'

'I've time for another.'

'Another time.'

* * *

Helen sucked in a deep breath, smoothed out a crinkle in her skirt and pushed on the doorbell of her mum's leafy Victorian manse. Stephen was next to her, he gave her an awkward looking smile. He was wearing a tailored tweed jacket and gave her a sheepish grin. She could hear what sounded like jazz music and chatter inside the vestibule. She was annoyed to find herself feeling nervous, as though she was about to step out on stage. Fingers crossed Mum hasn't gone crazy and invited half the town like she did last year. Twenty or thirty strangers wishing her a happy birthday, along with forced small talk, was hell.

She glanced over her shoulder, visions of this Button Killer copycat following her were constantly on her mind. Even driving here, she had taken the long way and parked down the bottom of the street.

Helen's mum pulled the door open and, letting them in, looked her up and down, the welcoming smile fading. 'You're not wearing the dress I got you.'

'No.' Helen did a twirl then lifted her foot. 'But I'm wearing the stilettos.'

'That top you're wearing . . . ?'

Helen leaned in and gave her mum a kiss on the cheek. 'I made it from the dress. It was too tight. Sorry, Mum.'

'You know, if you grew your hair out and put on a little makeup, you would look so pretty.'

Helen forced a smile. 'Thanks, Mother. I'll keep that in mind.'

A beat of silence. 'It suits you. Orange is your colour.' Her mum pulled the door open. 'Everyone's in the front room.'

'Everyone?'

'Go get yourself a drink, I'll be through in a minute.' She glanced at her watch. 'We'll eat at seven.' She turned her attention to Stephen, holding out a hand. 'This is a rare occasion.'

'What are—?' Helen interjected before she could be embarrassed further.

'Pineapple chicken.'

'Mum, I—' Helen trailed off as the doorbell went again.

'I'd better get that.' She gave Helen's arm a squeeze. 'Head on through and get a drink.' Her mum gestured to the living room door. 'There's some champagne and canapés.'

Helen exchanged an awkward look with Stephen as her mum went to the door and ushered in an older couple that she recognised from her mum's work.

'Right, shall we go through then?' Stephen said, touching the small of her back.

Helen forced a smile. 'After you.' She followed Stephen into the large front room and was hit with a wave of heat from the wood fire. If she was not mistaken, Mozart's *Symphony No. 6* was crackling from her mum's ancient wind-up gramophone. She glanced around the room, relieved to find only five people drinking from champagne flutes. She had no idea who two of them were, but they gave her a nod. They looked to be in their late fifties, so they were most likely friends of her mum's.

Helen plastered on her best smile and lifted a glass from the table. 'Cheers.'

'Happy birthday.' Stephen leaned in and kissed her on the cheek. She caught a whiff of his Hai Karate aftershave. Maybe this evening wouldn't be so bad after all.

'I thought you were vegetarian?' he asked.

'I am.' Helen smiled.

He cleared his throat. 'I got you a little something — it's nothing much.'

'You didn't have to.' She took the packet from him and peeled off the gold wrapping paper. It was a small jewellery box. She glanced up at him quizzically. 'You didn't need to bother.'

'Don't worry.' His cheeks flushed and he looked to the ground. 'I mean, it's not a ring or anything.'

She opened the box, revealing a set of silver Celtic earrings. 'Wow! These are—'

'You like them?'

'Lovely.'

'Are you sure? I'm never good at choosing gifts. If you don't like them, I can give you the receipt and—'

'No, they're lovely, thank you.'

'Are you sure?'

'Honestly, I love them.' She held one up to her ear and caught sight of herself in the mirror above the fireplace. 'Thank you.'

'They really suit you.' He huffed out a sigh. 'I feel terrible about this but I'm going to have to make a quick exit after dinner.'

'That's fine.' She drained the dregs of her glass.

'I'm working in the morning and have an urgent project I need to finish first.'

'Sounds interesting.'

'It's not really. I'm also flat hunting.'

'Oh, right. Whereabouts?'

'I'm not fussed, as long as it's close to the university, and cheap.' He smiled.

'Good luck with that.'

'You know, I'd love to do what you do; it must be . . . exhilarating.'

'I wouldn't exactly call it that.' She guided him over to the table, where she refilled her glass.

'I've been following it all in the papers,' he explained. 'I've even started reading Oliver Stanton's Button Killer book. They're saying that the Button Killer might've pushed him from the train, took exception to what he had written.'

'Are *they* now?'

'It's not my usual reading. Are you any closer to catching him?'

Helen put the earrings back into the box. 'I can't really talk about it.'

'He's left no forensics either — apparently that must make it really difficult. I think what they're saying is that an innocent man could be in prison.'

Helen's jaw tightened as she glanced around the room. Another couple of her mum's friends appeared in the doorway.

'I wish there was something I could do to help. I love a good puzzle. Can you imagine that — spending, what, fifteen years confined to a cell for something you haven't done?'

'This isn't a puzzle.'

'I didn't mean it like that.'

'He did what he's in jail for.' Helen glanced over at the phone. She'd call Randall later. They'd alerted all the taxi companies in Edinburgh of the potential danger, so all they could do now is wait and hopefully the extra patrols on the streets would work.

'Just thinking about it makes me break out in a cold sweat,' he muttered.

'What does?'

He looked at her and blushed again. 'Sorry. I never know when to shut up. I'm just nervous.'

Before Helen could respond the clock chimed for dinner.

CHAPTER FORTY-SEVEN

It was near closing time. He was propped up at the bar with his second whisky. He swilled it around in the glass. He had positioned himself so he was facing the door — that way he could keep an eye on everyone who came in. The place was a dive, a wee corner pub down by the docks that practically had sawdust on the floor, but it was cheap, and he wouldn't be noticed. He'd had a quick one in the Cask and Barrel earlier, but the place had been rammed with police. He had even seen Helen Carter in there drinking, looking like she hadn't a care in the world.

Two men in overalls pushed in next to him at the bar, trying in vain to get the attention of the barman.

'You hear about the murder of that lassie in town?' one of them was saying.

He kept staring straight ahead.

'Aye, they've not caught him.'

'I bet they'll probably no' either. You know what the polis are like. Aye, the papers are saying that the Button Killer is back.' He waved at the landlord. 'Give us a look at your newspaper?'

The landlord grunted as he chucked a rolled-up copy of the *Evening News* across the bar.

He couldn't help but smile.

The man flicked through the first couple of pages. 'Aye, this is what I was talking about. He could be targeting a taxi driver next.'

'Really?'

'Read that. They reckon he's recreating all the original murders.'

'We'll be walking home tonight then, I bet you'll no' be able to get a taxi now for love nor money.'

'If I was a taxi driver, I'd be taking the night off.'

'No' me.' The blond one proclaimed.

'What?'

'Imagine catching him,' the blond grinned. 'Bet there would be a reward and you'd be popular with the lassies, that's for sure.'

'I dunno.' His other pal laughed. 'I cannae imagine you doing that.'

His smile fading, he reached into his pocket and wrapped his fingers around the cold pistol. He would make an exception for that blond.

'Maybe they didn't put the right one away the first time.'

'Aye, well that wouldn't surprise me either.'

He listened to them bluff and bluster and become braver with each pint they glugged.

As he sipped the last of his whisky, the blond was now describing in detail what he would do to him.

* * *

Most of the guests left around an hour after Stephen did and Helen was now sitting in the icy little room next to the kitchen curled up on an armchair with a glass of red and a cheese sandwich. The news was on low in the background and when Mark Landis's picture appeared on the screen, she forced herself to look at him. In less than twelve hours she would be sitting opposite him. He had asked for her several times now and tomorrow he would get what he wanted.

She grabbed the telephone. Randall picked up on the second ring and sounded annoyed.

'Is there an update?' she asked.

There was a long pause and Helen could hear the rustle of papers. 'Nothing yet.'

She heard him sighing.

'We've got officers out driving taxis around the busier areas of the town. So far nothing. By now, he'll know were on to him. If he's smart, he'll lie low for a few days.'

The screen flashed with Helen's composite drawings of the suspect.

'I'm going off shift.' Randall said. 'Best bet is he gets into a taxi with one of our officers in it.'

Helen wasn't going to get her hopes up. 'I'll see you in the morning.' She hung up the phone and turned up the volume on the telly.

* * *

He wandered in the general direction of Leith Walk. He'd had no luck finding a taxi anywhere near the pub. If he couldn't get one there, he would head up to Princes Street and pick one up in the station — there was always a long line of them desperate for punters there.

He buttoned up his jacket against the wind and kept his head down, only looking up at the sound of an engine. Warnings of the Button Killer copycat had left the streets deserted.

The sky rumbled and he managed to get his hood up as a fat blob of rain landed on his forehead. He retreated into the bus shelter feeling unfamiliar anxiety grip him as he stood and waited in the silence for the storm to pass.

* * *

Too exhausted to drive home, Helen pushed open the door to her childhood bedroom. The room smelled like a museum, cold and dusty. It looked like one too, everything exactly as she had left it to go to university.

She went over to her dresser and wiped the dust from her favourite art book, tatty with use. The room was decked out in baby pink, including the carpets and frilly net curtains. Even her records, their sleeves now faded, were still on the shelf — Manfred Mann and Dave Clark Five, along with a selection of paperback novels.

Shaking her head at the posters of Dave Clark and his band, she flopped onto the bed, which groaned under her weight. There on the windowsill stood the clay figure her brother had made just before his accident. She screwed her eyes shut. She could almost hear him pounding on the door, asking her to let him in, whenever she had a friend over. She rolled over and curled up into a ball. Maybe that was why she had left everything as it was, she didn't want to banish the memories.

* * *

Something wasn't right. He could feel it as he walked across the darkened station concourse with a growing sense of dread. He glanced around and decided it was quiet. Too quiet. When he got around the corner and noticed a solitary taxi was parked at the rank, his heart began to hammer. He watched from a distance as the driver, a muscular-looking dark-haired man in his late twenties shooed away a couple who were hauling luggage, pointing them towards the bus stop.

His suspicions were confirmed that the man was police when he pulled out his personal radio as soon as the couple turned the corner. He clenched his jaw. Pity it wasn't DC Terry McKinley, that really would have killed two birds with one stone. A flicker of light in a car at the bottom of the road caught his eye — two men in a Cortina, one sparking up a cigarette. Police, he was certain of it.

He kept his head down and headed back towards the road, listening for footsteps or an engine firing up, voices, anything that would show he'd aroused suspicion. He quickened his pace, not daring to slip a glance over his shoulder. It felt like an age before he made it outside into the cool night air and could breathe again.

He broke into a jog, wanting to put as much distance between himself and the station, only slowing once he was on George Street. A clap of thunder tore across the sky, momentarily lighting the street around him. Another low rumble grumbled, releasing a torrent of rain. He was about to give up when a taxi rounded the corner thumping along the cobbles. He managed to get a quick look at the driver and decided it would be worth the risk.

'Where to, mate?'

'Here.' He handed the driver the folded-up slip of paper he had scribbled the address on.

'That's going to cost you.'

He merely nodded.

The taxi pulled out, its diesel engine chugging like a tractor. Enjoying the warmth, he sank back. His clothes smelled of damp and his arm ached from holding it so straight, thanks to the tyre iron wedged up his sleeve.

'I was about to give up on getting a taxi.' He took off his glasses and slipped them into his pocket. They helped him seem unassuming.

'Not many of us are working tonight. Not with all this Button Killer carry-on.'

'Terrible isn't it?' It would probably take them fifteen minutes to get across town, so they might as well make some small talk.

The driver blew out a breath. 'I mean . . . I didn't want to be out on these streets either.'

'No?'

'I need the money.'

He could feel the eyes of the driver on him, so he tried to smile as he reached for his leather gloves. 'Been a taxi driver long, have you?'

CHAPTER FORTY-EIGHT

'What do you remember about the Button Killer?' Helen took a sip of her coffee. The good thing about being back home was the fresh ground stuff. It was just gone seven and Helen was already on her second cup. Her mum had her head down, reading the morning paper. Helen caught a glimpse of the headline: *Local woman still missing.*

Her mum stiffened and kept her eyes on the page. 'I don't like talking about it.'

'I know, and I don't much either — but anything you remember about that time might be of help to me.'

There was a long silence before she answered. 'I remember it being a hard time for a long time.'

'I know. I mean—'

Her mum sighed. 'It was a difficult few years for us all, your dad especially.'

'I remember.'

'I stopped going out alone, you never knew where he was going to strike next. Everyone woman I knew was terrified. Your dad was never home. I didn't have a life, I felt like a prisoner in this house. It took me a long time to feel safe in here again.' She turned the page. 'I don't like thinking about it.'

'How was Dad sure he had the right man?' Helen leaned forward.

'Your dad was a good detective.' She paused. 'There was a time when he thought it might have been one of his own behind the killings.'

Helen set her cup down on the table. 'A police officer? I never knew that.'

'You probably wouldn't, he mostly kept that theory to himself.'

'What made him think that?'

'The way the killer evaded capture. He knew how the system worked and how to cover his tracks. We even got a few strange calls here.'

'Is that the time we moved out to Aunt Margo's for a while?' Helen remembered being woken up in the middle of the night and given a couple of minutes to grab what she could.

Her mum nodded. 'The Button Killer knew things about us, and your father could never explain how. He had no trouble getting our address or finding our phone number. There was a case not long before involving a police officer in America who turned out to be a killer. I think that was on your father's mind too.'

'Do *you* think Dad got the right man?'

Her mother seemed to be considering it. 'He was under a lot of pressure to make an arrest, I remember that much.'

'What kind of pressure?'

'Politicians, the public. His bosses.'

'Not surprising, I suppose.'

'He even thought the Button Killer might be two people but he could never prove that.'

'No.'

'He barely slept in those years. He began drinking. That was when things really changed.'

Helen looked away, remembering the struggles he had.

'It wasn't long after that he had his first heart attack.'

'I remember.'

'It was one of the reasons I was so shocked when you said wanted to join the police — you're surrounded by these horrible things all the time.'

'Good things too, Mum. I help people, I make a difference.'

'I'm glad.' She didn't look convinced.

'Mark Landis has said he is innocent.'

She dropped the bacon into the bin. 'I'd hoped I'd never have to hear that name again. He's all over the telly too and the paper.' She huffed. 'Are you going to stay for lunch? I thought we could go out somewhere later.'

'Can't, I've got to get to the station.'

'So soon?'

Helen nodded solemnly. 'I'm going to see him.'

'Who?'

'Mark Landis.'

Her mum's shoulders tensed. 'Be careful.'

'I always am, Mum.'

'Are you going to see Stephen again?'

Helen shrugged. 'We've made dinner plans.'

Her mum managed a small smile. 'I'm glad.'

CHAPTER FORTY-NINE

As they drove towards the blocks of dilapidated Victorian prison buildings that were separated from the rest of the town by a formidable wall, Helen felt like she was walking across a tightrope and could fall with one wrong step. She glanced at the rows of tiny white-barred windows and lines of chimneys puffing out wispy smoke into the morning sky. Despite its size, there was still a claustrophobic feel, and she couldn't imagine being one of the thousands of inmates that called these concrete cells home.

She sighed and slipped a glance at Randall. He was in the passenger seat flicking through a newspaper and hadn't spoken much during the one-hour journey. There had been no updates from last night either, which didn't help matters, along with the disappointment that they hadn't been able to apprehend the killer last night.

Randall threw his newspaper onto the dash, then gestured to the tower blocks that had sprouted up around the prison in recent years. 'I don't think I'd like to live so close to a prison,' he muttered. 'They put houses up anywhere nowadays.'

'I don't know. At least the area will be safe. Anyone managing to escape is hardly going to stick around, are they?' Helen came to a halt in front of the gates.

'Suppose not.'

The iron gates swung open and Helen drove slowly forward, gravel crunching under the tyres.

'What do you think Landis will be like?' she asked.

He shrugged. 'No idea.

'I thought you interviewed him?'

'When?'

'We found it in one of the reports.'

'Oh, that.'

'It was about a robbery, before he was convicted of anything.'

'That was a long time ago.' He turned up the radio, his signal for the conversation to end. The upbeat tunes of the Bee Gees filled the silence.

Helen turned her attention outside. She had read through all of the briefing notes about Landis, including his psychiatric assessments, most of which were inconsistent. Earlier reports described him as paranoid and resistant, displaying a reluctance to follow any course of treatment. The most recent ones practically described him as a saint who had found religion and a passion for art, particularly portrait painting. Having anything in common with him turned her stomach.

She had also spent a long time trying to dig into his background but the only facts she knew for certain were that he was born in London sometime in 1927 or 1928, and had spent time in a children's home, whose records were lost in the Blitz. Landis had consistently given different stories about where he spent his childhood, the name of his mother, his date of birth and never any mention of his father or any siblings.

'I've heard he can be a right charmer when he wants,' Randall said. 'He's had a lot of time to think about what he is going to say.'

Helen swallowed, trying to get rid of the burning feeling in the back of her throat. 'I'll keep that in mind. What about the taxi drivers?' she asked, changing the subject.

'A lot of them are going to carry on working. It looks like we're heading into a recession, they can't afford not to. A few said they were going to keep tyre irons on their passenger seats. So, we might get lucky.'

Helen nodded again.

'I think it was a good idea for the DI to send you.'

Helen frowned. 'How do you mean?'

'Well, if we know anything about him, we know you'll be his type.'

* * *

Helen winced at the sound of the metal doors slamming shut behind her. The sound was akin to nails on a chalkboard. She placed her bag on the table while a guard patted her down. Her mouth felt dry.

Randall was already through and waiting on the other side, looking bored.

'What are you expecting to find on me?' Helen asked the guard running her hand down the length of her leg.

'Oh, you can never be too careful,' the woman said.

She joined Randall, the chemical smell in the air growing thicker, irritating the back of her throat. Coughing, they were led down to a small holding room in the basement.

'You'll get used to the smell,' the guard stated. 'There's no plumbing in the cells, so the inmates have to empty their own mess.'

'Lovely.' Randall murmured.

It was musty with no natural light, and so small Randall had to edge his way along the wall to get to his seat. Helen was directed to a seat at the end.

'We'll be right outside,' the guard explained. 'There's a buzzer under the table and he'll be cuffed throughout.' There was a clock above their head whose ticking reverberated around the room. She and Randall sat waiting in silence for at least ten minutes before the door scraped open.

'Finally,' Randall muttered. Out of the corner of her eye, Helen saw him stiffen.

If Helen believed in the devil, he'd look like Mark Landis. The man who entered the room with his hands cuffed in front of him was nothing like the Landis Helen had imagined.

He lumbered in, looking a good three stone heavier than the pictures she had seen of him. He was taller than she had expected, too, over six foot. Despite his size, what took Helen aback was how unassuming he looked. He reminded her of her history teacher back in high school, though she wasn't sure why, and if he was nervous, he showed no sign of it.

'I hope I didn't keep you waiting too long.' His voice was soft, with just the hint of a gentle Scottish accent that Helen couldn't place.

'Take a seat,' Randall gestured.

'Thank you for coming all this way to see me.' He gave Helen a faint smile. 'I don't get many visitors.'

'You have information that will help us?' Randall asked.

'I would really like to help you if you could just—'

Helen cut him off. She had been warned he was good at dominating the conversation. 'Why don't you just tell us what you have?'

'Yes, of course.'

Helen hesitated for a moment then pulled the file from her bag and placed it on the table.

He leaned forward, chains clattering against the table-top. 'Let me have a look.'

'All in good time. What can you tell us about Oliver Stanton?' Helen asked, keeping control of the conversation.

'Are there photos in there?' He looked at the folder like a starving man in front of a three-course meal.

Instinctively Helen placed her hand on the folder. 'Tell us about Oliver Stanton.'

'Stanton . . .' He clicked his tongue. 'Oliver Stanton . . .'

Randall sat forward. 'We're not going to play games.'

'Ah, I remember now. He's that true crime expert. He wrote a book on the Button Killer.' He looked at Helen and smiled again. 'Is that the man, Helen?'

Hearing him say her name made her shiver. 'Did he ever come here to speak with you? Maybe in connection with his research?' Helen asked.

He nodded slowly.

'When was this?'

'It was over two years ago at least. I found him quite arrogant, as a matter of fact.' Again, he directed his statement to Helen. 'I think you'd find him the same. Did you come all this way to ask me about him?' He frowned. 'Why?'

'We believe he was pushed from a train,' Helen said.

'What does it have to do with me?' He smiled. 'As you can see, I haven't gone anywhere.'

'It's not your style either, is it?' Randall said.

'Oh, and what would my style be, Detective? I'm an innocent man. I would never—'

'He did go into your reasons for committing those crimes in some depth in his book,' Helen interjected, not wanting to lose him. She knew that as soon as he got bored or offended, he'd just end the interview.

He shrugged. 'The real killer is still out there. I'd hoped you'd see that.'

'Let's talk about Stanton's book.' Helen pulled out a bound copy of Stanton's thesis and dropped it onto the table with a thud. 'I'm sure you'll agree with me that it's hardly a flattering account.'

Landis shook his head with a look of pity on his face. 'He told me he'd come to see me with an open mind. He wanted to learn from me.'

Helen nodded. 'There was also a lot of debate in the book about your possible innocence—'

'There was.'

'In the end, he agreed with the police that you were guilty.'

'He was misguided.' He sat back in his seat. 'I do have a theory for you. One that might help you.'

'And what's that?'

'I bet you the *real* Button Killer got offended with what was written in that book.'

'Or someone is out there doing your dirty work,' Helen countered.

'I need some water. Helen, would you like some?'

'No, we're fine. How long did this visit last?' Helen said.

'Guard!' He smiled at Helen and held up a finger indicating for her to be quiet. 'Can we have some water, please? I don't mean to be rude,' he said after the guard had left. 'It's just that I'm prone to migraines.'

'Take your time,' Randall chimed in.

There was a long silence while the guard fussed with the jug and three plastic beakers. Landis took a long drink and sighed. 'Just what I needed.' He emptied the rest of the water into the two other beakers for Randall and Helen. 'What I could really do with is a pint of ale. I've not had one of those in over fifteen years. Fifteen long years. Still, I suppose it's good for my health.'

'That's one way of putting it.'

'I now put all my energy into painting,' he smiled. 'It's quite cathartic, isn't it?'

'You wanted to help us?' Helen prompted.

'I don't suppose you have a cigarette, do you?'

Helen shook her head and glanced at Randall, who took out his packet of Player's and handed one to Landis.

Landis put the cigarette to his lips. 'Oh, that feels good. Have you got a light?'

Randall made a show of patting his pockets. 'Sorry.'

'Pity.' He placed the cigarette on the table. 'There is one small mercy to be had from this.'

'There is?' Helen couldn't think of any.

'Well, yes. I read the papers, I read about his fall, and those other women, but it shows I didn't commit the horrific crimes I was sentenced for either.' His gaze bore into Helen, who longed to look away but by an effort of will managed to maintain the stare. 'All these years I've been warning you that the real killer is out there and will most likely strike again.' He looked pained.

'In that case,' Helen said, 'maybe you can give us your opinion on the recent cases. It would be interesting to get your take on them.'

'Certainly.'

'Have you ever seen either of these women before?' Helen pulled out two non-crime scene photographs, one of Ella and one of Vera.

'No, can't say I have.'

'Are you sure?'

'I've been locked away, in case you've forgotten. I am perfectly sure. Is there a connection between the two women?'

Helen had been watching him carefully while he examined the photographs. There was something in his eyes, a split second of a flicker.

Helen got to her feet. 'Thank you for your time, Mr Landis. We'll be in touch.'

He stepped forward, the chains at his ankles rattling. 'I'm not finished yet.' He stared at her. 'I've got more I can tell you.'

'I don't think so.' She gathered up the photos.

'You're related to DI Richard Carter.' He wasn't asking.

Helen nodded.

'He was one of the officers responsible for sending me here.'

'I know.'

The stare intensified. 'Do you believe he got it right?'

'What I think doesn't matter.'

'I'm an innocent man. The only thing I was guilty of was being in the wrong place at the wrong time. I'm not saying I'm perfect but—'

Helen clenched her fists. 'You haven't got a hope of getting out of here. Rather than continuing to protest your innocence, why don't you stop playing games and tell us where the—'

He turned his back on her, speaking directly to Randall. 'She doesn't like to listen, does she?'

'I do have a little theory. Do you want to hear it?'

'Tell me.'

'I don't think you worked alone.' Helen turned to face him. 'Do you have a brother?'

'A brother?' His brows rose. 'I'm an only child. Why are you asking that?'

Helen forced a smile. 'Good day.'

CHAPTER FIFTY

Randall ground his third cigarette into the ash tray and reached for another. 'Why were you asking him about a brother?'

They were now sitting in what looked like a large library come meeting room. Helen was just glad to be away from Landis and was flicking through the prison magazine, showing artwork created by the inmates.

'Oliver Stanton's wife mentioned a brother when Terry and I went to speak with her.'

Randall was nodding.

'We haven't found any evidence of one though. She gave us a box of notes and nothing, and she'd never met the man herself.'

Randall lifted the magazine and made a face. 'The world's gone mad, letting them do art and drama, that'll no' change a thing. Do you know they are even allowed to listen to music in their cells? An' wear their own clothes?'

Before Helen could answer the door opened and the prison guard entered carrying two mugs of coffee and a packet of digestives. He gave Helen a smile. 'Sorry it took me so long, but I have the details of everyone he was in contact with in the prison, as well as the people he's shared a cell with over the years.'

Helen took a mug from his hand. 'Thanks.'

'Quite a few of them have now been released.'

'Was there anyone he was particularly close with?'

The guard shook his head. 'He's always been a model prisoner, well behaved, but I'd say he's always kept everyone at arm's length.'

'We'll check them out anyway, thank you,' Helen said.

'Aye, of course.'

'How was he when he was visited by Oliver Stanton about the book he was writing?'

The officer considered this. 'I think he thought it would get him out of here and when that didn't happen, he became more depressed.'

'In what way?'

The officer shrugged. 'I think this Oliver Stanton made some grand promises that Mark believed.'

'What about his mail?' Helen asked, sipping her drink.

'We check through all the mail before the prisoners get it. I'll warn you though, he gets plenty of fan mail.' The guard rolled his eyes.

'Fan mail?' Randall asked.

'Oh aye, he's always been popular with the ladies.'

Randall shook his head. 'What about visitors? Do any of his *fans* come to see him?'

The guard blew out a sigh. 'He hasn't had many recently, but I'll get the list for you. There's a couple that were what you could call "regulars".'

'Thanks.'

'What a backwards world we live in,' Randall remarked. 'Kill a load of people and you get more fan mail than the Beatles and have to fight off the lassies. I don't know.'

'He's had his share of marriage proposals too,' the guard said. 'I've lost count of them by now.' He said it like he was bragging.

'How romantic,' Helen remarked sardonically.

'Oh aye, and good-looking women too,' the guard said, addressing Randall. 'You should see some of the pictures.'

It was a strange phenomenon. It happened with death row inmates too. Helen had found that these women had often been abused in the past, and felt safe giving their love to someone behind bars who couldn't hurt them.

The guard went away to fetch the list.

'It doesn't seem fair,' Randall said. 'I'm twice divorced and my new girlfriend is already getting bored, complaining about my poor wages and the long hours I work. I missed her brother's wedding last week, and she was livid. I should've taken to crime.'

The officer returned. 'We check all the letters before they are handed to the inmates.' He pointed to three large crates that took up half the room. 'It's my job to go through all this lot. There's no guarantee that the women are using their real names. I mean, I wouldn't, would you?'

Helen smiled. 'I can't say it's something I've thought about doing.'

'Love makes you do crazy things, I suppose. Landis has had a few letters this week and we've kept them in here as you requested.'

'Is there anyone who writes to him regularly?' Helen asked.

'There used a to be a few but they've died off lately, if you'll excuse the pun. Once he realised that book wasn't going to help him, he's refused all visitors and letters.'

Helen smiled faintly. 'We'll let you know if we need anything else.'

Still smiling at his own joke, the guard left them to it.

'How far back in time are we going?' Randall asked.

Helen shrugged. 'Suppose we start from around the time Stanton died and go from there?'

'What did you think of Landis?' Randall asked. 'Was he what you expected?'

Helen considered this. 'I wasn't sure what to expect.' She put her pencil down. 'If I never had to speak to him again it would be too soon.'

'I've thought a lot about when I interviewed Landis after you mentioned it.' He shook his head. 'Landis didn't stand out. He had a rap sheet as long as your arm, conning old ladies out of their pension and the like, but there was never anything to suggest he was involved in murder. I mean, you've read the statement, it'll all be in there. I'll need to get McKinley to give me a copy of that too, to refresh my memory. Though from what I remember his victims always handed money over willingly.'

'It's on my desk.'

'He wasn't exactly memorable, put it like that. Why don't we just go through this lot and get out of here?' He reached for an envelope.

CHAPTER FIFTY-ONE

Helen started the car and set off for the station, Mark Landis's words repeating themselves in her head. Still on edge, she decided to take a detour to Ella White's property and look at it again with fresh eyes. She expected Randall to be annoyed at the delay but he didn't seem to mind.

A stray strand of police tape across the entrance flapped in the wind. When Helen opened the door the smell of bleach had gone. The air was icy and stale, and all the lights were out. She felt around the wall for the light switch.

'What do you think we're looking for?' Randall asked, following her in.

'I don't know. I just think there is something about Ella we're missing. We know she was running from something but we still don't know what.'

Randall looked like he was going to say something but changed his mind.

'I'll take upstairs and you check down here, OK?' Helen said.

Randall nodded.

The air in the bedroom felt thick. Sunlight leaked though the pink curtains, turning the whole room pink. She decided to start by looking under the bed. Nothing. She stood up slowly, her left knee aching. They were probably wasting their time listening to what Landis had said. Sighing, she went over to the wardrobe. Dust had started to collect on the shoulders of the colourful outfits. She slid her hands into all the pockets. Empty. Damn! The shelf above was empty too.

She went onto the landing and called down to Randall, 'Any luck?'

'Not yet.'

The shelf above the bed was too high for her to reach all the way back, so she climbed onto the bed to get a better look. Finding nothing, she went over to the window and pulled the curtains back to let in some light. The floorboard under the radio creaked when she put her foot on it, and she could feel it bounce.

She knelt down and found that the carpet wasn't completely tucked into the skirting board, and she was easily able to peel it back. The floorboard looked shorter than the others, and slightly loose. She managed to insert her hand round it and prised it open. Her fingers brushed against something cold and hard.

'Randall, I think I've found something.'

A moment later he was at her shoulder, peering over at what she was doing.

She pulled up the floorboard and snatched away her hand. Bloody splinter in her finger. She tugged it free and stared into the space beneath the floorboard. She could just make out what looked like a shoebox.

* * *

He reckoned that in another life he would've enjoyed being a taxi driver. Surprisingly, he found the drive meandering across Edinburgh relaxing, and it gave him time to think about his next steps. He kept finding himself going back to Helen Carter. She had impressed him, going back to her flat despite the risk. There was more to her than he'd initially thought.

He drummed his fingers on the steering wheel as he slowed for a bus on Princes Street. The rain had stopped and the sun had come out. He slipped a glance behind him. The cab was also surprisingly spacious. Practically speaking, there was plenty of space on the back seat to lay out a body. The occasional muffled sound — a gurgle, a faint scratching — reached his ears through the glass partition every once in a while, but they weren't loud enough to spoil the morning. He even found a pair of aviator glasses and slipped them on. Nice, very nice indeed. They complemented his leather driving gloves and made him feel different, more confident somehow.

They passed the police station, his heart doing that little fluttery thing he liked. He imagined Helen Carter inside trying in vain to track him. He leaned forward and reached into the dash and found the man's licence papers. He frowned when he noticed a couple of yellowed photographs of the taxi driver and his family. His stomach lurched as he looked down at the happy faces.

'So, your name's Anthony then?' He swallowed, his mouth suddenly dry.

The taxi driver grunted. He lay struggling against the rope that bound his wrists and ankles, his face pink with the exertion.

He adjusted the rearview mirror to get a better look. 'Who are they?' He held up the photograph.

'My children.'

'How could you have been so reckless, eh?' Anger bubbled in his gut. 'What were you doing out last night? How do you think this makes me feel, eh?'

'I need the money.' Anthony was still struggling, still trying to break free.

He thumped the dash with his fist. 'That won't do you any good, you know,' he warned. 'We're just going to go for a little drive, all right? So you might as well relax.'

'There's money in my wallet,' the taxi driver rasped. 'Take it. Take the taxi, take the lot. I'll no' say anything, just let me go.'

'I won't keep you long. We need everything to be just right.'

CHAPTER FIFTY-TWO

'What have you got?' Randall asked.

'I'm not sure exactly.' Helen was sitting on the bed with the box on her lap. 'There's some letters and newspaper clippings.' She squinted, trying to read one of the letters. Most of it was impossible to make out — the writing was yellow with age and the paper brittle.

'Can you tell who they're from?'

Helen shook her head. 'They've been written in pencil, the words just scrawled, and the sentences look like they run into one another.' She could just make out a couple of words per page. 'We need to get these back to the station and see if Forensics can tell us what they say.'

Her thumb connected with something cold and solid at the bottom of the box. She pulled out a small bronze button.

'What about the newspaper clippings?' Randall was asking.

'They're all about the Button Killer. There's hundreds of them, even going back to before he was caught. What the hell was she doing with them hidden under the floorboards?'

'Let's get all this back to the station.'

* * *

He turned into the drive, and she motioned for him to wind the window down with her index finger. Her face was twisted in annoyance. The thought of reversing out and driving away crossed his mind. Instead, he gave her a thin smile and did as she commanded.

'You're late.' She reached into the cab to touch his cheek. 'I've been waiting for ages.' She was dressed all in black and had hair half-tied up. He noticed a large leather bag at her feet. 'It's freezing out here.'

He pulled away then killed the engine. 'I went as quick as I could. You've seen the papers, haven't you?'

'That's no way to treat me.'

'You've no idea how hard this has been, do you?' He snapped back. 'The police are all over the place. I nearly got caught.'

'Do you think anyone followed you?'

He shook his head.

'Well then, the more attention we get, the better it'll be in the end for us. All that matters is that you've got him here.' She smiled as she pulled open the taxi door with a clunk. 'We'd better hurry, we don't have much time.' She slipped on a pair of leather gloves.

* * *

When Helen got back to the station, Terry McKinley looked busy reading through all the letters Mark Landis had received in prison, along with the lists of visitors he'd received.

'How are you getting on?' She headed towards the kettle. She hadn't had a coffee since the prison one.

He wiped his forehead with his sleeve. 'Nothing so far. He had a lot of visitors in the early days but then they tailed off. I am checking if any of them match our list of known criminals.'

'Good plan. What about the taxis?'

He shook his head. 'I'm starting to think we've scared him off. How did the prison go?'

'Waste of time.' Helen spooned some instant into her mug. 'I felt like he just wanted to see where we were in the investigation.'

McKinley's brow twisted in concern.

'I'm fine though.' She forced a thin smile. 'I asked him if he had a brother. He denied having one but I'm not sure.'

'I'll keep digging.'

'Thanks.' Coffee in hand Helen set down the box on her desk. 'Let's see if he makes any calls in the next few days too.'

'I thought you would've been back a while ago.'

'We took a detour.' Helen gestured to the box. 'We found this in Ella White's house.'

McKinley pushed away from his desk. 'What is it?'

'There are letters that need to go to Forensics.'

'I'll sort that.'

'Can you fax her photograph to the prison and ask them if she ever visited Landis? Do the same for Vera too.'

McKinley nodded. 'Will do.'

Before Helen could take a sip of coffee her telephone rang. It was DC Bell.

'What can I do for you?' Helen asked. She had the receiver balanced on her shoulder and used her free hand to give McKinley the box.

'Is the DI there?'

Helen tensed. She could tell by his tone something was wrong. 'No. He has a budget meeting.'

'We need him. There's been another call.'

'What kind of call?' The room felt like it was spinning.

'He said he's killed a taxi driver. He didn't call 999 this time.'

'Who did he call?'

'Jim Savoy. Told him to put it on the front page of the news.'

'Shit.' She fumbled for her pen as Bell rattled off the address.

CHAPTER FIFTY-THREE

Helen got out of the car and put her foot straight into a deep pothole. Icy water sloshed into her boot. *Bloody brilliant.* Out of the corner of her eye she could see Randall smirking. He shut the car door and headed towards the crime scene. The sun was just starting to come up.

'This is the kind of place the Button Killer used to take his victims to,' he said.

'That's what I was thinking.' Her boots sinking into the mud, she trudged towards the scene. 'If this is the copycat, our victim will be a taxi driver with dark hair, mid to late thirties.' She glanced up. The sky was just starting to turn pink. At least it would be light soon. Randall was now a few steps ahead and not doing much better than her, having managed to get mud all over his jacket. The woodland they had been called to wasn't far from a sprawling estate of identical newly built houses.

'There's a good chance that someone saw something,' Helen said.

Randall shrugged. 'I wouldn't bet on it. They don't like to talk to police around here.'

The path into the woods was evidently well used but steep. The air was clammy. Another bout of rain wasn't far off. Helen stepped up onto the embankment followed by Randall. It would be difficult to get any forensic evidence out here — the rain would have washed it away. That was probably why the Button Killer left his victims in places like this, and how he'd managed to get away with killing as many as he had.

Helen ducked under the cordon and approached the body, which was only partially hidden by leaves and twigs. She grunted. It was a pretty half-arsed attempt to conceal him.

No matter how many times she came across scenes like this, they never seemed to get any easier. It was probably a good thing, she supposed. It kept her instincts sharp. He was lying on his stomach, his fingers covered in soil. She could see the white mark on his index finger where a ring had been. He was wearing a knitted jumper and jeans. The jumper was torn at the sleeves and stained with blood. Helen could see purple rope marks at his wrists.

'Sergeant Carter, so nice to see you again and so soon.' Winston, the pathologist, kept his eyes on the body. The dead man's skin looked rubbery under the lamps.

'Likewise.'

Two scenes of crime officers rolled him onto his back, groaning with the effort. The victim's eyes were wide open, so dark they looked black. Congealed blood glimmered on his thinning brown hair and his jaw was pitted with acne scars. He appeared to be in his mid-thirties, slim — almost thin — with narrow shoulders.

Helen crouched next to the prone figure. 'So, who are you then? Do we have an ID?'

The pathologist shook his head. 'Not yet.'

'Any keys on him?' she asked.

'No keys, no wallet.'

'We believe whoever murdered him could be someone copying the Button Killer. If it is, our victim is probably a taxi driver.'

'It doesn't look like he's been dead long,' Winston said.

'This is a well-used path,' Randall said. 'It doesn't look like they made much effort to try and hide him either.'

'What are your thoughts?' Helen said to Winston.

'Well, his skull is fractured.' He turned the hands palm upwards. They bore cuts and were covered in grit. He made a face. 'No sign of any defensive injuries.'

'Do you know what he was hit with?' Randall said.

'Could it have been a tyre iron?' Helen asked Winston. 'That's how Landis murdered that taxi driver.'

'Yes, that would do it,' Winston said. 'He has a cylindrical indentation near the base of his skull.'

'Is that what killed him, do you think?' she said.

Winston nodded. 'I don't think he succumbed to his injuries straight away. You see there.' He pointed to some track marks in the boggy ground. 'I think he crawled here before he died.'

The wind whipped the trees that surrounded them, blowing Helen's hair into her mouth. She brushed it aside.

'He was found by a dog walker, a local man who didn't recognise him.'

'Great,' Helen muttered. 'I think we should contact all the taxi companies and see if any drivers are missing.'

'Obviously,' Randall said, sounding impatient. 'Is there anything else we need to know?' He and Helen had been on duty nearly twenty hours now, and it was beginning to tell.

'Could this be the work of a single person?' Helen asked.

'Hard to tell.' Winston shrugged. 'I'll know more at the post-mortem.' He snapped his case shut and stood up. 'I'll get my assistant to call you.'

'Thanks.' Helen and Randall headed back through the woods. The going was tough — thick roots jutted from the rocky ground, which was overgrown with shrubs, weeds and vines. A perfect place to discard any evidence.

A uniformed officer was frowning and speaking into his radio as they got to where they'd parked the car. Helen could just make out the word "taxi". She exchanged a look with Randall.

'An abandoned taxi has been found in a multistorey car park,' the officer said. 'The driver — an Anthony Reynolds — matches your victim's description. His wife reported him missing this morning.'

'Well, it looks like you were right. We are dealing with a copycat then.' Randall got into the car.

'Wait!' The officer was waving at them.

Randall sighed. 'What now?'

CHAPTER FIFTY-FOUR

The officer jogged up to them, red faced and panting. 'We've spoken to a couple of the locals. They said that last night there was a woman at the bottom of the lane stopping traffic from going any further.'

'Why?'

'Apparently she was saying there had been an accident and the road was blocked.'

'Has any accident been reported?' Helen asked.

'That's what I was just checking, and there hasn't,' the officer said.

'Good work.' Helen exchanged a look with Randall. 'Who did you speak to?'

'That house on the end there. The one with the broken plant pots out front.'

'You go up and speak to them,' Randall said. 'I'll try the houses around the other side.'

* * *

'Mr Sam Wiley?' Helen asked.

'Aye, that's me.'

Helen held up her warrant card. The man she was speaking to was in his late fifties and wore thick-rimmed glasses and faded brown overalls. His cottage was the first one at the bottom of the lane. The other two seemed to be deserted as far as Helen could tell.

'Do you mind if we ask you a few questions about the woman you saw in the lane last night?'

The man frowned. 'I suppose you'd better come in then.'

They followed him to his front room. Helen took her notebook from her pocket.

'The funny thing is that when the woman flagged me down, I wasn't even going up the lane. I only use it to turn round in. So when she said I couldn't continue, I wasn't bothered.'

'Did you see if she had a vehicle?' Helen asked.

'Nah, didn't see one. Mind you, I wasn't really looking. I was keen to get home. I'd just come off a twelve-hour shift, you see.'

'What do you do?'

He smiled. 'Nothing fancy. I just work in the building trade. I was probably a bit earlier than usual, now that I think about it.'

Are you the only person living in this row?' she asked.

'Aye. The rest moved out a long time ago. The council says repairing these houses is "not viable". Even the lead's been stripped from the roofs of the other ones.'

'So, this woman. What did she say to you?'

'Ach, no' much. Just what I told you. I said it was fine and went on my way. Like I say, I wasn't bothered.'

'What did she look like?' Helen asked, biro poised.

'Hard to say. She kept her head down and she was wearing a hat and glasses. I wouldn't recognise her if I saw her again.'

'Was she young? Old?'

He shrugged. 'Around the same age as you, I reckon. Same height and maybe a bit thinner.'

'What was she wearing?'

'Now, let's see. Dark clothing. Trousers, I remember that.'

'What about her accent?'

'Scottish. She sounded local,' he said.

* * *

Helen caught up with Randall, who had gone to speak to other potential witnesses.

'How did you get on?' he asked.

'Waste of bloody time. You?'

'If it's a copycat, he's not working the same way, is he? The Button Killer never had a female accomplice, he was always alone,' Randall said.

'We need to consider it as a possibility though. It's hardly likely there'd be any other reason for stopping people going up that lane.'

'Maybe we're dealing with a woman working on her own.' Randall shrugged. 'It is the twentieth century.'

CHAPTER FIFTY-FIVE

Pulling their gloves on, Helen and Randall approached the black cab. All the doors were open and a forensics officer, a young man with cropped ginger hair, was busy inspecting the vehicle, looking like he would rather be anywhere but here.

'Found anything?' she asked.

'Nah. Taxi's been wiped clean,' he said.

'Hardly surprising,' Randall remarked. 'If the killer left the car out for us to find, he would have wiped it clean first, wouldn't he?'

The driving licence in the glove box belonged to a man called Anthony Reynolds, thirty-three, with an address in east Edinburgh. She found a tatty leather wallet in the foot-well, with over twenty pounds still inside, along with some dry-cleaning receipts. She looked sadly at a weathered-looking photo of Anthony with a smiling woman — presumably his wife — and two young boys.

'Robbery wasn't a motive then,' Randall said.

Helen shook her head. 'Robbery was believed to the motive for the original Button Killer murder of a taxi driver.'

'Sergeant?'

Helen stiffened. She recognised the voice immediately. She plastered on a smile and turned to face the speaker.

Randall muttered something under his breath that Helen didn't catch.

'Mr Savoy.' Helen had been warned about the journalist, who was trying to manoeuvre around her to get a look at the crime scene. He was flanked by a skinny man with a camera around his neck.

'What have you got for me?' Savoy asked. 'If you want us to keep holding back what we already have, then I need something good.'

Craven had often referred to Savoy as a shark and she could see why. She stepped in front of him to block his view. 'You are quick off the mark. How did you hear about this?'

'The call came into our office. Someone — they wouldn't say who — told us that the Button Killer was back, and he had murdered a taxi driver to prove a point.'

'What point?' she asked.

Savoy shrugged. 'He hung up. I did ask him to identify himself but got no response. In the end I wasn't even sure if I was talking to a real person. It might have been a recording.'

'How do you mean?' she asked.

'For one thing they spoke in a monotone, then there was this weird static or interference on the line. He didn't answer any of my questions and the voice was distorted. I couldn't even tell what accent he had, just that it was a man, that's about it.'

'I don't suppose the call was recorded, was it?'

He shook his head. 'Look, I have been reasonable with you lot. I held back the piece about the Button Killer being back like Craven asked.'

'I understand.'

'But if I don't get something, my editor will have me out of a job.'

'Whoever is doing this wants to spread fear. Here's what you can do. Run the story but don't mention the Button Killer,' she said.

'I'll see what I can do, but I can't make any promises,' Savoy said.

A group of onlookers had started to gather, and a uniformed officer was moving them back.

'Sergeant, we've found something,' a forensics officer called.

Helen turned to Savoy. 'You'll get your story. We just need to be careful how we do it.' She moved around the taxi, keeping her back to him so that he wouldn't see the scenes of crime officer hand her a clear plastic evidence bag containing a silver button. It looked genuine, vintage, with a swirled pattern in the centre. She could see a small piece of plum thread in the loop, as though it had been tugged off rather than let fall. It looked like it belonged to an item of women's clothing, possibly a jacket.

'What else have you got?' Savoy was still hanging around. 'Come on, you need to give me something to go on. People are getting scared. The Button Killer prowled the streets of Edinburgh for more than ten years, though you might no' remember that, Sergeant.'

'I do.'

'There's a man in prison that many people believe is innocent,' he said.

'The right man is in prison, there's no doubt about that,' Helen replied. 'We're dealing with a copycat here.'

Savoy frowned. 'The original Button Killer never contacted the press.'

'Well, he knows we're not playing ball, doesn't he?' Helen turned her back on Savoy and said to Randall, 'We'll need to get Anthony Reynolds's wife to identify him.'

Randall hesitated. She knew he didn't agree with speaking to the press, but it was out of his hands. She thrust her hands in her pockets and turned towards the car, stopping when she saw DI Craven drive up.

He wound down his window. 'Savoy is looking for an exclusive,' Helen said. She tilted her head in Savoy's direction. He was staring after her and walking towards Craven's vehicle.

'Don't worry about Savoy, I'll deal with him,' Craven said.

'Like I said to your sergeant,' Savoy began, 'I am holding off on a hot story and if I don't publish something, I'll get my hands burned.' He reached into his pocket and pulled out a packet of Player's, offering it to Craven, who shook his head. 'Not like you to turn down a cigarette. On one of them health kicks, are you?'

'Something like that.'

Savoy lit a cigarette and took a long drag. 'I've requested to speak to Landis for an exclusive. Do you know he's got a woman, some hippie freedom fighter? Claims she has proof of his innocence, and that he's been the victim of some police cover-up.'

'Rubbish.'

'Hey, don't shoot the messenger. I'm only telling you what I've been told.'

'We're dealing with a copycat,' Craven said. 'Someone that feeds off the attention and the thrill. A man in his twenties to forties with an interest in photography. Could be someone you'd least suspect of being a killer.' Craven left out the fact, based on his evident knowledge of police procedures, that he suspected the killer to be a security guard or a retired police officer. It was the last thing he wanted Savoy to know.

* * *

He wiped down the taxi driver's wedding ring and placed it in the box with all his other trinkets. It was just a cheap-looking faded gold band, nothing valuable, but it made a nice memento. He had the radio on listening out for reports on the death of Anthony Reynolds.

CHAPTER FIFTY-SIX

You can do this, Helen told herself. *It's just a nice drink, that's all.* She made her way to the bar, conscious that she was tottering. Why did she have to wear these stupid heels?

Stephen was wearing a light denim shirt with the top button undone. His blond hair was slicked back and she could see the glint of a gold chain peeking out from under his shirt. He looked completely different from the history teacher she'd met at the college. She wasn't sure she liked it.

He got up from the bar stool and put out his hands to embrace her.

'Helen! You look . . . I mean, it's so good to see you again.'

She gave his shoulder a squeeze. 'Good to see you.'

'Can I get you a drink?'

'Babycham.'

'I was surprised to hear from you, but I'm glad you called. I was worried I put my foot in it the other night.'

She smiled. He had but she'd decided to give him another chance. Taking him to her mother's hadn't been the smartest idea.

'Did you manage to find a place?' she asked, wanting to change the subject.

'What?'

'The flat hunting?'

His blue eyes sparkled. 'Oh, that. I did, up on Guthrie Street, perfect for the college. I move in next month.'

'That's great.'

He glanced around the pub, evidently not much impressed with the place but not liking to say so. He gestured towards two men at the dartboard who were laughing and talking loudly. 'I take it this is where the local constabulary come at the end of their shifts.'

'How can you tell?'

He shrugged. 'Oh, I don't know, I guess I'm just perceptive.'

Helen had picked the place because it gave her an easy way out if things didn't go well. Someone from CID was bound to come in, giving her an excuse to invent a work issue and disappear back to the station. Terry was also at the hospital tonight, so she wasn't likely to run into him in here. Her stomach did a little flip. They hadn't really talked about things either.

She sipped her glass of Babycham and to her surprise found herself relaxing. She could see from the way he was leaning forward and smiling that he was too.

'So, tell me, Miss Carter. What made you join the police?'

'Oh, I'm sure you've heard that story from my mother.'

Stephen waved his hand dismissively. 'I did. But I want to hear your version.'

'I was rebellious, I guess. Mum wanted me to go to art school. I wanted to be a psychologist.'

'What happened then?'

She pointed to the thin chain around his neck. 'What's that?'

He smiled. 'Oh, it's just something from one of my digs. It's supposed to bring the wearer luck.'

'And has it?'

'I think so.' He met her eyes.

'So, what about you then? Why go into teaching?' she asked.

'What's that old saying? Those who can, do. Those who can't, teach.' He shrugged.

'I'm sure that's not true.'

'I'll have to have a lot more to drink before I can tell that story.'

Helen found herself smiling again. 'Well, I'd like to hear it.'

* * *

The telephone rang as Helen was peeling off the heels from hell. It was only the second time she'd worn them and she was rather surprised not to find a pool of blood in them. Sucking through her teeth, she stepped onto the soft carpet. It had only been a couple of drinks but enough to make her feel woozy and warm. She had needed the distraction after today. Tonight was the first time in a long while that she'd been able to let herself relax and she was determined not to become like her father.

'All right, hang on, I'm coming, I'm coming.' She lifted the receiver.

'Helen it's me.'

'Terry! This is a surprise.' She crossed to the window and pulled the curtains shut. 'What time is it?'

'Where have you been?'

The tension in his voice caused her to stiffen. 'What's going on?'

'I've tried calling you a couple of times, but never mind that. You'd better just turn on the telly.'

'The telly? Why?'

'Just do it. ITV. Seriously. Now.'

'Shit.' Helen got on her knees in front of the television, fiddling with the knobs. 'I'm trying, give me a minute.'

The telly, along with nearly everything else in the flat, was ancient. Helen thumped the top of it, knocking the aerial onto the floor. To her surprise, that seemed to do the trick because a woman with long grey hair and a blue floral dress had come into focus. She was explaining to the talk-show host that Mark Landis was an innocent man. *This was all they bloody needed.*

'She's a lawyer,' McKinley explained, still on the line. 'A good one, apparently. She specialises in helping people who've been wrongfully convicted.'

'Oh, God!' Helen turned up the volume.

'Mark has been languishing in prison for over thirteen years and an innocent man has lost most of his young life,' the woman was saying.

'Huh! What about all his victims?' Helen said. 'They lost all their lives. Spending the rest of his life in prison was the least he deserved.'

'Today, there has been another Button Killer killing. A young taxi driver. Murdered right under the polices' noses. Murdered, I should add, in similar style to the original murders. Yet the man who supposedly committed those atrocious crimes is in prison? How could that be?' She paused, frowning, for dramatic effect.

Helen felt suddenly sober.

'When Mark was arrested,' she carried on, *'He had a long history with the police, and is the first to admit he was no saint, but he had never committed a violent crime. He was an easy target for the police, one who would be convenient to get off the streets, and that is exactly what happened.'*

Helen turned the volume down. The woman was still talking but she had heard enough.

'What do you think?' McKinley asked.

'I'm not surprised.'

'Helen, what if he gets out of prison?'

She shook her head. 'I can't think about that.'

She jumped as there was a knock at the front door.

'What was that?'

'Someone's at the door.'

'At this time of night?'

Helen clambered to her feet.

'Are you going to answer it?' McKinley asked.

Whoever it was knocked again.

* * *

'What are you doing here?' She'd made it quite clear earlier that she wasn't ready for anything more, especially not in the middle of a case, not while Ted was . . .

Stephen took a step back. 'Sorry. I didn't mean to startle you, but you left this.' He held up Helen's purse.

'I'm sorry. I didn't even realise.'

'I just thought you might need it,' he said.

'How come you know where I live?' she asked.

'Your address was on a dry-cleaning slip in the back. I hope you don't mind, I just wasn't sure when I'd see you again.'

She took the purse and put it on the side table. 'Thank you, I appreciate it. I hope it didn't take you out of your way.'

He smiled. 'It's all right. I wanted to bring it.'

'I'd invite you in but . . .' Helen forced a smile. 'I'm just right in the middle of something.'

'I understand.' His lips thinned and Helen could see he was disappointed.

'I'll make it up to you, another time.'

CHAPTER FIFTY-SEVEN

After getting past the first chapter, Helen thumbed through the rest of the book. She didn't understand Stanton's appeal as the "real true crime tsar", as the bold statement on the back of the glossy cover described him. On the front was the creepy police sketch of Landis, an image that had often featured in her childhood nightmares.

There was very little substance in this volume, few hard facts, which was surprising given the research he'd put into the book. She supposed it had been edited down for the masses. If she hadn't needed to read it, she would have dumped it straight in the bin. Stanton seemed to suggest that the Button Killer's victims deserved what happened to them. He described one victim as an "experienced lady of the night", and detailed the number of boyfriends another was supposed to have had. Helen skimmed through until she got to the chapter entitled, "Mark Landis, Murderer or Victim of the System?" The first couple of pages detailed Landis's hard life growing up in care, and the difficult time he'd had adjusting after serving in World War Two, where he nearly died from a serious shrapnel injury.

The next chapter caught her attention. It went into more detail about how he was caught. He had served in the army with one of his final victims, Ada Campbell. Ada had been attacked and left for dead, but against all odds she had survived and identified Landis as her attacker. He had also apparently told her the names of several other people he had murdered. Helen sighed at the way Stanton cast doubt on Ada's testimony.

Landis had also been in regular trouble with the police. He had been arrested for assaulting a police officer, PS John Mills, breaking Mills's leg in the scuffle, leaving him with a permanent limp. Mills had been reassigned to desk duties before being sent home on early retirement. The author speculated on the reasons why the police took such an interest in Landis as a suspect. The final piece of evidence concerned the fingerprint found at two of the murders that hadn't belonged to Landis.

She slammed the book shut. She had read enough for one evening.

* * *

At the reception desk, Police Sergeant Robert Keaton had his head down, writing something in a ledger. Helen was tempted to sneak past, but then asked herself why she should. Keaton had been a detective sergeant in CID before his drinking problem had put him back in uniform, and he, along with others — his drinking buddy, Randall, for one — believed that Helen had stolen his job. Keaton had been in the police nearly thirty years now, and was still a font of knowledge when he wanted to be. The fact that he thought she'd stolen his job was his own childish problem.

Helen adjusted her satchel, which was packed full of files and beginning to hurt her shoulder. She cleared her throat.

Keaton raised his head. 'Detective Sergeant Carter. What can I do for you?'

She approached the counter and put her satchel down. 'It's about the Button Killer,' she said. She could see his jaw tighten. He carried on writing.

'Right.'

'I know you're busy, so I'll be quick.'

'Good. So, how can I help?'

'I wanted to ask you about a former police officer named John Mills.'

'Who?'

'It's from a while back — John Mills left the force in 1966. But it's related to the Button Killer investigation. When Mark Landis was arrested for suspected burglary, John had his leg broken in the scuffle.'

'Aye, I remember that. Vaguely.'

'Were you there?' she asked.

He made a clicking sound. 'In sixty-six, I was in Traffic. I heard what happened after.'

'So, what did happen?'

He shrugged. 'Why don't you ask Randall?'

'Why?'

'John and him, well, they were close back in the day. Look, I have hundreds of these reports to finish. The joy of being back in this role,' he muttered.

'I'll do that, thanks.' She took a steadying breath and pulled open the double door leading to the stairwell.

* * *

Helen waited until Randall had finished his customary mug of builder's tea and bacon roll before asking him about Mills. She had gone off meat after attending a fire back when she was a WPC. An old woman had died after leaving a lit cigarette smouldering in her bed, and the place had smelled like a barbecue.

Randall looked up, barely bothering to hide his annoyance, so Helen wasn't about to drag it out.

'Why didn't you mention before that you know PS John Mills? The officer injured when—'

'Knew. I knew him.'

'Fine. So why didn't you mention that you knew him?'

'He died over ten years ago.' Randall raised his eyes to the ceiling. 'Am I supposed to give you a list of everyone I know now? Because that's going to take all day.'

Helen sighed. 'Of course not. I was just speaking to Robert, and he says you two were close.'

'We were, but it was a long time ago.'

'It must've been hard seeing Landis again then.'

'No. I suppose you want to know why.' Randall's eyes flashed with animosity.

Helen nodded.

'Because that day probably saved John's life.'

'I don't understand,' she said.

'He was left with a horrible injury, but it was a wake-up call. He stopped drinking, lost weight . . .'

Helen nodded again.

Randall glanced away. 'He retired no' long after. Had a great time, travelled all over the world. Had a heart attack in the end.'

'I'm sorry to—'

'I mean, come on. Landis didn't even recognise me, did he?'

True — or if he did, Landis hadn't shown it.

'And he was arrested for those murders a few years later. Now, do you mind, because I need to get back to this.' He motioned to a report on his desk. 'And I need to get ready for shift handover.'

'It was just that Robert mentioned something about what happened after,' Helen said.

'Aye. What happened is what I already told you. Before the other day I hadn't seen Landis in over twenty years. All right?'

'Of course.' But Helen wasn't convinced. Randall was holding something back, and she needed to figure out what.

* * *

234

After searching up and down the station, Helen finally found McKinley in the canteen, chomping through a morning sandwich.

'I need you to do something for me,' she said, pulling out a seat opposite.

'Aye?'

'I need you to dig up everything you can on John Mills.'

'John Mills?'

'Keep this between us, all right? I don't want Randall finding out.'

'Is there something I should know?' McKinley frowned. 'Why mustn't Randall find out?'

'It might relate to him.'

'I'll see what I can find.'

CHAPTER FIFTY-EIGHT

Helen got back to her desk later that afternoon, large coffee in hand, and found a message on her typewriter telling her to phone the prison. She glanced around. Randall was at his desk doing his usual two-finger typing and DC Bell was at the other end of the office sifting through one of the metal filing cabinets.

'Is that the note to call the prison?' Randall asked, not bothering to look up.

'It is.'

'No need to bother with that.'

Helen rubbed her forehead, feeling the usual tension build. 'What do you mean?'

'I called them. I saw the note about an hour ago.'

'And?'

'Well, as we could be looking for a female accomplice, I thought she might've visited Landis in prison. I suppose you saw the news last night, along with most of Scotland—'

Helen didn't like where this was going but before she could say anything, Craven appeared in the doorway of his office. He didn't look pleased. She had seen the news and Landis's interview from prison. 'We've expected Landis to make some noise.'

'It's more than noise,' Randall shook his head. 'Way he's been going he'll be out next month.'

'Has something happened?' Helen met eyes with Craven.

'We've been informed that Landis got some suspicious mail this morning,' he said.

'Who from?' Helen looked from Craven to Randall.

'The Button Killer — or so it says, anyway,' Randall said flatly.

Shit. 'What did it say? What do they want?'

'You'd better have a look.' Craven beckoned to Helen, who, followed by Randall, went into his office.

'There's a copy of the letter on the fax machine.'

She picked it up, trying her best to stop her hands trembling and failing miserably. The first page consisted of a typed letter, the second a scan of two Polaroid photographs.

'Read the letter,' Craven muttered.

The letter began by stating that a copy had been sent to the press so the public would know the truth. It also said that they knew Mark Landis was innocent and had been fitted up by corrupt police officers who had framed and planted evidence on an innocent man to make themselves look "good". The room began to spin around her. She could hear Randall and Craven talking but couldn't make out the words.

> *I take objection to someone being in prison for my work, taking the credit for the things I did. It is disrespectful to have books written about me but using Landis's name instead of mine. It is disrespectful to think I'd be so stupid as to be caught and left to languish in some prison like a caged animal in a zoo.*
>
> *Signed, the Button Killer.*

'Helen.' Randall was tapping her arm. 'Are you even listening to me?'

She shook her head. If she didn't sit down, she'd be sick.

'Helen, this is serious.'

'How do you mean?'

'There are also bank statements that show that your father was paid four-figure sums on the day Landis was arrested and when he was convicted.'

'That's not possible.'

'Look for yourself.'

'Where . . . where did they come from?'

'They came in with the letter.'

'That doesn't mean they're real.'

'They don't look like they been forged.' Randall stated. 'I'm waiting for the bank to confirm.'

'Paid by who?'

'We don't know yet.'

Helen slumped onto a seat and put her head in her hands. 'Even if it were true that he received money into his bank. There's no proof that my father was bribed to have Landis convicted. Why would he? It doesn't make sense.'

'No, but it plays in Landis's favour. It casts doubt.'

'This makes no sense.'

'His appeal looks like it's going to go his way.'

Helen was winded. 'Jack, my dad was far from perfect. I just don't understand why this has all come up now. I know he wouldn't have put the wrong man in prison for money.'

'Landis's appeal has been in the works for a long time,' Craven said.

Helen shrugged. 'So, all of these supposed Button Killer murders couldn't have happened at a more opportune time.'

Craven nodded. 'I'm going to be honest with you, Helen. It does not look good.'

'Landis is guilty,' Helen stated.

'The evidence is mounting that he's not, despite what we may think,' Craven said.

Bile rose in Helen's throat. 'There is so much to this that doesn't make sense. We . . . we went to Ella White's property and found letters under the floorboards, newspaper articles on the Button Killer. There's something going on there. Landis gets a lot of female attention. I don't know, maybe Ella was one of them.' She knew she was grasping at straws. 'Sick and bizarre as it is, Landis has a lot of fans, female admirers, whatever you want to call them. What if one of his fans is a serial murderer? Maybe they're committing these murders to win Landis's admiration and his freedom? And that's why they're pretending to be the Button Killer.'

'Fax the images of Ella or Vera to the prison and see if anyone recognises them,' Craven said. 'If we don't find something to nail on Landis, he could be out in a matter of weeks.'

CHAPTER FIFTY-NINE

'Right. Sorry, I have it somewhere . . .' Helen had the telephone wedged between her neck and shoulder and was searching her desk. Her head was thumping and she couldn't concentrate. The pathologist had called her looking for some further information. She pushed papers around on her desk, trying to find what she was looking for. Every time she went out, more documents seemed to be added to the pile, which was becoming increasingly disordered as the hours went by. She was sure Randall was going through her files, but she had no way to prove it.

Damn! One of the folders landed on the floor with a thud, spilling its contents across the carpet. She knelt to gather them up and her temple connected with the corner of the desk.

Shit. She nearly dropped the telephone, just managing to catch it before it hit the floor.

'What was that?' Winston asked, sounding annoyed. 'Sergeant, I don't have a lot of time here.'

She picked up the last photograph from the floor, a close-up of Ella White smiling standing outside the shop where she had worked. Helen let go of the photo. Panic rising. She staggered to her feet and rifled through her pedestal. They were here somewhere, she was sure.

'Looking for something?' Randall peered over his typewriter, two fingers poised above his keys and a cigarette dangling from his lips.

Helen swallowed hard. Not taking her eyes off the photo, she shook her head. 'I'm going to have to call you back.'

'Helen, I must—'

She slammed the phone down.

'Sure I can't help?' Randall began to get up from his desk.

She shook her head and fumbled through the drawer, pulling out paper, pencils, books, her brother's final school photograph. She avoided looking at it most of the time yet couldn't bear not having it near.

She piled everything onto the table. A couple of the pencils rolled to the ground. No luck. She pulled out the entire drawer. *Please don't say I've lost them.* She'd put them in here, she was sure of it. Sweet wrappers. Polo packets. Tissues.

Finally, her fingers connected with the box. Meanwhile, Randall was now on his feet. Her heart was hammering in her ears, her hands felt clammy. It took her a couple of tries to prise it open.

She emptied the earrings out onto the desk next to the photograph. Yes, they were the same. The earrings Stephen had given her were exactly the same as the ones Ella White was wearing.

Her blood ran cold. The DI wasn't in his office and McKinley was down in records. *There's no way Stephen can be involved in this*, she told herself. *It has to be a coincidence.*

She grabbed her jacket from the back of the chair, picked up the box and headed for the door.

'I'll phone Winston back then, shall I?' Randall called after her.

* * *

'Terry?' The lights were out in the records room. Where the hell could he be? She dragged a hand through her hair and looked down at the box in her hand. She knew Stephen worked late at the university on a Thursday, so he was probably there now, though he wouldn't be for much longer. She could take Randall with her, but if she was wrong, it would blow up in her face. She turned to close the door and walked straight into McKinley. She dropped the box.

'I've not found much yet.' McKinley said reaching down for it.

'It's not about that,' she said.

'What is it then?' He took off the giant pair of headphones he'd been wearing. She could hear the tinny sound of music from his Walkman but couldn't make out what he was listening to. She could see the growing look of concern on his face.

'Where have you been?' Helen asked.

'Randall asked me to pull out some records for him. Didn't he tell you?'

'No, he didn't. What records? Anyway, it doesn't matter right now.'

'Helen, what's going on? Has something happened?'

'I need your help. I'll explain on the way.' Helen started down the corridor.

'You know the story that Randall gave you about John Mills?' he said.

'Aye.'

'As far as I can see, it's not true.'

She stopped in her tracks. 'How do you mean?'

'Mills was pensioned off for his drinking issues and was working in a supermarket when he died of a heart attack. He was destitute, living in a grotty old flat.'

Quite a different picture from the turnaround Randall had painted.

'I also went over all the previous Ella White incidents — you know, when she called the police about someone breaking into her home and when she said she had a stalker. On two of those occasions, she specifically asked for Randall.'

This was all she needed, but she couldn't think about it right now. She needed to get to Stephen. She would get Terry to radio the DI and update him once they were in the car.

CHAPTER SIXTY

Stephen was at the back of the classroom stuffing papers into a briefcase. He had his tweed jacket draped over his arm. All the chairs had been stacked on the desks.

She rattled on the door to get his attention, clenching her fists to stop them shaking. Terry McKinley was waiting in the car. She hadn't given him the full story, otherwise he'd never let her do this alone.

Stephen looked up and smiled, but it faded when he saw her face. 'Helen, this is a nice surprise. Are you going to join the art class?'

'Not tonight.'

'If you want to go for a drink, I . . . Is everything all right?'

'No.' She took a step forward. 'Everything is not all right.' She was surprised at how level her voice sounded.

'OK.' Stephen's face fell. 'I'm just packing up here. I've been reading about this little French place that—'

'This isn't a social call.'

'No?' His eyes widened. 'I don't understand. Are you here about your case?'

Helen nodded. 'That's exactly why I'm here.'

'It's terrible what happened to that girl. Are you any closer to catching the person responsible?'

'Am I looking at him?' she said.

'What?'

She said nothing, continuing to stare at him.

'Helen, I don't understand, but if that's a joke, I don't find it funny.'

She took the box of earrings from her pocket and put them down on the desk in front of him.

He looked at them. 'Don't you like them?'

'I thought they were lovely,' she said.

'I'm pleased.'

'I also thought they looked familiar.'

'What is going on here?' he folded his arms.

'Do you recognise the name Ella White?'

'She was on the news, I think.'

'Well, these—' she tapped the box — 'are the very earrings that Ella White is wearing in the photograph that's in all the papers.'

'I don't understand.'

'Now, why would you give me those earrings?'

'Helen.' He stepped forward and put his hands on her shoulders. 'Surely, you don't think I would, I don't know, murder someone then give the police officer investigating the case something that belonged to the victim? That would be madness.'

'Or thrilling?' Her gaze bore into him. She took Ella's picture from the back of her notebook and placed it next to the box. 'Take a look for yourself.'

'You can't seriously think that, or you wouldn't have come alone. May I?' he pointed to the photograph and Helen slid it closer it to him.

There was a long moment of silence.

'No. Maybe they're the same style, but they're not the same earrings.' He handed her the photograph back. 'The shop where I got them has probably sold dozens of them.' He sighed. 'They were on sale. I got them from the department store up on Lothian Road. I must have bought them about a month ago.'

Helen felt sick. That was the shop where Ella worked.

'I thought they were nice, and the assistant said they were popular.' He began to rifle through his briefcase. 'I'm sure it's in here somewhere . . . Here.'

He took a slip of paper from his briefcase. 'I even kept the receipt.'

'Stephen, I feel terrible.'

His brows lifted. 'I don't earn much on a teacher's salary but I'm not a thief or . . . some crazed killer.'

Helen shrugged and met his glare. 'Then you'll have no problem accompanying me to the station.'

'This has got to be a joke.'

'I'm not laughing.'

'If that's what you want to do, then let's go. I need to clear my name.'

CHAPTER SIXTY-ONE

Sitting by the ancient gramophone, he put a cigarette to his lips and listened to the singer crooning. The song was called "My Echo, My Shadow and Me." It was one his mother used to sing to him, a lifetime ago now.

He despised smoking but he did it anyway. He could hear his mother saying, *'It's a grubby and disgusting habit and it'll stunt your growth.'* It was disgusting, but no matter how hard he tried he found himself puffing away, taking one long drag after another like it might save him from his grief. Blowing out smoke, he glanced around the room that used to be his safe space.

Now that Vera had gone, emptiness had seeped into everything, dragging him down. Colours that were once luminous had dimmed, the world just that shade darker. Even the rose on the windowsill had wilted, shedding its leaves onto the carpet. He picked one up and ground it to dust between his fingers.

Well, there was no point wallowing. He went over to the gramophone and lifted the needle, scraping the record. At the door, he shrugged on the jacket Oliver Stanton had left on the train. He was ready for the next stage.

* * *

Helen had insisted they weren't to use one of those stuffy windowless interview rooms. That left the meeting room next to CID. Stephen had refused the offer of coffee. Unable to participate in the interview, owing to her personal connection to the suspect, Helen had decided to wait it out in the canteen, while Craven and Randall questioned him. She couldn't keep her eyes off the big bloody clock above the counter, watching the minute hand move forward so slowly she could swear the thing had stopped.

She had two empty cups of coffee in front of her and bit into a Fry's chocolate bar and closed her eyes. If there ever was a time for comfort eating, it was now. She liked Stephen — he was nice, a history teacher. She had gone out for drinks with him, he'd been at her birthday do. She'd met him at her mum's wedding for goodness' sake! *Shit*. Surely, she would have known.

'Helen.'

She opened her eyes.

Stephen slumped down on the chair opposite. His tie was undone, his jacket slung over his arm.

'Well, that was a first. I've never been interviewed by the police before, never even got a parking ticket. And before you ask, I've been cleared of any wrongdoing. I can honestly say that this has been the worst day I've ever had.'

'I can only imagine.'

He stared at her. 'Can you?'

'Stephen, I want to apologise.'

'Luckily I was on a college trip when one of the murders took place, and I had a — what's the word — an alibi for the others.'

'I hope you can see my side of it.'

'That's why I'm here now. It's why I haven't just walked straight out of the station.'

'I'm glad.' She said quietly. 'Let's go for a drink, let me make it up to you. There's that lovely French place not far from here.'

He looked like he was thinking about it, then shook his head.

'Maybe another evening then, let me drive you home.'

'You thought that I was capable of those horrible things? That's what you thought of me?'

Helen could see he was angry but trying his best to hold it in.

'I didn't . . . not really. I just don't know what I am doing anymore. A cold-blooded murderer is going to be let out of prison and there is nothing I seem to be able to do about it. I don't blame you,' Helen muttered. 'I can't even begin to imagine if I was in your position.'

'No.' He glared at her.

'I feel terrible, Stephen. I hate that I hurt you.'

He was nodding.

'I hope we can move past this,' Helen said hesitantly. 'Start again.'

'I just don't think this kind of life is right for me, Helen. You see so much of the bad in the world, and if you can't also see the good, then—'

'I understand.' She let out a long sigh. 'I'm never going to hear the end of this from my mum.'

Stephen smiled. 'I won't tell her if you don't.'

'I'll hold you to that,' Helen said with a pained smile.

His smile faded. 'I hope you catch whoever is doing these horrible things. I've never had anyone think so badly of me before. I mean, you thought me capable of murder.'

'I'm sorry.'

'We live in different worlds. I like you, Helen, I really do. But can I ever believe you really trust me? I'll always wonder what's going on in your mind when you look at me.'

'It was just those earrings. They looked so much like Ella White's. Can you understand why I jumped to the conclusion I did?'

He rose from his seat. 'I hope you find who you're looking for.'

Not long after, Helen stood in front of the mirror in the bathroom, splashing her face with cold water, her eyes stinging from tears. She sucked in a long, shuddering breath. After Stephen had left the station, Helen had gone up to CID. She hadn't even got near the door when she'd heard Randall and Bell having a good laugh at her expense. Why did she have to be so rash? She slung the earrings into the bin.

CHAPTER SIXTY-TWO

Unsurprisingly, the CID office was buzzing, stuffy and over-heated. Every available officer had been tasked with going through the visitors' books and contacting everyone who'd visited Mark Landis during his years in prison. She knew in her gut Landis was too smart and they'd be unlikely to get any leads. She looked up from her papers as Bell slammed his phone down and was shaking his head. She looked back down — she only had a couple of minutes before she was due to brief the DI, and she wasn't sure what she'd tell him. He probably wouldn't be pleased that she had wasted his time too. Her head was still spinning from the conversation she'd had with Randall and Craven, and the news that Landis would probably be freed before long. And if he was, he'd pick up straight where he'd left off and kill again. Not to mention how much she'd hurt Stephen.

'There're protesters,' McKinley commented, coming into CID. 'They're down in reception. Keaton has his hands full.' He jabbed his thumb in the direction of the door.

'What?' Bell rose to his feet, rolling up his sleeves.

'Aye, I had to come in through the back door.'

Could this day get any worse? Helen kept her head down. She wasn't up to talking and was determined to knuckle down and get through her backlog of paperwork.

'What do they want?' Randall asked.

'Landis to be released.'

'Of course.' Randall got up from his desk. 'Well, they'll probably get their wish soon enough. Let's go down and have a look,' he said to Bell, who was moving to the door.

'How many are out there?' Bell asked.

McKinley puffed out his cheeks. 'A dozen, but I wouldnae be surprised if there's not more turn up. It looked like it was being organised by that hippie lawyer that was on telly the other night.'

'Let's see how they'd like a night in the cells,' Bell spat.

McKinley parted the blinds. 'It looks like there's a mob out there now.'

Randall let out an exasperated sigh. 'I'll make the DI aware.'

'Are you OK?' McKinley asked Helen when it was only the two of them in the room.

'Never better.'

'I've gone through every letter he's had, every visitor, for the last two years.' He shook his head.

A headache was building behind her eyes. 'How many are we talking about?'

'I've lost count.'

Helen crinkled her nose. 'What's that smell?' It was a bit like a mix of rubbing alcohol with a hint of lavender.

'Oh, that. You stop noticing it after a while. The writers of some of the letters to the prison had sprayed them with perfume.'

'I've also gone through all the records all the records for Ella's time in children's homes too.'

'Anything?'

'Most of the records had been destroyed in a fire like we were told. ' He shook his head and sank into the empty seat next to Helen. 'I saw Stephen go.'

'Did you?'

'Are you all right?'

Helen shrugged. 'I don't know how I feel.'

'Well, your shift's over for a start.' He reached behind and grabbed the newspaper from Randall's desk. 'You need cheering up. Have a look at what's on at the pictures.'

'I don't know.'

'I'll even buy you an ice cream.' He smiled. 'And I'm not going to take no for an answer.'

Helen rose from her chair. 'I can't. This Button Killer copycat apparently has proof of my dad being paid large sums of money. I need to try and find out the truth.'

CHAPTER SIXTY-THREE

The next morning Helen sat at her desk, with a strong coffee in her hand, staring at a report but unable to focus. She didn't get much sleep last night. All she could think about was what had happened with Stephen and the fact that Mark Landis would likely be free soon. She'd gone through her dad's old accounts with a fine-tooth comb and found nothing there either.

Randall was on the telephone. He had a habit of shouting even if the line was clear. The radio on the windowsill was spewing out some annoying disco tune, which wasn't helping either. She was tempted to turn it off, but decided it wasn't worth the aggro.

She had finally finished the last pile of reports when her phone rang. Glad of the distraction, she snatched it up on the first ring. 'Sergeant Carter here.'

'Hiya. It's Jim.'

'Jim?' The headache that had come on yesterday was still niggling.

'Aye, the prison officer from Barlinnie prison.'

'Hi, Jim, what can I do for you?' She flipped her notebook open with her free hand. 'Did you get my fax all right? And the pictures?' Where the hell had all her pens gone? She looked up and noticed Randall, still talking, one of them in his mouth.

'Aye. Well, I got the photographs you sent through. Sorry I've not got back to you. I've just got back on shift.'

'No problem.' She pulled open her pedestal drawer and rummaged about in it, finally coming across a pencil.

'The thing is, I recognised one of them.'

Helen's heart quickened. 'Which one? Who did you recognise?'

'Er . . .' She could hear him rustling papers while she sat on the edge of her seat, wanting to shout at him to hurry up. 'I wasn't sure at first, she hasn't visited in over a year.'

'Yes?'

'But I looked back through all the records . . . Just to be sure, like.'

'Who did you recognise, Jim?' She was clutching the receiver so hard her knuckles were white.

'I didn't connect at first, she was using a different name back then.'

For the love of God! 'Who was?'

'Ella White.'

Helen dropped the pencil and scrabbled to pick it up. 'Are you sure?'

'Aye, I remember her clearly. Really nice wee lassie, softly spoken. Her hair was a bit different, a bit longer, a bit lighter perhaps.'

'Why was she visiting him? Was she one of his fans, do you think?'

'I would say so. Used to write to him regular too.'

'How often did she visit?'

'Every month, like clockwork,' he said. 'Before he started refusing all visitors, of course.'

'Did she come alone?'

'I think so.'

'What name was she using?'

'Hang on. Got that somewhere . . .'

'OK.' *Come on!*

'Andrea Sutton.'

'Are you sure?'

'Certain.'

It was after two thirty by the time by the time McKinley emerged from the records room with a box of files, his shirt marked by dust and his sleeves rolled up to the elbows. Helen was standing at the incident board where Ella White/Andrea Sutton's photograph had been pinned. Bell and Randall were down in the canteen and DI Craven was sitting at McKinley's desk going through some of the files.

'So, this Ella White disappears from the flat, and someone calls the police telling us that she has been murdered. The flat has some of the hallmarks of the Button Killer murders,' Craven said. 'Except our victim spent the last couple of years visiting our killer in prison.'

Helen nodded as she picked up the copy of *Sybil* that she found in Ella's bedroom. 'I don't know if it's worth visiting Landis in prison again. He enjoys playing with us, but maybe we will get something out of him now we know about his connection to Ella White.'

'We both know he'd like to see you again. I'm coming with you, this time.'

CHAPTER SIXTY-FOUR

Craven had been right about Mark Landis wanting to see her again. He sauntered into the interview room looking pleased with himself and not taking his eyes off her. Helen wanted to look away, but there was no way she was going to.

'If I feel you're not saying something useful, I'm ending this,' Craven warned him.

'Sergeant Helen Carter, it's good to see you again. Though I do hope you don't mind me saying but you are looking a little tired.'

'Sit down,' Craven commanded.

Landis's mouth twisted but did as he was told and sat opposite Helen, splaying his legs. 'I'm glad you came back. I wanted you to, but I expect you never got my messages.'

Helen opened the first file. 'You want to help me with this investigation?'

'I do.' He threw up his hands and the chains that bound his wrists clattered. 'It's in both our interests.'

'Is it now?' Craven stated.

'What do you need?' Landis asked, ignoring Craven. 'Did you read what my solicitor said in the paper?'

Helen took the photograph of Ella and placed it in front of Landis.

For the briefest moment, Helen saw a flicker in his eyes. She leaned forward. 'We know Ella or Andrea, whatever you want to call her, used to be a regular visitor here.'

'Oh, really.' His face remained friendly, but she could tell he was surprised that they had managed to piece that together. 'Visiting me?' He frowned and lifted the photo. 'I suppose you know how many letters I used to get?'

'We have them all.'

'I thought you might. I stopped accepting them.' His lips thinned. 'There are some sick people out there. I just want to focus on the future and getting out.'

'Why did you deny knowing Ella?'

'I didn't . . .' He slid the photograph away. 'Like I say, I used to get a lot of visitors. If I remember rightly this woman was . . . a fan of the Button Killer. I'm not him, so there was no need for her to visit.'

'I've got better things to do.' Craven made a move to stand.

'I'll be out soon Helen.'

Him saying her name sent a shiver down her spine. 'I wouldn't bet on it. Whoever you are working with will be joining you behind bars soon.'

'You should let me help you. I was so worried when I read the killer struck right across the road from where you live. It seems to me that you are being targeted,' he said with a shrug.

'And why do you suppose that is?'

'Maybe whoever is doing this is angry that your father put an innocent man away behind bars.' He held up his hands. 'It's only what I can guess from what I've heard in the papers.'

* * *

Back at the office, bleary eyed with a coffee and sandwich from the canteen, Helen stopped in the doorway. Ted was standing by the desk where all the case files and photographs were stacked, and it didn't look like anyone else was around. She cleared her throat. He pulled his hand away.

'You're not meant to be in here.' Helen said.

'I tried calling.'

'Who let you up?' Helen shrugged off her jacket and draped it on the back of her chair.

'The front desk.' He gave her a smile. 'Have I caught you at a bad time?'

'What can I do for you, Ted?'

'I wanted to see how you were getting on with the files I gave you.' His smile faded. 'This has brought back a lot of memories. I want to get justice for Simone.'

'There's nothing new . . . Or I would've phoned. Sorry.'

'Of course.' There was a long silence as Helen sank into her chair.

'It keeps going through my mind,' he said. 'I remember that day so clearly. It never gets any easier.'

She could understand that. She still had flashbacks of her neighbour who was murdered by the Button Killer. She had spent most of her childhood sleeping with the light on.

He moved towards the door then stopped. 'How was the prison visit?'

'How did you know about that?'

'Keaton . . . You know what this station is like for gossip.'

Helen sighed. 'He's confident that he'll be released soon.'

'I'm sorry, Helen, I know that would've been hard to hear.'

'I expected it.'

'Still, wouldn't have been easy.' He smiled. 'You know where I am if you need me.'

'Thanks . . . if there's any developments, I'll let you know.'

'I know . . . I just feel so helpless.'

'Why don't I give you a call later?' Helen said.

* * *

McKinley followed Helen into DI Craven's office. 'I've found no trace of an Andrea Sutton.' He puffed out his cheeks. 'It seems to be a name she picked out of thin air.' He started to list with his fingers. 'I've tried homeless hostels, hospitals.'

Helen wasn't surprised. Ella probably had a long list of fake names that wouldn't be traceable.

'And I've liaised with Strathclyde and Grampian,' he carried on.

'Sounds like you've been thorough.' Helen perched on the radiator, looking at the evidence bag in her hands. 'There haven't been any reported sightings for her either.'

Craven pushed away the report he was reading. 'So, we're not any further forward.'

'We did find a set of keys in Ella White's flat.' Helen held up an evidence bag. 'They look like house keys — maybe they're for wherever she's hiding out.'

'Trouble is, we don't know where that is,' Craven said.

'I think I have a plan,' Helen stated. A crazy plan, one that was going to cost them — resources, a huge overtime bill — and might not lead to anything in the end. 'We need to smoke her out. It's the only way.'

'How?' McKinley asked. 'We've no idea where she is.'

'Well, we know that Ella or Andrea or whatever she wants to call herself is keeping an eye on the press, along with whoever she is working with, right?'

'Aye, they've been trying to use it to make sure Landis's appeal goes his way,' Craven said.

'We can use that.'

'How?'

'We need to turn the tables on them. We need to control what they print. We do that and we can send her a message.'

'What message?' Craven asked.

She smiled. 'Something enticing. Something that makes her desperate to see Landis.'

'So, we use the press to entice her to see him, and if she does—'

'We'll be there to arrest her.'

McKinley was nodding. 'What if we make it medical, say he's had a heart attack, something serious?'

'That might work,' she said.

Craven shook his head. 'Not with his appeal coming up, it's too risky. They might find out it's not true and it'll backfire on us.'

'So, what if we say there's been a fight on his wing and he's in a critical condition? We don't explicitly say its Mark Landis but say a man Landis's age, height, build—' she counted these off on her fingers — 'has been taken to the infirmary.'

'What if she just phones the prison?' Craven said.

'Then we make sure Mark is not available to take that call.' Helen stood up. 'If she is as much in love with Landis as she seems to be, she won't be able to stay away. I know I wouldn't.'

'Perhaps.' Craven shrugged.

'We can have officers at each of the hospital reception areas and others posing as visitors near the intensive care ward.'

'We know she's working with someone else, a male,' Craven added. 'He might smell a rat. He's got knowledge of how we operate.'

'So, we do this differently.'

Craven relented. 'Fine. If it's all we have then it's worth a try.' He lifted his phone and dialled the number. 'Savoy, it's Jack Craven. I've got that tantalising story I promised you . . .'

A few hours later, the story was going out on the front page of the morning paper. Helen had an early typed copy on her desk. She read it again — it was a good feeling, finally it seemed like they might be getting somewhere.

'I think this might work, Helen,' McKinley said, holding out a coffee.

'If it doesn't, my head's on the chopping block.'

She glanced back down at the newspaper. Helen now had a couple of days to get to the bottom of her dad's finances.

CHAPTER SIXTY-FIVE

Two days later

Sitting on a hard plastic chair in a little side office. Helen couldn't imagine why she'd wanted to be a nurse when she was younger. She hated hospitals — the weird chemical smell, the sound of machines beeping, trolleys rattling about, and sickness. Even the ward door flapping open and scraping shut every couple of minutes was getting to her. She hated it even more now that she was a nurse named Maisie, responsible for making sure the giant metal tea urn was topped up with hot water and that there was a constant supply of little white cups. She stood and tugged at her uniform. It didn't help that the thing was a size too small. She had been stationed near the reception desk closest to the room where Landis was supposed to be and hadn't seen anyone all day. They were on the floor above the intensive care wards, which hadn't been used for some time.

'We don't have enough nurses,' Randall had said with a smirk. Besides Helen, they had also managed to rope in some WPCs from other departments to cover various strategic points around the building. There were also uniformed officers stationed outside the room Landis was supposed to be in.

Helen sighed and stretched out her neck until it gave a satisfying clunk. 'I need to stretch my legs,' Helen said to the woman who was heading her way. 'Do you mind covering for me?'

The woman smiled. 'Not at all.'

Every now and then she caught sight of McKinley pushing wheelchairs and moving gurneys. He was wearing baggy white overalls and looking like he'd rather be anywhere else. Helen gave him a nod as she headed down the corridor. They had been here more than eight hours now, and so far, nothing.

She stopped in the stairwell and looked out the window. From here, she had a good view of the car park. Randall and Bell were parked somewhere in the sea of cars. She could imagine what Randall would be saying, that he was against this plan and expected it to fail. She carried on down one flight of steps and followed the signs for the fire exit. The hairs on her arms bristled — this part of the hospital was freezing and looked abandoned. The paint on the off-white walls had started to peel in places and was badly scuffed, and a few of the chequered floor tiles has been ripped up.

She pushed open a second set of double doors into another disused section of the hospital. Most of the overhead lights had been blown out and from the brown staining on the ceiling, it looked like water damage. Rusted trolleys lined the corridor, along with ancient wheelchairs and various metal apparatus and broken machine bits. She paused in front of a plaque that had the names of hospital staff who had died in World War One in gold lettering.

A thump made her jump. Adrenaline rushed through her body, yet she was frozen to the spot, watching as the double doors slowly swayed to a stop.

* * *

Randall was on his second cigarette in ten minutes, which was probably a bad idea as his mouth felt dry. There was a greasy spoon across the road — it would only take a minute to nip across and get something. He slipped a sideways glance at Bell, who was frowning at the crossword in the paper on his lap.

'How are you getting on?' he asked.

'Four across – Very Eager.' Bell sighed and threw the paper onto the backseat. 'I give up.'

He jabbed a thumb towards the café. 'I need a drink.'

'Aye.' Bell stretched his hands above his head. 'My back's killing me, sitting here.'

Randall nodded. Visitors into the hospital had been few and far between and he still felt that sitting here was pointless.

A rattle on the window startled him. He turned to see a young skinny lad with black hair. He looked no more than twelve years old and was gesturing for Randall to wind the window down.

He did as asked.

'Are you two cops?' the lad questioned as he peered into the car.

'Can we help you?'

McKinley's voice coming through on the radio gave the lad his answer. Bell turned it off.

'If you're wanting to speak to police, the station is down the road.' Randall made a move to put the window up.

The lad put his hand in the gap. 'I've got something for you.'

'What?' Randall said, not hiding the impatience in his voice.

'I was asked to give the two cops this.' He held up a folded piece of paper in his free hand.

Randall peeled it open. '"I don't like games?"' It was typed in faded ink.

'What the hell does that mean?' Bell asked.

'Who gave you this?' Randall clambered out of the car, his eyes darting everywhere. A car pulled out. A couple of decorators headed into the café. His grip on the car door tightened. 'Who gave you this!'

The boy looked up at him like a deer in the headlights. 'Wait, I'm not in trouble, am I?'

'The person that gave you that might have hurt a lot of people.' Then again, he told himself, it could just be someone playing a joke. He could tell from the panic in the lad's eyes that he was sincere. He took an evidence bag from his pocket and slotted the letter inside.

'He . . .' The boy swallowed and pointed to the main road. 'He . . . he was up at the phone box. He gave me a tenner and told me to hand the letter to the two police officers in the brown car.'

Randall exchanged a look with Bell.

'Should we go after him?' Bell asked.

Randall shook his head. 'No. He'll be long gone.'

'Did you get a look at him?' he asked the boy.

'Am no' sure, sir, he had a hat and glasses on. He just looked . . . normal.'

Randall huffed like the air had been knocked out of him.

'What are we going to do?' Bell asked.

'Keep a hold of him.' Randall gestured to the lad.

'Oh, no. Please, I've no' done anything wrong!'

'Come on, son.' Bell ushered the lad into the back of the car.

'This . . . this is a distraction.' Randall glanced back at the hospital. 'Get back on the radio and warn them. If he's trying to distract us, then I bet she's inside. Stay with the boy, I'll go in.'

* * *

'Shit,' Helen murmured. She patted down her pockets. Her radio. She'd left her radio upstairs. She forced herself to suck in a deep breath, telling herself that the noise she had heard was probably the wind. Making herself move, she pushed open the door with her trembling hands.

As she advanced into the passage, she was relieved to find this corridor had a thin strip of window the length of it and the morning sun flooded through, giving her a good view all the way along. She strained to hear any noise. Her heart quickened as she heard another thud in the distance. She had reached the end of the passage when she heard the tap of footsteps behind her.

'Are you all right?'

Helen whipped around, coming face-to-face with Terry McKinley, his forehead creased with concern. 'Sorry, I didn't mean to scare you.'

Helen stepped away from him. 'What are you doing down here?'

'I was worried.'

'So you followed me?' She said quietly.

'Sorry.'

'I've heard some noises. I think someone is down here.'

'Are you sure?' His shoulders tensed. 'I mean, it's probably just a rat or something,' he whispered.

'No.' She put a finger to her lip to silence him. 'A rat can't open a door.' Helen frowned as she tried to open the door to the abandoned ward as quietly as she could. The lights were completely out in this section, and it took a few moments for her eyes to adjust to the darkness. She could feel McKinley's arm next to hers. 'I've left my radio upstairs.'

He took his from his pocket. 'I'm not getting an answer.'

Helen tapped him on the arm to let him know she was going to investigate further. In this area there were a couple of beds set up with the curtains around them. She pulled them back. They were empty.

'I don't think anyone's here,' McKinley murmured.

'Try the radio again?'

This time static burst through and she could hear Bell.

'Where's Randall?' McKinley asked.

Before Bell could explain Helen heard a noise that sounding like a gurney being moved. There was someone there, she was sure of it. She took off running towards the noise.

* * *

She shouldered through another couple of doors until she was in a narrow hallway that felt like it was leading her back around the building, her heart hammering. She pulled open a door to the stairwell and listened for any indication that there was someone there. Nothing, except darkness and dust. Gasping for breath. Helen lent on the banister for support. What had she been thinking running off like that? Anyone could have been out here waiting for her. Icy realisation gripped her. She slipped a glance over her shoulder, partly surprised that McKinley hadn't followed. Composing herself, she turned back towards where she had left him. When she got back to the disused ward where she had left McKinley, she found Randall, who looked equally surprised to see her.

'Where the hell were you?' Randall said, looking annoyed. He had his radio in his hand and his collar was torn. 'I've been trying to contact you.'

'I thought I heard something.' She looked him up and down. 'I went to check it out.'

'What, alone?'

'What happened to you?' Helen asked.

'I got her.' He grinned. 'She's on her way to the van with DI Craven.'

'Her? Was she alone?'

He nodded. Still, it was a breakthrough.

'I found her on the stairwell back there — she put up quite a fight.'

'That's good.'

'Did you leave young McKinley all alone?' His smile was gone.

'Only for a minute.' Her body tensed. 'Why?'

'You shouldn't have done that.'

'Where is—?'

He jabbed a thumb towards the concrete. As soon as Helen noticed the blood on it. Her mouth went dry.

'Well, it's good we're in a hospital.'

'Is that Terry's blood?'

'Where's your radio?'

Helen swallowed. 'Where's Terry?'

* * *

Helen didn't want to face him. How could she have been so reckless? Her heart jumped when she spotted him being examined by a nurse. He was conscious, and that was something at least, but it looked like he had a head wound.

'Terry, I'm so sorry.' Helen sucked in a raspy breath 'Are you all right?'

'I've been better.' McKinley grimaced. He was sitting on the edge of a bed. The nurse was at the other side, and it looked like he was getting stitches. She could see flecks of red in his blond hair.

'What happened?' She blinked away the warmth she felt behind her eyes.

He sucked through his teeth as the nurse moved his head. 'It's nothing.'

'It doesn't look like nothing.' Helen looked away, her eyes filling with tears.

'Ach, I don't remember.'

'I shouldn't have left you. I got carried away.' She stepped forward, wanting to touch him, but hesitated.

'You could've been hurt,' McKinley warned her. 'Running off like that.'

'I . . . I wasn't thinking. I just wanted to stop them before they could hurt anyone else.'

'I get that but—'

'What happened?'

He shook his head and winced. 'Never saw it coming.'

Helen's stomach squirmed. 'Are they going to keep you in?'

'No, like I've said. I'm fine.'

Helen met eyes with the nurse.

'He should take things easy,' the nurse said. 'He's been very lucky.'

'It doesn't feel like it.' McKinley gave a pained smile.

'Believe me, it could've been a lot worse. Anyway, that's me done.' The nurse dropped the needle into a metal pan with a clunk, then gave his shoulder a squeeze. 'Take things easy and remember to take the painkillers.'

'I'll drive you home.'

'No.' McKinley eased himself up from the gurney. 'I'm going back to the station.'

CHAPTER SIXTY-SIX

Helen's chest ached as pulled out a seat opposite an ash-en-faced Ella in Interview Room One. She had been left to stew for over an hour in the hopes she'd become more cooperative.

DI Craven sat in the other chair and made a steeple of his fingers. 'It's a pleasure to see you alive and well, Miss White — or would you prefer Miss Sutton? We've all been very worried about you.'

Ella snorted. Her solicitor, a plump man in his late fifties, sat next to her, looking like he'd rather be anywhere else.

Helen stared at Ella. The young woman in front of her looked unrecognisable from her photos. Her hair was shorter and blonde, though her dark brown roots had started to come through. She seemed smaller too, but that was probably because of the baggy jumper she was wearing.

'So, tell us, you clearly weren't murdered in your flat. We found blood, so who was?' Helen asked.

'No comment,' Ella said with a shrug.

'You assaulted one of my officers,' Craven said flatly.

A grunt.

'You'll be pleased to know he'll make a full recovery,' the DI continued. 'And that's lucky for *you*. So, why don't we start at the beginning, eh? You staged your home to make it look like something bad had happened to you. Why?'

Ella's emotionless gaze met Helen's.

'Are you going to tell her she's not doing herself any favours?' Craven said to the solicitor.

'I've already advised my client of her rights.'

'Working in a shop wasn't enough excitement for you?' Craven jibed. 'Or maybe you just felt . . . what's the word . . . invisible? Inconsequential perhaps? Lonely?'

Ella's eyes snapped towards him.

'You've spent years calling the police, making up imaginary stalkers, fake intruders. Everyone saw past that, didn't they? They all saw what was right in front of them, a boring little girl with nothing better to do and no one who cared.'

She shrugged again and started picking at a chip in the table with her thumb.

'You're going to be a lot more bored in prison — and you'll go away for a long time,' Craven warned. 'And you'll be alone.'

'I'm not scared of that.'

'What are you scared of?' Helen asked.

'I'm not scared of anything.'

'We know you're not working alone. Who's helping you?' She gestured to the ring Ella was wearing a gold band on her index finger. 'That's a lovely bit of jewellery,' she stated. 'Who gave you that?'

Ella flexed her fingers, then slipped her hand under the table.

'A lot of people have been really worried about you. Your next-door neighbour spoke very highly of you.'

She gave the ghost of a smile. 'I thought he would.'

'What happened, Ella?' Helen asked.

'You can't prove I've done anything.'

'We can. Do you want to know what I think? I think you got in way over your head and now you don't know what to do.'

'How do you work that out?' Ella straightened in her seat. 'Do I have to be in here?' she asked her solicitor, who nodded in response.

'This is only the beginning. It's time you started to help yourself,' Helen said. 'Otherwise, you're looking at a very long stint in jail.'

'Do you really think that would bother me?' she scoffed. 'I've been through worse.'

Helen leaned forward. Ella White might talk a good game, but she could see the fear in her eyes. 'Do you actually know what prison's like?'

'I don't need to worry about that, I've done nothing. I left to go on holiday, it's not my fault if you lot think I'm missing, is it?'

'I want to help you Ella. Is whoever you're protecting really worth throwing your life away for?' Craven said.

'I'm not protecting anyone.'

'We know you didn't do all this on your own,' he added.

'I don't know what you're talking about.' She turned again to her solicitor. 'I'm done answering questions.'

'Is this going anywhere?' the solicitor chimed in.

Helen took a different tack. 'You have put a lot of effort in for Mark, haven't you? More than most women would. I'm impressed at your dedication.'

'I don't know what you're talking about.'

'Killing two innocent people isn't a small thing.'

Ella's eyes widened. 'I didn't.'

'Then tell us who did then. Help us before they hurt someone else.'

'I don't know who's doing it.'

'When did this obsession with the Button Killer begin?' Helen asked. 'Was it because he was safe? Behind bars, so he can't hurt you?' It will be a different story when he gets out. You'll just be another one of his victims.'

'I haven't hurt anyone.'

'You expect me to believe that? You even staged your own disappearance, so we'd believe you'd been murdered by the Button Killer.'

'I told you, I just needed to get away.'

'Why?'

She sucked in a shuddery breath.

'Who phoned the police?' Helen asked. 'If you went on holiday? Who would do that?'

'Probably someone playing a prank, you know what that estate is like.'

Helen smiled. 'We can go down this road if you want, but I have the records of every incident you've reported to the police over the past few years.'

'So?'

'You've reported being followed, stalked, beaten. You've had someone break into your home. But none of the officers who came to investigate ever found a trace of anything untoward.'

'I was telling the truth.'

'Truth is, you're a fantasist.'

'Think what you like.'

'It was all just cover to help Mark Landis. Even your neighbours, your employers, they all thought you were running from someone. That's the picture you wanted to present, isn't it?'

'No, that was the truth.'

'On two occasions you even asked for my colleague, DC Randall. Why was that?'

Ella shrugged. 'He was nice. He listened to me. Not all of them did.'

Helen exchanged a look with Craven. 'I bet Mark Landis promised you the earth, didn't he? He's smart like that. I bet he told you everything you wanted to hear.'

'It's not like that.'

'Well, tell us how it is.' Craven wasn't doing a god job of hiding the annoyance in his voice.

Ella scoffed.

'You don't really think he would keep you around when you were no longer useful to him, did you?' Helen said. 'He needs to kill.'

'Mark would never hurt me.'

'Ella, for goodness' sake, wake up! You don't mean anything to him.'

'He loves me.'

'Love? He's incapable of it. You're not special to him, you were just someone to pass the time. One of many, by the way,' Helen said. 'Judging from the letters.'

'Who's playing games now?' You know nothing about us.' She gave Helen a hard stare. 'Someone like you could never understand what we have!'

'Enlighten me then. I can only go by what I've read.'

'Huh. You lot are all the same.'

'As a matter of fact, I do understand, but I don't think you do. Have you seen what he's capable of?'

'He's innocent. You lot framed him.'

'That's not true. Why don't we look at some of his hand-iwork. I'll warn you now, these are graphic.' Helen took the folder containing the photos from her bag and laid them out on the table like a deck of cards. 'Take a good look.' She spread them out, sending some of them to the floor. 'Here, see for yourself. He likes to inflict a lot of pain and he enjoys doing it.'

Ella recoiled. 'This wasn't him.'

'Look at them.'

'No. I can't. Take them away.'

'It's enough to give you nightmares.' Helen showed her a bloody photograph of Gary Anderson, the Button Killer's original taxi-driver victim. 'This man here was only thirty-two years old and had three children under the age of five when he was beaten to death with a tyre iron. Or what about this poor woman—'

'Stop!' Ella put her hands over her ears. 'I can't listen to this, I won't.'

'You need to, this is who you've done all this for. Surely you want the whole picture? I know I would.'

Tears streamed down Ella's cheeks. 'Stop this, please.'

'Fine,' Helen relented. 'I'll put them away. Why don't we read some of his love letters? He's written to hundreds of women over the years, and he's repeated the same rubbish to you. He's not much of a wordsmith though. "You're my star . . . the only light in my life."'

Craven snorted. 'He didn't write that, did he?'

'Oh aye, he used that same line to three different women in the space of a week. There's more too.'

'I might keep that one for next time I'm down the pub,' Craven said.

'I don't believe you. You're lying.' Ella kept her eyes averted from the pictures.

'I can let you read them if you like.'

'I want to go home.'

'You won't be going home for a long time,' Helen said. 'Why don't you tell us about his brother?'

'Brother?'

'That's who's helping you, isn't it?'

Ella turned to Craven. 'I don't want to speak to her.'

'Ella, you look tired,' Craven said, playing good cop. 'Can we get you something to drink? A cigarette?'

Ella looked at the table and shook her head.

'What about something to eat?'

She shook her head again.

He tapped Helen on the shoulder and gestured to the door. Helen followed him out into the corridor.

'You're not going to get anywhere with her,' he said.

'I am.'

'No.'

'I was close, I could feel it.'

'You risk breaking her, then we'll have nothing.'

'What do you suppose we do?'

'Get Randall down here, have him turn on the charm. She likes him, so let's use that.'

'OK.' Helen blew out a sigh.

'Once this is over—' Craven looked like he was carefully choosing his words — 'we're going to need to talk about what happened in the hospital.'

CHAPTER SIXTY-SEVEN

Helen sat at her desk staring into space, too tense to work. She slipped a glance at McKinley, who was working at his desk. She felt so guilty, having left for him to get hurt, and it was obvious that he was putting on a brave face.

She looked back down at her notes. The office was sweltering. It looked like someone had finally got around to fixing the window. Her head was thumping. The interview with Ella kept going round and round in her mind. She understood why Craven had pulled her out, but at the same time she resented it. Craven was right, Ella was easily charmed, so maybe the two men would get more out of her. And if anyone could, her money was on the DI.

She'd grab a coffee then tackle the forensic report in her in-tray. She noticed a new report on the top of the pile, dealing with the murder of Anthony Reynolds. McKinley got up and crossed to the trolley they had purposed as a tea and coffee station and dropped a teabag into his mug.

'How's the head?' Helen asked.

'Hardly notice it.' He gave her a pained smile. 'Listen, Helen, I know what you're like and I know you will be beating yourself up over this, but it's nothing. I've had worse, believe me.'

'Easier said than done.' She returned his smile.

McKinley put a coffee on her desk as Helen flicked to the last page in the report. She stopped in her tracks, staring down at the enlarged grainy image of a button. It was silver with a swirl pattern, but badly scratched and faded. Helen frowned. She was certain she had seen it before.

She took the photo over to McKinley. 'Terry, take a look at this.'

McKinley nodded, brushing some custard cream crumbs from his mouth.

'Does this seem familiar to you?'

'I'm not sure.' Making a clicking sound, he headed for the spare desk where they had all the Button Killer records spread out. 'Give me a minute . . .'

He held up another photograph. 'Aye,' he muttered. 'The button is badly discoloured and aged, but I think it could have come from Simone Langford's jacket.'

* * *

'There's no doubt about it,' Ted said flatly. 'That's Simone's. I bought that jacket for her.

'Are you sure?' Helen asked. The jacket was dark purple, a particular shade she knew was Ted's favourite colour. He had a few ties in the same colour.

A shuddery sigh escaped him. 'I had the jacket specially made as a birthday present.'

'I'm sorry.'

He nodded and handed her back the evidence bag. 'She loved that jacket . . . Clematis flowers were her favourite. Anytime, I see that colour . . .'

'You don't need to explain.' Helen said.

He'd gone pale and she thought there was a chance he'd faint. 'It's hard seeing this again.'

Helen rubbed the evidence bag with her thumb. She felt at a loss for words. What could she possibly say that would make any of this Ok?

'Someone kept that button for over thirteen years, and it was found in the taxi,' he said, as if to himself. They had taken him down to the canteen for some quiet, and McKinley was on his way to the table with a tray of teas and biscuits.

Ted looked up at Helen. 'Surely, this means that who-ever . . . did what they did to Simone was the same person who murdered that taxi driver this week?'

'We can't rule that out,' McKinley said, setting down a tea in front of Ted. 'The only thing we know for certain is that it's not Mark Landis.'

'Whoever did this is still out there on the streets,' Ted said.

'Ted, we are going to do everything we can to find out what happened to Simone,' Helen said.

'I know you will. If anyone can, it's you, Helen.' He sat up straighter, as if he'd come to a decision. 'I'll need to go and let Simone's mum know.'

'Are you sure?'

He nodded. 'I don't want her to hear this on the news. She's very fragile and . . . well, I think this could finish her off.'

Helen remembered from having spoken with her.

'I don't know how I'm going to do it.'

'You can take time to think about it.'

'No. The drive will do me good, give me time to think about how I'm going to put it.' He moved his cup aside.

'Ted, take some time, this has been a shock.'

'I . . . Look, I know it's not fair for me to ask you, but would you be able to come with me?'

Helen could feel McKinley's eyes on her.

'I can't face going there by myself,' Ted added. 'You know what, I shouldn't have asked you, it's not fair.'

There was a long silence before Helen spoke again. 'My shift's almost over, I just need to get my things. Can you wait here?' She turned to McKinley. 'I should be back home by nine.'

'Are you sure?' McKinley frowned. 'Have you seen the weather forecast? It's meant to snow.'

'I'll be fine, can you call me then to keep me updated with any developments?'

'What developments?' Ted asked. 'Have you got a suspect?'

'Nothing I can talk about . . . yet.' Helen was concerned that the news might send him back to drinking, like it had after his dad died. He was sitting with his hands resting on the table, gazing out of the window at the fields beyond. It looked like he was using all his strength to keep himself together.

'I would appreciate you keeping me up to date.'

'Of course.' She reached out and gave Ted's hand a squeeze.

'Thinking about it rationally, I knew she must be dead after all this time, but there was always this little bit of hope that she was off somewhere living the good life, drinking cocktails out of coconuts.' He smiled dreamily.

She touched his arm. 'I'll help you any way I can. You won't need to do this alone.'

'I can't face telling Simone's mother. It will break her heart. She's such a fragile woman, it feels cruel to do it to her. Though if I don't tell her, she'll only hear it on the news or somewhere. These things always have a habit of getting out. Can you imagine her finding out like that?'

CHAPTER SIXTY-EIGHT

Helen wasn't entirely convinced that Mrs Langford had fully understood what Ted had told her. She had insisted that they both stay for food. Having had nothing to eat all day, Helen was grateful for the offer. It was a long drive back home in the dark.

She took another piece of shortbread from the plate. 'These are lovely.'

Ted leaned over and squeezed Simone's mother's hand. 'Yes, it was. I'll do the washing up.'

While he gathered up the plates, Helen gestured to the mantelpiece. 'You have some lovely photos, Mrs Langford.'

'They are, aren't they? Those are my favourite ones, and I have a photo album around somewhere.'

Helen got up to take a better look. She picked up a gold-framed picture of Simone and Ted skiing. Another showed them scuba diving. It reminded Helen of the holiday brochures Ted used to bring her, despite her telling him she'd been terrified of water ever since the tragedy involving her brother. It was one of the things that had been a constant source of tension.

'She's so pretty, isn't she. My Simone.'

'Yes.'

Mrs Langford chuckled. 'Ted's always been an adrenaline junkie, and Simone loves skiing. I don't think anything can faze either of them.'

Her heart sinking, Helen said, 'Not me. I can barely swim the length of a pool.' And she had only learned to do that in the last couple of years.

'He's done so well for himself, hasn't he?' Mrs Langford smiled. 'I'm so proud.'

'Yes, he has.' Helen agreed.

'Finished at the top of his class. He's got a bright future ahead of him. Well, you'll know all that, won't you?' A look of confusion clouded her grey eyes. 'Remind me dear, are you a friend of Simone's?'

Helen drew a breath to speak.

'I forget things sometimes. He's gone through a lot you know.'

'Ted?'

'Oh, yes. Things haven't always gone well for him.'

'I'm sorry to hear that.'

'He wasn't well.'

Helen frowned. 'In what way?'

'He spent a long time with a psychologist,' Mrs Langford said. 'I didn't approve.'

'What didn't you approve of? Who saw the psychologist, Mrs Langford?'

'Teddy.'

'Ted?'

'It was a shame what happened to him, wasn't it?'

'What happened to him?'

'He found out the truth.' Mrs Langford's face darkened. 'He died recently.'

'No, Mrs Langford. Ted's fine. He's right in the kitchen.'

'Not Teddy.'

'Then who.'

'Oh, I can't remember.'

Helen placed the photo back on the mantelpiece. 'Can I get you anything? Do you need to rest?'

She shook her head. 'It's come to me now. It was all over the news. I saw it on the telly.'

A shiver trailed Helen's spine. 'What did you see?'

'The accident on a train. That was who Ted had been doing his therapy with.' A look of worry crossed her face. 'I wasn't supposed to tell anyone that. Ted has been so good to me over the years, paid for my care, this home.'

'I won't tell.'

'Won't tell what?' Ted asked with a smile. He was standing in the doorway watching them.

* * *

After giving Ella time to read Mark Landis's correspondence with other women, Randall and Craven resumed the interview.

Randall gave Ella a knowing smile. 'It must've been horrible reading those letters.'

Ella sniffled.

'And seeing all those horrible photos.' He drew an anguished breath. 'I heard my colleague rammed them in your face.'

'She did.'

'I guarantee you'll end up a photo like that if you carry on down this road. And I don't know why you bother with Landis. A lovely lassie like you could have any fella she wants.'

'I don't know about that.'

'Aye, well, listen to me. I know what am talking about.'

Ella blushed and looked down at the table.

'Come on, what has he promised you? Is it worth throwing your life away for?'

'It's not like that.'

'Then tell us how it is. Do you think he'd want you to spend the rest of your life in jail? If he cares for you as much as you think he does, then he'd want you to tell us.'

'When he gets out, he says he's going to take me travelling round the world. I've never been abroad before.'

'How's someone who's been stuck in prison for years going to afford that?'

'He's got connections,' Ella said.

'His brother?'

Ella's eyes shot up.

'Who's his brother, Ella?'

CHAPTER SIXTY-NINE

Helen placed a hand on Mrs Langford's shoulder. 'She doesn't want to let you know that she's tired.'

'This afternoon has been a lot,' Ted agreed.

'I think we should look at heading back up to Edinburgh now.' Helen took her plate into the kitchen.

Ted followed and stood by the Aga. 'I do feel bad leaving her alone though.'

'We must go sometime. How about you phone her when we get back?'

Ted started spooning coffee into mugs. 'Yes, you're probably right.'

'I hope she's not been boring you.'

'Not at all.' Helen assumed her politest "everything's fine" smile.

'She says a lot of things, she gets confused,' he said.

Helen scraped the remnants of her meal into the bin. 'On the contrary. She's been telling me all sorts of interesting things.'

'Oh? About what?'

'Just bits about your love of skiing and adventure.'

'I've not done that in ages.' He stirred the coffee slowly.

Helen could feel his eyes on her. She was starting to think he'd heard more than he was letting on. She had to get him out of here. If she could just get back to the station . . . 'I'll be back in a minute.'

Suddenly gripped with an icy fear, she went out into the hall and snatched up the telephone. The line was dead. She clicked the receiver switch a couple of times. Nothing. 'Ted—' she tried to keep her voice steady — 'I need to call the station, but the phone's not working.'

'Sorry, forgot to mention it — the last heavy winds broke the line, and we've not got around to fixing it yet. It's a big job, apparently. I hope whatever it is can wait.'

'I'd like to get an update from the station.'

'I'm almost done here.'

Her hand shaking, she set the receiver back in its cradle. 'Well . . . I might just wander down to the High Street and see if I can use the public telephone.'

'Can't it wait?'

'No.' She surprised herself with how strong her voice sounded. 'I just want to see what's going on at work.'

He glanced up. 'I thought your shift had ended.'

'It did, but I'm never really off the job. You should know that.'

He appeared in the hall with a smile. 'I'll come with you.'

'It's all right. I could do with the fresh air.'

'Don't be silly. I'll show you where it is.'

'I saw one on the way here. I'll manage.'

'Well, come to think of it, I could do with phoning the office,' he said. 'Are you all right? You seem—'

'I'm just tired.'

He nodded but his look told her he wasn't convinced.

'Is the bathroom upstairs?' she asked.

'First on the right.'

Helen ran up the stairs two at a time, her heart pounding. At the top, she stood and listened for any indication that Ted had followed her. Nothing. Good. She was probably worrying for no reason. Was she jumping to conclusions again, like she had with Stephen? She could hear Simone's mum and Ted chatting. That would give her a bit of time. She certainly wasn't going to confront him with her suspicions when they were out in the middle of nowhere with an elderly lady. At least McKinley knew where she was. He'd probably phone her flat tonight — he usually did, to make sure she got home safely or give her some update on the case.

She locked the bathroom door and went over to the window, where she tugged at the latch. It refused to give, locked. She swiped at the bottles on the windowsill but there was no sign of the key.

Shit. Shit. Shit. She sat on the edge of the bathtub and put her head in her hands.

She had no idea how long she'd been sitting like that when someone rapped on the bathroom door. She saw the door handle move back and forth a couple of times.

'Everything OK in there?' Ted called.

She jumped up and turned on the tap. 'I'm fine. I'll be out in a second.'

'Why don't you come out now?'

'I'll be a minute, Ted.'

'Helen. I hope you are not trying something stupid in there, or I'll kill that old woman before any of your little colleagues can get here.'

CHAPTER SEVENTY

Groggy from the pain medication and pounding headache, Terry McKinley sat hunched over his desk, trying and failing to go through witness statements. The DI and Randall were still in interviews, so he had the office mostly to himself and he didn't want to even think about going home until he'd heard from Helen.

He glanced up at the clock. Gone nine thirty. He sighed and decided to try her home phone on the off chance. No matter what was going on, even if she was having the time of her life and that Ted bloke had swept her off her feet, she would have phoned for an update, especially after what had happened today and how guilty he knew she felt.

No answer. He dialled the number they had for Mrs Langford. He tried twice but it didn't even ring. All the numbers he had for Ted were the same — no answer.

He didn't have a good feeling about this. In fact, he was seriously worried. He knew he should've insisted on going with them. Not that she would have likely agreed to it anyway.

He went over to the evidence board. The sketches Helen had made were pinned up. He pulled one off the board.

* * *

'What do you want from me, Ted?' The bathroom door had given way easily to his weight against it. He took her roughly by the arm, pulled her downstairs into the hallway and shoved her back against the radiator.

'You'll find out soon enough.'

'You wouldn't hurt me.'

His grip tightened. 'I will if I have to.'

In the front room, Mrs Langford was hunched over in the armchair.

Helen gasped and made a move towards her. Ted stepped in front of her. 'I haven't done anything to her, I just slipped a little something in her drink so she wouldn't be a problem.'

'Why are you doing this?' She kept her gaze on him, refusing to give in to her fear. 'It was you. You worked with Ella White to murder those people. *You* murdered those people. *You* took those Polaroids!'

'Don't say it like that.'

'For goodness' sake Ted, how would you put it?'

'We're going to take a little drive,' he said.

Helen shook her head. 'I'm not going anywhere with you.'

'Have it your way then.' He took a handgun from his pocket and aimed it at Mrs Langford.

'Don't! Ted, this isn't you.'

'If this is how you want to play it.'

'OK, OK . . . On second thoughts, going for a drive sounds like a . . . a cracking idea. Just put the gun down.'

* * *

Like someone lost in a huge stormy sea, waves of panic threatened to overwhelm her. She struggled to catch her breath. Tears stung her eyes but she was determined not to let them fall. He wasn't getting the satisfaction of seeing her cry. She kept telling herself she'd been in worse situations, though she couldn't quite remember when.

He took her arm and dragged her towards the car. She considered making a run for it but there were no trees, no cover, and he was still brandishing the gun.

'You wouldn't get ten yards before I put a bullet in your spine,' Ted growled, as though reading her mind.

'I'm not going to do anything.'

He gave her another shove and her hip connected with the car boot. He chucked the keys at her and levelled the gun at her head.

'Open it.'

'Ted. No, please.'

'Are you deaf as well as stupid? Open the boot or I use this. Your choice.'

Her trembling hands were clammy, and it took her a couple of tries to slot the key in the lock and open the boot. She was relieved to find it full of boxes and tools. She'd never be able to fit in there with all that stuff.

'Take a look,' he said. 'Go on, pick it up.'

The camera felt cold and heavy in her hands. Every bone in her body told her to drop it and run but the cold barrel of the gun pressed hard into the nape of her neck. He pointed to a small oak box at the very back of the boot. 'Open that one.'

She reached in and did as she was told. The box was full of Polaroids. *No. It can't be.* She turned the first one over and recoiled.

'Ted, no. I don't want to see any more. Why are you doing this?' All the while, her relationship with Ted flashed through her mind. He had proposed to her, they had planned to move in together. The weekends away — hell, even the time spent in front of the telly, that couldn't have been fake. Her jaw ached with the effort of trying to sound calm. 'If you're going to kill me, stop playing games and just get on with it.'

'You're brave. I'll give you that. It's something I've always admired in you. No, I'm not going to kill you — yet. There's something I need you to do for me first.'

* * *

A sickening feeling was building in Terry McKinley's stomach. He was rummaging through Helen's desk pedestal on the off chance there was a photo. This felt wrong. As he pulled out notebooks and packets of Polo mints, throwing them onto the desk, he looked up, expecting her to walk through the door at any minute. He was about to give up when he spotted a bit of colour under a police manual. Bingo.

A photo of Ted and Helen smiling arm in arm. It had been folded in half. He smoothed out the creases as he walked back to his desk and placed it next to the pencil sketch, comparing the two. He shook his head and winced at the sudden movement. What was he thinking? Maybe the head injury had affected him worse than he thought. The nose was similar, the jaw not so much.

'What are you doing?' Bell asked. 'I'd put all that back if I were you.'

'I want your opinion on something.'

'Aye? Well, I was just about to head for a drink. Don't suppose it's a good idea wi' your head, but if you fancy it.'

'Never mind a drink. Just come here, will you?' He could see Bell was taken aback by his tone but did as he asked. He moved aside. 'Do you think he looks like the sketch?'

Bell was silent for a moment, then made a face. 'I don't think so, I mean if we're honest, the sketch could be any man really. Wasn't it done based on a description in a phone call?'

'I suppose you're right. How is Randall getting on?'

Bell threw up his hands. 'They're still in there. Listen, pal, you look like death. Go home, get some sleep.'

'Aye, maybe you're right.' McKinley lifted the picture and folded it. 'I have an idea and I'll need you to drive.'

CHAPTER SEVENTY-ONE

'Don't look at me like that, Helen. I'm not a monster.'

'Oh no?' Helen glanced at her hands, bound together in her lap. Her ankles, too, were tied together. With the seat belt keeping her in place, she was unable to move, so she leaned her head back against the headrest.

He slipped her a sideways glance. 'Don't be like that. You've left me no choice. You know you have.'

'Me?' The Bentley reeked of stale alcohol and smoke, burning the back of her throat. She swallowed. 'You're bloody mad.'

'I didn't want to hurt her.'

'Didn't want to hurt who? Vera, or—'

'I've only done what I've had to.'

'No, you haven't.' They weren't going too fast. Just under forty miles an hour. She thought about getting the door open. She could probably get the seat belt undone but there was no way she'd be able to pull up the lock. Helen's body sagged as she looked at the gun on Ted's lap. Her thoughts went back to when she'd first met him. She had been a WPC and he was the solicitor in a case she had worked on, one that she would never forget. He had been the friendly face she'd needed. She hadn't taken to him at first, but he had won her over. Had this been his plan all along?

The car jolted forward, pulling her from her thoughts. The road had straightened, so he had picked up the pace. Helen shuddered. Where was he taking her?

'Are you feeling a bit calmer now?' Ted asked.

'What do you think? Your girlfriend is in custody, you know.'

'She's not my girlfriend.'

'She's quite talkative. She'll be pouring her heart out right about now.'

'Where is Mark? Is he in hospital?' Ted asked.

'Why d'you want to know? Scared you're not going to get an autograph before he croaks it?'

'Autograph? What the hell are you talking about?'

The penny dropped. 'It was all a ruse, wasn't it?'

His Adam's apple bobbed.

'You're the brother. You're the Button Killer's brother.'

* * *

'What's so important that you need to interrupt?' Randall's face was etched with annoyance as closed the interview room door. 'I'm right in the middle of wearing her down.'

'It's important,' McKinley said. He took the photograph from his pocket.

Randall snatched it from his hands. His brows lifted. 'You've interrupted to show me a picture of Helen and that dippy solicitor boyfriend?'

'Ask her if she knows him.'

Randall rolled his eyes.

'Do it. Please.'

CHAPTER SEVENTY-TWO

Helen's head was spinning. She swallowed down the sick feeling. 'I met your mum and dad. I met your older brother. How can you be related to the Button Killer?' They were lovely people, and as far as Helen was aware, he'd had a picture-perfect childhood.

'I was adopted. Mark is my real brother.'

'You were raised in a loving family. They put you through private school, law school.'

'Yet, there was always something missing.'

'You didn't have to kill. You don't have to. He can't be worth all those lives. He wasn't worth throwing your life away. You had everything. You could have done anything you wanted.'

'I didn't have a choice,' he said, not looking at her.

'There's always a choice. How long did you know about him? You know what, it doesn't matter. You do have a choice and it's still not too late to make the right one. Ted, I know that somewhere inside you there's a good person. I know, I've seen it.'

'I know what I have to do.'

'You gave Simone's mother that house in Coldstream, you didn't have to do that.'

'Of course I did.' He took a breath. 'I wanted to make it up to her somehow. I couldn't make things right, but it was something.'

'It was a caring thing to do. That's who you really are.'

'Am I?'

'Was . . . was it an accident?' she said tentatively.

He shook his head.

Helen struggled to catch her breath. 'I don't believe you.'

'I hadn't planned it. It's not as simple as that. It's a question of family, Helen.' His glance at her was scornful. 'Something you'll never understand.'

'Make me understand.'

* * *

Randall emerged from the interview room.

'Well?' McKinley asked. 'She recognised him, didn't she?'

As soon as McKinley got a look at his face, he had his answer.

'She denied it.' Randall shrugged. 'But I don't believe her.'

'Ted was at the station earlier — he left with Helen.'

'When?'

'Late this afternoon.'

'Have you tried to call her?'

'Several times. I've tried Ted too.'

Randall huffed. 'Do you know where they were going?'

* * *

Helen shimmied closer to the door, allowing her to get a better look at Ted. His face was expressionless.

'Was Oliver Stanton the trigger?' she asked.

'Him. Well, he deserved everything he got. Guess who funded his research for his book?' He pointed at his own chest. 'I funded all that stupid propaganda. He used me.'

'Why do that?'

'He was meant to help me prove my brother innocent. That's what he promised to do. My adopted parents sent me to him as a child, he was supposed to help me with "my problems", as they called it, and for a while it worked.'

'What kind of problems?'

'Getting rid of the family pets . . . fighting in school . . . I enjoyed setting fire to things.' He smiled.

'No . . . I don't believe you.' The Ted she knew drank too much and struggled with his demons but she'd never think he'd be capable of hurting anyone.'

'I was adopted when I was six years old.'

'Then what happened?'

Ted laughed bitterly. 'He approached me a few years back, told me he could get my brother out.'

Helen shook her head. 'How could I have been so stupid as to get together with you?'

'Do you remember meeting me?' he asked.

Helen felt a tear roll down her cheek. She nodded. 'What about Simone? Do you think she deserved what she got?'

'No. I loved Simone. She was . . . I don't know, collateral damage. Believe me, I didn't want to hurt her.'

'Oh, sure.'

'I did love her.'

'You're delusional.' Helen struggled against the restraints. She was beginning to feel lightheaded.

'I needed one of the killings to happen when Mark was already in prison, so it would cast doubt on all the other killings he was accused of. Anyone with half a brain would put two and two together and realise the Button Killer was still out there.'

'It didn't work though, did it?'

'No. Thanks to your father.' His mouth was a tight line. 'He was hell-bent on putting someone away, it didn't matter who.'

'The right man is in prison and will stay there. And you'll be joining him.'

'No.'

'Why did you leave that picture of Coldstream?' she asked.

'Because that was where Simone was from. I wanted you to realise she was one of the Button Killer's victims. I knew you'd never piece all the clues together on your own.'

Helen watched the road. Despite her situation, she wanted to laugh. He was still driving like some old granny. 'You've hurt people and you've got yourself in a whole lot of trouble for nothing.'

'You intrigued me, Helen. I wanted to know everything about you, about the person who destroyed my life.'

'Oh, come on. I didn't destroy your life. I didn't do anything to you. What? After five years you still can't believe that?'

'I often thought about killing you.'

She laughed. 'Just what everyone wants to hear from their ex-fiancé.'

Ted shrugged. 'Being with you gave me access to your dad's files, to his office.'

Her dad's office had been in the family home. No wonder he had been so keen to stay over. It was locked but he would've known where the key was. Helen no longer felt like laughing. All the nice times she and Ted had spent together flashed through her mind. They were together for years, how was it possible she hadn't seen this part of him before? How bad a cop must she be not to have realised?

'What are you planning to do with me then? You don't want to hurt me, not really.' How could this be happening? This was Ted. She took a breath. 'I'm going to call the station and we'll both go in together.' Even as she said it, the words sounded lame. She wasn't convincing anyone.

'You, my dear Helen, are going to be my collateral. My plan B.'

With a laugh, he put his foot on the accelerator. Helen's head jerked backwards. Her vision was becoming blurred. 'You put something in my drink too, didn't you?'

'Don't worry, you'll come round soon enough.'

* * *

Helen's flat showed no signs of life, and neither did Ted's. After banging frantically at Helen's door, her neighbour confirmed that he hadn't seen her for a couple of days. In Coldstream the local police had visited the address that Helen was meant to be at, but there had been no sign of them there either. They had found Simone Langford's mother inside. She seemed disorientated, so they had taken her to hospital to be checked out.

McKinley put his hands to his mouth as he stood outside Helen's. He looked up at the darkened window. His mouth was dry, and he had trouble swallowing. Ted was capable of anything, and he was alone with Helen.

'Come on. We're no good to anyone here.' Bell grabbed his arm and tugged him towards the car.

'I . . . I don't know what to do.'

'I do. We might as well go and see Bert List.' Bell started towards the Rover.

'What good would that do?'

'Ted was acting as his solicitor, and I remember List mentioning that he saw Ella with a man a couple of times.' He pulled open the car door. 'Well, are you coming or not?'

'I'll radio the station on the way, see if we have an update from Randall.'

'If anyone can get the information we need, it's him. He's been in CID right from the start. He's the best copper I know.'

* * *

After bringing Randall up to speed, Terry McKinley was now frantically banging on the door of Bert List's home, while Bell rattled the front-room window.

'We know you're in there,' Bell bellowed. 'We only want to have a quick wee word.' About a minute later, an annoyed-looking List pulled open the door. He was wearing the same tatty dressing gown as before.

'What do you pair want? I've had enough of you lot to last me a lifetime.'

Bell smiled. 'Like I said, we'll be quick.'

McKinley held up a photograph. 'Have you ever seen this man with Ella?'

List's features grew darker.

'We know he's your solicitor, but did you ever see him with Ella?' McKinley demanded. 'We have reason to believe he may have taken one of our colleagues, and we need to find him before he does her any harm.'

There was a long moment of silence.

'He could hurt her; do you want that on your conscience?'

'Do you think he's hurt Ella?' List asked.

'We would need to find him to know.'

List finally nodded. 'I did see him with Ella, and I don't think he saw me.' He glanced around as if someone might be listening.

'Why didn't you tell us this before?'

'I didn't put two and two together until he came to see me,' he added.

'After your first visit to me when Ella went missing. He came to offer his help for free. He told me Mark Landis, the Button Killer, got fitted up and he was going to make sure the same thing didn't happen to me.' He stepped back into the house and took a business card from the hall table. 'He said I could go and see him at this address.

CHAPTER SEVENTY-THREE

Ella looked exhausted. She had been in the interview room for over six hours now, and despite the warmth, she had refused all offers of water. She was prettier sitting in front of him than her pictures, though she was too skinny with small eyes that held a lot of sadness.

'Do you know while we've been chatting, Ella, other officers have been out searching. They've been to Ted's house. If I was you, I would start talking. You know he's a solicitor. He knows how to talk his way out of anything. You're going to get all the blame.'

Her eyes flickered.

'I'm doing my best to help you here.' Randall held up his hands. 'But there's only so much I can do.' He decided to try a different tack. 'I didn't agree with what he said about you . . . at first.'

'What does that mean?'

He shrugged. 'Just that you weren't the sharpest knife in the drawer.' He made a move to stand. 'I think we're done here.'

'It was his idea.' She exchanged a look with her solicitor. 'If I tell you, I want to see Mark in return.'

'I'll do my best to sort that for you,' Randall said. 'But I can only do that if you help me, Ella. Think about it — once Ted starts talking, I'll not be able to do any favours for you. When Ted starts talking you will never see Mark again.'

'I was lonely. I hated my job. I hated my life. I read this article about prison pen friends, so I wrote to a couple and Mark was the only one who wrote back.' Her shoulders sagged. 'I was stuck in a horrible marriage, and I was miserable. I didn't think anything would come of it, it was just a . . . I dunno, a distraction at first.' She swatted a tear away. 'He made me feel special. It was . . . well, it was not long after that, that I met his brother.'

'Ted?'

She nodded. 'He told me all about how Mark was framed by this bent copper. The injustice and all that, and they wanted me to help them. They said if we could convince you lot that the Button Killer had returned then you lot would have to let him go. His brother has a lot of money, you see, and he promised me a new life.'

Randall looked down at his notes. He could see Ella believed this, but he was certain they would have killed her as soon as she was no longer useful.

'We spent a long time planning me going missing,' she explained.

'Why did you go to the hospital? Surely that was risky?'

Ella gave a small shrug. 'Ted wanted us to do it . . . Is that copper all right?'

'He's going to have a headache for a few days but aye, be all right.'

'I'm glad.'

Randall didn't believe that. 'What about these keys? Where are they for?' He slid the evidence bag across the table.

'I've never seen them before.'

'They were found in your house, Ella, and I'm getting tired of playing games. If you don't give me what I need right now, I guarantee you will never see Mark again.'

She sighed. 'They're for Ted's house — well, a place he owns.'

'This man has abducted one of our officers.'

She looked at the floor.

'You know what he'll do to her, don't you?' Randall said.

She shrugged. 'I don't know the address, I just know it's some old family home in the middle of nowhere.' She dragged her hands down her face. 'I've told you everything.'

* * *

When Helen came to, it took her a moment to remember what had happened to her. Then the fear and pain came rushing back. The car had stopped. She was alone. Where was she?

She sat up, eyes darting around. It was too dark to see anything. There were no lights, no sound, nothing. She heard someone's approaching footsteps and suddenly she was blinded.

Whoever it was had aimed a camera flash at her. She recoiled and blinked away spots. She closed her eyes as hot tears stung the back of them. She had no idea where she was, no idea how long she'd been out for.

The door whipped open, and she was blasted with icy air.

'Morning, sleepyhead. Hope you haven't been awake too long. I was just making some final preparations.'

'Where are we?'

'A place where we won't be disturbed.' He grabbed her above the elbow, hard, and hauled her out of the car.

Oh, God! They were in the wilderness. All she could see was dense woodland everywhere she looked. He pulled her up a path to a small house with smoke billowing from its chimney and iron fencing around the perimeter.

As he pulled open the gate, Helen could see that it was not a house but a small church in a graveyard where most of the headstones had been laid flat. Nausea threatened to overwhelm her. The building was deceptively large inside and looked like it had been converted into a living space during the war, with a small kitchen area, tables, chairs and sofas. He gave her a shove. She squealed as she thudded onto her knees in front of the crackling fireplace.

Her heart told her he was beyond reason, but she had to keep trying.

'Ted, please think about things. Ella's in custody, she is talking. CID will know everything. I bet they're tearing your house apart right now.' Helen forced herself to stand. 'How long do you think before they know about this place?'

It looked like a hunting cabin, with large knives on the wall and a stag's head above the door. The place was dingy and dirty and illuminated by candles. Not the kind of place she ever thought she'd see Ted in.

'Helen, you can be so dense sometimes.' He shoved her onto an ancient, overstuffed sofa. 'I knew Mark wasn't in that hospital, but it was an opportunity.'

'What are you talking about?'

'Come on, I knew that was a plant, so I went along with it. I know you better than you think.' He tapped at his temple.

'I was the target? You didn't need to go to all that trouble.'

'You like to make everything about you, don't you?' His lip curled into a sneer. 'You weren't the target, that Terry bloody McKinley was. Do you think I'm blind, Helen? I can see the way he looks at you.'

'God, you're mad!'

'I knew if anything happened to him you would blame yourself, and it was an easy chance for him to get what he deserved. Only she mucked it up.'

'I don't see a way out of this for you, Ted. You think you are so smart — but you must realise the best way is to turn yourself in.'

'I'm never going to go to jail.'

'You could've got away, why did you take me to Coldstream?'

'Once I knew Ella was in custody, it was only a matter of time before you would be after me. You're my safety net, they won't be able to hurt me if you're with me.'

'I think you give me far more credit than anyone else does.' Apart from McKinley and the DI, most of the department would be glad to see the back of her.

He pulled the gun from his pocket and aimed it at her. 'And if you're thinking of trying anything, don't forget I have this.'

'You don't need to point that at me, Ted. I'm hardly going anywhere.'

He slumped down into the armchair. 'Sorry.'

Helen laughed. 'Sorry?'

* * *

When McKinley had finally got through to Randall on the radio, it wasn't good news. Ella knew Ted had a small house in a remote location, but she didn't know where, perhaps somewhere in the Borders. He had his map book spread out on his lap and was trying to rack his brains. He couldn't recall Helen mentioning a place that Ted owned.

He popped a couple of aspirin as Bell pulled up in front of the townhouse Ted had been staying at. Detective Inspector Craven was already there, along with a couple of uniformed officers. They were forcing the door with a baton and Craven was on his radio, presumably with Randall.

Bell whistled and wrenched up the handbrake. 'That Ted must be rolling in it.'

'Ted is renting the place from a colleague. It's not his.'

'Still.'

McKinley forced a thin smile and pulled on gloves as he approached the property. He could see the DI groping the wall for a light switch with a gloved hand. McKinley followed him inside, and the uniformed officers took them upstairs.

Craven dragged a hand through his hair, then made a beeline for a console table by the door and lifted a stack of envelopes out of a holder. 'These are all for the owner.'

'I'll take the front room,' McKinley said.

Craven bunched the envelopes back into the letter holder. 'Ted keeps his victims for at least a few days before he murders them.'

'That's right. Two to three days.'

'There's no way he does that here. It's too open.'

'What about close to where the taxi driver was found?' McKinley asked.

A radio chirruped behind them. Randall was standing in the doorway. 'According to the Land Registry, Ted doesn't own any property in Scotland, and neither do his parents.'

'What about Mark Landis's family?' McKinley asked.

'See what you can find,' Craven directed Randall.

Randall turned to leave then changed his mind. 'I don't want to state the obvious here, but are we certain that Helen didn't leave with him of her own volition? Weren't they engaged?'

'Helen broke that off.' McKinley stepped forward.

'Maybe that's what she told you.'

'I can't believe that you are questioning if she went off with a killer.' He looked at Craven for backup and the DI moved between them.

'I'm sure Randall didn't mean it like that,' Craven said. 'Anyway, I spoke with the police in Coldstream. They've found Helen's Mini abandoned and there are signs of a struggle.'

Randall shrugged. 'I was just expressing a suggestion.'

'Aye? Keep things like that to yourself.' McKinley was surprised at how steady and strong the words came.

Randall held up his hands in mock surrender. 'I'll go see what I can find out.'

Craven nodded. 'Tell the Coldstream officers to speak to Simone Langford's mother, again, maybe she'll know where he's taken her.'

CHAPTER SEVENTY-FOUR

'If you're even a little bit sorry then loosen these.' Helen held up her hands. 'My wrists are killing me. I can't feel my hands.'

'I can't do that.'

Helen sighed. 'Then what about some water?'

Ted's face hardened.

'Please, Ted. What harm will a small glass of water do you? I'm not going anywhere. You've got me tied up like Houdini.'

He rolled his eyes, then pushed to his feet.

As soon as his back was turned, she patted her trousers pockets. Ted hadn't taken it. The little screwdriver keyring that Terry had given her. She twisted round further until she could just get a couple of fingers into the pocket. Gritting her teeth, the restraints tearing at her wrists, she pushed further until she her fingers closed around the keyring, then she bent her fingers until she could get the screwdriver through the middle of the knot. She twisted, and twisted, and twisted some more. *Come on.*

She caught movement from the corner of her eye and threw her hands back onto her lap. She put her leg over the screwdriver as Ted returned with the water. 'Thanks.' She took it from him and glugged it greedily.

'Better?' He held out his hand for the empty glass.

'Thanks.' She gave it him and wiped her mouth with the back of her bound hand. 'What's the plan, Ted?

'You don't need to know that.'

'You can't just keep me here.'

'Are you warm enough?'

'I'm fine.'

Ted moved to the fireplace and threw another log on the fire. While he had his back to her, Helen wrapped her fingers around the screwdriver.

'Why did you take my photograph?' she asked.

'What?'

'When I was in the car.'

'It's how I want to remember you.' He had his hands on the mantelpiece, his shoulders slumped.

Helen pulled and twisted at her bindings, ramming the screwdriver into the knot. It felt like it was taking for ever but she now had more movement in her right wrist. With one final tug, she managed to wriggle her right hand free. She slipped it back inside the loosened hole. She didn't want Ted to realise what she'd managed to do.

* * *

Terry McKinley was back in the Viva with Bell. They were heading towards Coldstream and waiting for Uniform to call them back.

Bell gave McKinley a sideways glance. 'How are you holding up?'

'I'm fine.' That was a lie. His head felt like it was about to explode, and his eyes were blurry, but there was no point in letting Bell know that. He had the road atlas on his lap. 'Take a left here. That'll get us on the right track.'

The radio bleeped. McKinley snatched up the receiver.

'It's Constable McArthur here.'

'Receiving you.' McKinley winced as his head was shoved back into the headrest. They were now on open roads and Bell has his foot down as far as it would go, despite the darkness and the flakes of snow gathering on the windscreen.

'We've tried a couple of times to speak to Mrs Langford. She's on her way to hospital.'

'What's wrong?'

'She's complaining of chest pains.'

'Did you get anything out of her?' The line went silent apart from a couple crackles. 'Are you still there?'

'Still here. Sorry. Just trying to get the information.'

McKinley rubbed his eyes. His vision was getting worse.

'Sorry for the holdup, the ambulance has just taken her away. She's a nice woman but she's not all there.'

'Did you get anything out of her?' McKinley repeated.

'I did. She said Ted loves to spend time out in nature. There's a place he used to take Simone. She gave us the address.'

* * *

Ted drained a glass of whisky in one, then refilled his glass. He was trying to hide it, but Helen could see the tremor in his hands.

'What?' Ted sneered. 'Why are you looking at me like that?'

'Thought you had given up drinking?'

'I've had a hell of a day.'

'You were adopted by wonderful parents that gave you the world and this is how you end up?'

His sneer twisted into a smile. 'My adopted parents tried and tried to have their own child and couldn't. I guess that's why they turned to adoption. Only as soon as they got me, Mother ended up getting pregnant. Can you believe that, eh? They got their dream child and ended up stuck with me.'

'They never saw it like that.'

'I was the problem child. My adopted brother the perfect one.' He put his empty glass on the table next to him.

'You can still make this right, Ted, it's not too late. Please let me help you.'

'I saw a lot of myself in you,' Ted remarked.

'Rubbish.'

'You were a constant disappointment to your parents.'

'No, I wasn't.'

'Especially when you joined the police.'

'I'm nothing like you.'

'They had the perfect child too, didn't they? Your perfect little brother.'

'Stop it.'

'I understand you, Helen, better than you'll ever know.'

He went back to the kitchen area, opening and shutting cupboards. It sounded like he was going to prepare food. Helen used the chance to work on the rope tying her ankles together. It was thin but tough, something he used for fishing, Helen guessed. She slipped off her boots. It wasn't working.

She swallowed back the rising panic, forced herself to take a couple of deep breaths. She wasn't going to let it end like this. She had to fight.

The room fell silent apart from the howl of the wind. From the corner of her eye, it looked like Ted was opening a can. This might be the last chance she'd get to free herself. She stabbed at the rope with the screwdriver with all her might, trying to be as quiet as possible.

'Are you hungry, Helen?'

Helen froze. 'I lost my appetite when you put a gun to my head.'

'I'll make you something anyway.'

That sounded like the old Ted. She swallowed back tears. No, the old Ted was gone. No — not gone — he had never existed.

Helen let out a shuddery breath and managed to release her feet. The clink of crockery filled the void. It felt like an age before Ted was walking towards her with two plates in his hand.

This is it. Now or never.

As he bent over to hand her a plate, she aimed a boot into the side of his knee with all the force she could muster. He screamed out and collapsed to his knees.

Another kick, this time to the ribs. The plates were lying upside down on the ground. She grabbed one and smashed it onto his shoulder.

She scrambled past him. Pain shot up her leg as he grabbed her ankle and pulled her to the ground. She landed with a thud on her arm and all the air escaped her body. Wincing, she twisted around and kicked out again.

Pulling herself to her feet, she tried the door handle. It didn't budge. *Shit.* The keys. Where were they?

Something shiny caught her eye. Ted, on all fours now, looked down, Helen following his gaze. The gun lay on the ground just beyond his reach. She made a move, snatched it up and pointed it at Ted, somewhere near his shoulder. The gun shook in her trembling hands.

Ted was smiling. He held his hands up. 'You're not going to shoot me.'

Helen's heart hammered. 'I will if I have to, so stay where you are.'

A thump at a door made Helen jump. For the briefest second, she thought she was saved. She imagined CID on the other side of it, about to burst in. Then realisation dawned on her, as it happened a second time, that it was coming from inside. There was someone else in the house.

Ted stepped forward, snapping her from her thoughts. 'I told you not to move. Who's behind that door?'

'Come on, Helen.' He hobbled forward again. 'I didn't want to hurt you.'

Helen's eyes darted around the room until they alighted on the telephone. An old-fashioned candlestick rotary phone. 'Don't come any closer.'

'Helen, please.'

She backed away and grabbed the phone, keeping the gun aimed at Ted. Her heart sank. The line was dead.

He lunged towards her. Helen pulled the trigger.

* * *

'What was that?' McKinley leaned forward in his seat.

'I'm not sure I heard anything.' Bell had a tight grip on the steering wheel. They had slowed to a creep on the narrow single-track road.

'It sounded like a car backfiring. How much further?'

'I'm not sure.'

'Pull over here, let's walk the rest of the way. I don't want him to hear the car approach and hurt Helen.'

* * *

Helen shuddered and looked down at the warm gun she was clutching, the bang still echoing in her ears. Ted was sprawled on his stomach. Was he breathing? She couldn't see.

She swallowed and forced herself to approach the door that she had heard the noise coming from. With one hand, she pushed it open and raised the gun in the other. She found herself at the top of stairs.

'Hello? Is someone down here?' She started on the steps. 'I'm a police officer.' She touched the wall to ease herself down. There was no handrail. The room was soundproofed — the bloody thing was padded. Helen shivered, terrified of what she was going to find.

At the bottom, she caught sight of a shape lying on the floor in the corner. It was a person, female, with long, dark hair. She was lying on her side with her back to Helen. 'Can you hear me?' Helen took another step forward. 'I'm not going to hurt you.'

She struggled to think. After the taxi driver, the Button Killer's next victim had been an estate agent. Rose somebody. Rose McDaid.

'Are you OK?' Helen called out. 'Don't worry, I'm going to get us out of here.'

Her eyes darted around the room. The back wall was filled with metal shelves and boxes, the only other thing an old horse blanket crumpled on the floor. She knelt next to the woman, relieved to find a pulse. Her lips were dry, and her face pale. Helen covered her in the blanket. 'You're going to be all right, just hang on, I'll get us out of here.'

Helen had gritted her teeth so hard she could taste blood. She stepped back. Her gaze fell to the tin box on the bottom of the shelf. It stood out of place compared to the others and it was the only one with a thick rusted padlock on the front. Helen squatted down to get a better look. All the other boxes looked new but not this one. This one looked like it had been green at one point but most of the paint had chipped away over time. She ran a finger along its blistered edges.

'I wouldn't touch that.' The voice was soft and raspy. 'He doesn't like people touching his things.' The woman had turned over and was tightly gripping the blanket.

Helen had to haul the woman up the stairs and was struggling for breath by the time she got to the top. Ted was still in the same position, except Helen could now see blood pooling around his torso. She guided the woman to the sofa. She felt tears on her cheeks as she reached into Ted's pockets for the keys to the front door.

Outside, the air was now arctic cold, making it hard to breathe. They pushed forward towards the gate. Snow had covered the cemetery, concealing the path. Helen took a step forward and slipped, landing hard on an upturned headstone. The woman had landed hard too and was now sobbing.

'I'm sorry, but we have to keep going.' Helen fumbled to her feet but the woman wasn't moving.

'Helen!'

For a moment, Helen wasn't sure whether she had imagined his voice. Then she felt Terry pull her to feet and draw her close to him.

'Are you all right?'

Bell knelt next to the woman. Helen closed her eyes. A sob burst from her throat and tears flowed. She watched as Bell went into the house.

'Where's Ted, Helen?'

'I . . . I've shot him. I think he's dead.'

Her knees buckled but McKinley kept her from falling again.

'He's not dead yet.' Bell appeared in the doorway. 'He's lost a lot of blood, but he's breathing.'

'The ambulance is on its way, Helen. It should be here any minute.'

CHAPTER SEVENTY-FIVE

According to the doctors and nurses, Helen had been lucky.

Being forced to shoot her ex-fiancé — lucky wasn't exactly how she was feeling. They were keeping her in over-night for observation, though her injuries were what the stern matron had deemed "superficial". Apart from a couple of broken ribs that the painkillers numbed, she felt like one giant bruise. All she really wanted was a long, hot shower, her own bed, and a massive hot chocolate.

Groaning, she hauled herself up in a seated position on the bed and shoved the paperback on her lap aside. After reading the first page ten times, she'd given up. She looked up as the curtain that separated her from the rest of the ward parted.

'Good to see you awake.' It was DI Craven. He looked exhausted. The work and his personal life were taking its toll — he was in his late forties, though the gloomy strip lights easily added another ten years to that.

'What time is it?' Helen asked, giving him a pained smile.

'It's just gone eight. Are you up to visitors?' He held up a brown bag. 'Grapes. These are traditional, aren't they?'

'How did you manage to get in before visiting time?'

He grinned. 'I have my ways.'

'Please.' Helen gestured to the chair next to her bed. 'How is the woman I found? I didn't get her name.'

'Tracy Blyth.' He put the fruit next to her. 'Doctors think she'll make a full recovery, though she's badly dehydrated.'

'Has she started talking yet?'

Craven shook his head. 'Not said a word since she arrived.'

Helen was hardly surprised considering the state she'd found her in. They sat for a moment in an awkward silence, both chewing on grapes. Helen wanted to ask about Ted, but she was too scared of the answer. Deep in her gut, she felt a stab of sorrow.

'I don't know if you'll be happy about this but Ted's out of surgery and stable.'

'I . . .' Helen felt a sudden chill in the air. 'This might surprise you, but it's a relief to hear that he'll live. I didn't want to be responsible for taking his life and he deserves to go to prison for the rest of his life — that's where he belongs. Him dying would be the easy way out.'

Craven looked like he was considering it. 'I'm not sure I would feel that way.'

'Ted was—' She stopped herself. What was she going to say? That somewhere buried deep inside was a good man. 'I don't know. I've barely slept. I keep trawling through every interaction I've had with him, looking for any sign that I might've missed, but there wasn't any.'

'Don't. You'll drive yourself mad if you go down that road.'

'I can't help it.' She dragged her hands down her face. 'He had been desperate for me to leave the police, but I think that was his way of protecting me.'

'Or helping himself,' Craven countered.

'In the basement I found some boxes, what was in them?'

'Enough evidence to put Ted away for a long time. All his trophies from his victims, photographs mostly.

'Good.'

'We found all his tools too, claw hammers, tyre irons . . . The man had more knives than a butcher.'

'He'd drugged me too.'

Craven nodded. 'We found methaqualone, enough of it to take down a small army.'

That would do it. Helen knew that was a powerful and dangerous sedative.

'Where's Terry?'

'He . . . well, he's going to be OK.'

'His head?'

'It's got worse . . . nothing to be alarmed about but they are going to keep him in hospital for observation.'

CHAPTER SEVENTY-SIX

Two days later

Discharged from hospital and back at her flat, Helen had just got off the phone and was at a loss for words. She was certain it had been the first time in her life that her mum had uttered the words "I'm proud of you." There were many times she'd come close to it when Helen had got her first job at the greengrocers on a Saturday morning, graduated from university, and when she'd won her first of many art competitions. For years, she had longed to hear those words but now she just felt empty.

Sitting on the sofa, she shivered and wrapped her blanket around her shoulders. The telly was on low, mainly for background noise. Some science fiction film about a submarine crew that had been shrunk. She glanced around the lounge from its dated décor and her stuff still in boxes. She had packed a lot of stuff when Ted had asked her to move in with him and had never bothered to unpack them.

She heard the front door open and smiled as the smell of fish and chips hit her.

'Hurry up, Terry, you're missing the film.'

He appeared in the doorway looking windswept, clutching a carrier bag. 'Sorry I got sidetracked.'

'What's happened?'

'We heard from the prison that when Landis found out that he wasn't going to be released after all, he started a fight and came off worse. He died from his injuries a couple of hours ago.'

Helen's shoulders sagged. 'What about Ted?'

'Faced with a long prison sentence, Ted is singing like a canary. We also found photos of Oliver Stanton in the train station — it was clear Ted was stalking him.'

'He's admitted that Landis was the Button Killer and says he knows where the victims that weren't found are likely buried. We're likely looking at more victims than he was originally tried for.'

'I can't believe it.'

'There's more. Ted's fingerprints were the ones found at one of the earlier crime scenes. He said that he was with Mark Landis at some of the killings.'

'He would have been a teenager.' Helen shook her head.

'Mark had tracked him down at a young age apparently and basically gave him an apprenticeship in murder.'

Helen put her hand to her mouth. 'The blood found in Ella's house. I know Ella wasn't talking—'

'Ted had told us that Ella tried to copy one of the Button Killings. He cleaned up the scene.'

'Do we know who's blood it was? Do you believe him?'

'Not yet.' McKinley shrugged. 'I mean we're still working on him. I'm not sure I'd ever truly believe anything Ted says. I mean practically everything you know about the man is a lie and he's very good at it too.'

'The only positive I can take from this', Helen said, 'is that hopefully, it will give some of the families closure. I can't believe Ted did all that just to get his brother free.'

McKinley sat down and put his arm around her shoulder. 'I don't think he did all this for his brother — he was in it for the thrill too. He may have even been involved in the early murders with his brother.'

'My father never discounted that two people could've been involved.'

McKinley blew out a sigh. 'When are you back at work?'

'In a couple of days . . . Mind you, my ribs are killing me.'

He rubbed her arm.

'How's your head?' she asked.

'They said it might take a few weeks for the concussion to heal but don't worry about me. Anyway, our fish and chips are getting cold and we're missing the film.'

* * *

On her first shift back, Helen was in the DI's office, finally having made up her mind. She had been dreading this moment for weeks. 'I'm going to be honest with you, Jack, because it doesn't sit right with me not to be.' She had walked in without knocking, and now she was standing in front of Craven's desk with no real idea of what she was going to say next.

Looking almost as surprised as she was to find herself here, Craven stopped writing and put his pen down. 'Honest about what?'

'I do know who gave information to the press. I've known about it for a while. I wasn't sure what I was going to do about it, but after everything that's—'

'And?'

She looked away and let out a sigh.

'Well, you can't not tell me now.'

'It was Terry McKinley. But I've dealt with it.'

'OK.'

She stared at him but couldn't make out what he was thinking. 'He got drunk and made a mistake, that's all.'

Craven was nodding.

'I know he regrets it, and before you say anything, he didn't do it for some easy cash. He just got caught on a bad day after Sally left him, got drunk and said too much.' In her opinion, it was something that could have easily happened to any one of them.

'Fine,' Craven said. 'You're in charge of this department and if you say you've handled it, I'll go along with that. But if it happens again—'

'It won't.'

He stared hard at her. 'Are you willing to take responsibility for that?'

'I am.'

After she left Craven's office, she approached Randall's desk. He was typing up a report with a cigarette dangling from his lips.

'Why did you lie?' Helen asked.

'About what?'

'About PC John Mills?'

'Oh . . . that.' He took a deep drag of his cigarette. 'I didn't see the harm. He had nothing to do with this.'

'Still.'

'I didn't want his name dragged through the mud.'

EPILOGUE

'Can I take you up on your offer to stay?' Helen smiled at McKinley. 'Power's out again at my place.' No way did she want to be alone, not tonight, not after everything that had happened.

Without saying a word, he pulled the door wide.

She slung her bag down in the hallway. The building was a couple of hundred years old and there had been a lot done to the interior since, with new lavender flock wallpaper and thick lime-coloured carpets. McKinley regularly succumbed to temptation and rented or bought all the new gadgets he could get his hands on. He was the only person she knew with a personal computer, a big colour telly, and a digital watch that he only wore on special occasions.

'I hope it's not too cold, I left the windows open,' he said.

'It's fine.'

McKinley shoved open the mahogany door to his bedroom. 'You can stick your stuff in here.'

She raised an eyebrow at him. Smiling, she did what he said, her bag landing with a thump on the bed.

McKinley headed for the kitchen and began rummaging through the cupboards. 'I would have done a shop if I'd known I was going to have company.'

Helen stood in the doorway and watched as he pulled out a packet of digestives, a couple of packets of crisps, Texan bars and bags of nuts. 'I thought you said you had nothing in?'

He gave a small shrug. 'I wouldn't exactly call this food.' He tugged open the fridge and made a face. 'I've got some tins of those salad things. I've developed a right taste for them.'

'Just pass me one of those chocolate bars. And the crisps and the biscuits as well.'

McKinley chucked one of the bars in her direction and tore the other one open. She didn't feel like eating but couldn't remember the last time she had, and no doubt it would be another long night.

They both chewed in silence.

'I had no clue about Ted. In all the time we were together, I never suspected a thing.'

McKinley considered it. 'Do you know what? Sometimes people are good at hiding who they really are. He was a clever, successful solicitor with all the money he wanted, the last person you'd think would be holding some dark secret.'

Helen looked down at the carpet. 'I thought the problems went as far as him drinking too much. And I practically accused Stephen of being a killer.' She put her head in her hands, cringing at the memory.

A smile played on McKinley's lips. 'You didn't practically accuse him. You did.'

She looked up. 'Hey, aren't you supposed to be making me feel better?'

'I'm sure he'll come round.'

'I don't think I want him too.' She leaned forward and kissed him. 'Here.' She grabbed the newspaper from the coffee table and dropped it into his lap. 'Find us something on at the flicks — you're buying the popcorn. And no horror films, or—' she waved her hand in the air, searching for the right words — 'crazy sadistic killers. And especially not killer solicitors.'

'You don't make it easy, do you? *Star Trek* it is then.'

THE END

THE JOFFE BOOKS STORY

We began in 2014 when Jasper agreed to publish his mum's much-rejected romance novel and it became a bestseller.

Since then we've grown into the largest independent publisher in the UK. We're extremely proud to publish some of the very best writers in the world, including Joy Ellis, Faith Martin, Caro Ramsay, Helen Forrester, Simon Brett and Robert Goddard. Everyone at Joffe Books loves reading and we never forget that it all begins with the magic of an author telling a story.

We are proud to publish talented first-time authors, as well as established writers whose books we love introducing to a new generation of readers.

We have been shortlisted for Independent Publisher of the Year at the British Book Awards three times, in 2020, 2021 and 2022, and for the Diversity and Inclusivity Award at the Independent Publishing Awards in 2022.

We built this company with your help, and we love to hear from you, so please email us about absolutely anything bookish at feedback@joffebooks.com

If you want to receive free books every Friday and hear about all our new releases, join our mailing list: www.joffebooks. com/contact

And when you tell your friends about us, just remember: it's pronounced Joffe as in coffee or toffee!

CPSIA information can be obtained
at www.ICGtesting.com
Printed in the USA
BVHW040722170523
664253BV00007B/357